Five

Jane Blythe

Bear Spots Publications
Melbourne Australia

bearspotspublications@gmail.com

Paperback
ISBN: 0-9945380-7-3
ISBN-13: 978-0-9945380-7-9

Cover designed by QDesigns

I'd like to thank everyone who played a part in bringing this story to life. Particularly my mom who is always there to share her thoughts and opinions with me. My awesome cover designer, Amy, who whips up covers for me so quickly and who patiently makes every change I ask for, and there are usually lots of them! And my lovely editor Mitzi Carroll, and proofreader Marisa Nichols, for all their encouragement and for all the hard work they put in to polishing my work.

PROLOGUE
FIVE YEARS EARLIER

11:34 A.M.

Eliza Donnan walked down the street toward her house. The eighteen-year-old college freshman's mind had already switched from her schoolwork to what she would be doing this afternoon.

She hadn't seen her boyfriend, George, in almost four days. He'd gone home to visit his family because his grandfather had been in a car accident. After she ate lunch, she'd call him so they could catch up; she hated being away from him for long. They'd been dating for almost a year, and Eliza was sure that he was her one true love.

She slowed down to let a car back out of a driveway and noticed a man next to a car at the side of the road. The hood was up, and the man seemed to be examining the engine.

He looked up and saw her watching him. "Excuse me, miss, do you happen to have a cell phone on you? The battery's died on mine." He gave her a warm smile. He had amazing bright blue eyes that stood out in contrast to his pale skin and curly, black hair.

Looking nervously up and down the street, there was no one else around. Eliza knew better than to walk up to a stranger. She'd been taught at a young age, as all children were, never to talk to strangers. She knew the dangers. She knew that, as a young woman, she was particularly vulnerable. This man could be a robber or a rapist or a murderer. He didn't look evil or psychotic, but that didn't mean anything. Looks could be deceiving.

Taking a tentative step toward the man, she glanced cautiously

1

inside the car where she saw a tiny baby asleep in the back, and a little girl of about four sitting in a car seat, twirling her finger around the end of one of her pigtails.

Put at ease by the sight of the small children, she walked the rest of the way toward the car. Obviously, someone had seen enough in this man to marry him and have two children with him. A woman would know if her husband and the father of her children was some sort of psychopath.

She fished around in her bag for her phone, then finally finding it, she held it out to him. "Here you go."

The man gave her another warm smile. "Thanks. They always seem to die just when you need them."

He reached out to take the phone and introduced himself. "I'm Malachi, and that's Bethany." He pointed to the four-year-old, then indicated the infant, "And that's Hayley."

"I'm Eliza; they're cute." Eliza adored children and was an early childhood education major at college.

"Nice to meet you, Eliza. And thanks, they are cute, except when they wake you up in the middle of the night," he joked, laughing.

Eliza smiled, then stood back to give him some privacy as he made his phone call. She turned back around when he was finished.

"Thanks. You live around here?" Malachi asked as he handed her the phone.

"Yeah, just down there a little way." Eliza pointed down the street toward her house.

Too late she noticed the cloth coming toward her.

She struggled in vain as Malachi held it firmly to her mouth. Her limbs began to tingle, her head began to swim, her vision blurred, and her knees buckled.

Malachi caught her as she slumped forward. Her phone dropped from her hand and shattered on the ground. She was vaguely aware of him lifting her into his arms and placing her inside the car before everything went black.

* * * * *

Eliza's head was aching and she felt as though she were spinning. Spinning and spinning and spinning. The sensation was making her horribly nauseous.

With sheer force of will, she attempted to focus.

It felt like she was in a car, but that couldn't be right. She had been on her way home from college and … she kept drawing a blank.

She forced herself to concentrate.

This was important. She could feel it.

Someone was crying somewhere nearby.

Who? Who would be crying?

Then her memories came back in a sudden rush that left her feeling more nauseous than before.

That man, Malachi, had drugged her and put her in his car.

Eliza forced her eyes open and saw that she was indeed in a car. Her head rested against the window. The baby, Hayley she thought Malachi had said her name was, was asleep in a baby seat next to her, and the other little girl, Bethany, was crying quietly in a car seat next to the other window.

This couldn't really be happening. Could it?

Had she really just been kidnapped?

Fighting to keep calm, Eliza took several deep breaths. If she was going to somehow get herself out of this, then she was going to have to keep a straight head.

Casting a careful glance at Malachi, it seemed like he was preoccupied with driving wherever it was he was going, wherever he was taking her. Lifting her hand cautiously, she moved it slowly toward the door handle. The car didn't seem to be going too fast, and Eliza thought that if she opened the door she should be able to jump and then make a run for it.

Slipping her other hand to unclick her seat belt, she released it as slowly and as quietly as she could. Stealing another glance at Malachi, he didn't seem to be aware of what she was doing. Curling her fingers slowly around the door handle, she waited until they slowed to turn a corner, then pulled the handle.

She bumped against it when it didn't open.

"Child lock is on."

Looking up, she saw Malachi's reflection smiling at her in the rear-vision mirror. Terrified by his eerie calm, Eliza found herself rapidly losing control of her emotions and giving in to the terror that threatened to engulf her.

"Where are you taking me?" she screamed, hearing the hysteria in her own voice.

"Quiet, please; you'll wake the baby," he reprimanded as though he were admonishing a disobedient child.

Anger began to trickle in through her fear. "You can't just drug me and drag me off somewhere."

"I can, and I did."

Fueled more by anger than common sense, she ripped her seat belt away and lunged forward, grabbing at Malachi's face. If she could get him to crash the car, she would have a good chance of getting away. The two little girls were safely strapped into their car seats, so they should be safe enough. All she had to hope was that she didn't sustain serious injuries. Still, so long as help got here quickly, she should be okay even if she were incapacitated.

"I wouldn't do that if I were you."

Freezing mid-lunge when she saw the gun, Eliza slumped back into her seat, defeated. This man had covered everything. He wasn't going to let her go. "What are you going to do to me?" she whispered.

Malachi ignored her and returned his attention to the road. Bethany was still crying, so she reached over the baby and put her hand on the little girl's shoulder and squeezed gently. The child immediately grabbed onto her hand, clinging tightly. Terrified blue eyes looked back at her, and Eliza got the uneasy feeling that the little girl had suffered the same fate that she herself had.

Had Malachi kidnapped Bethany, too?

What about the baby?

His? Or another victim?

Attempting to give the child a reassuring smile, she knew it did little to ease the girl's terror. Nor did it do anything to relieve her own. The tears that she'd been holding back began to fall, sliding slowly down her cheeks. Eliza laid her head against the window and sobbed.

NOVEMBER 3RD
9:00 P.M.

9:04 P.M.

"Just hold on, cupcake, we won't be long," Ryan Xander promised his wife.

Sofia had been sick with the flu for the last week. And, of course, she'd been overdoing things. Between bouts of vomiting, she had tended to their two young children. Ignoring headaches and chills and coughs, she had cooked meals, done laundry, driven their five-year-old daughter to school, and basically just pushed herself too far. He had tried to step in, insist that she rest, but every time he turned his back, she was out of bed doing something.

Then, ten minutes ago, she had collapsed.

He had been in the kitchen having dinner with his older brother Jack and Jack's wife Laura, when his wife had come in to get a glass of water. Ryan had just been reprimanding her for getting out of bed to get it herself instead of calling for him when she had fainted.

Ryan had scooped her up and bundled her into the car, ignoring her protests that she was fine and didn't need to go to the hospital. Jack had offered to drive them, so Ryan was in the back seat with Sofia lying beside him, her head in his lap.

"I'm cold." Sofia was shivering.

"I know, honey." Ryan wrapped the blanket tighter around her. "You have a fever; you're getting chills. We'll be at the hospital soon."

Sofia gave a half nod and let her eyes flicker closed again. Ryan stroked her hair and cast a glance at his sister-in-law. He was concerned about Sofia, but he didn't think it was anything too serious—dehydration if he had to guess. She'd been too nauseous to eat or drink much the last few days. Adding the vomiting to that, it was a fair guess.

Laura, on the other hand, was a completely different story.

His sister-in-law suffered from severe agoraphobia as a result of a violent attack many years ago. She had improved the last few years. She could go outside now, but she usually needed time to prepare herself, and she didn't do well with large groups of people. Coming with them to the hospital was probably not a good idea.

This was not a planned outing, and Laura was already looking stressed. Her eyes were clenched shut, her head rested against the closed window, and she was breathing too quickly.

"Jack, maybe we should drop Laura off at your place," he said softly. "She's not looking so great."

"I'm fine," Laura said through clenched teeth.

She sounded anything but. Laura was more like his sister than his sister-in-law. Ryan and Jack had known her their entire lives. They'd grown up together; her family had lived across the street from them. They'd played together, gone to school together, and Jack and Laura had even dated all through high school, while he had had a major crush on her. Back then, Laura had been vibrant and adventurous and full of life—until an attack that had almost killed her had completely changed her.

"I'll drop you guys off at the hospital, take Laura home, then come back." Jack's gaze kept darting from the road to his wife.

"No." Laura forced her eyes open. "I can do this. I *want* to do this."

Jack took a hand off the wheel and took hold of one of Laura's. "Honey," he began.

"No, Jack. No honey, and no being bossy and ordering me around. I'm going." Laura turned her head back to the window and closed her eyes once more.

"I'm not bossy," Jack muttered with a frown and Ryan couldn't help but laugh. His big brother was well known for his bossy attitude.

"Yeah, you are, honey." Laura smiled.

"She's right, Jack, you are, and you know you are," Ryan agreed cheerfully, pleased that Laura had at least been momentarily distracted.

Sofia groaned. "I think I'm going to be sick."

Jack glanced in the rear-vision mirror. "You want me to pull over?" he asked.

"Yeah." Sofia struggled to sit up.

Jack immediately parked the car at the side of the road, and Ryan helped Sofia out. She dropped to her knees and retched. Her stomach was empty, so nothing came up but a little liquid. He knelt beside her, holding her hair back from her face and rubbing her back.

"All done?" he asked, once her shoulders stopped heaving.

Sofia nodded, her whole body trembling. Ryan gathered her up and climbed back into the car. This time he set his wife in his lap, hoping he could help to keep her warm until they got to the hospital.

"Almost there," Jack announced. The shiver that wracked through Laura at Jack's words was bigger than the ones that kept rippling through Sofia.

"You can stay in the car, angel." Jack took Laura's hand again. "You don't have to come in."

"I do have to. I do. I do," Laura murmured, sounding like she was trying to convince herself as much as them.

"Honey, you really don't." Jack was looking concerned. "If you can't handle it, that's totally fine, no one is—"

"Stop, Jack, stop. I can't listen to you right now." Laura pressed her hands to her ears.

Jack frowned, but chewed on his lip to refrain from saying

more. A couple of minutes later, they pulled into the hospital parking lot.

"Here we are, cupcake." Ryan opened the door and climbed out, balancing Sofia in his arms. "I got you, honey," he assured his wife as her eyes flickered open.

"It's all right, Laura, I'm right here," Jack was saying as he helped Laura from the car, keeping an arm around her waist to steady her.

Leaving Jack to deal with Laura, Ryan quickly carried Sofia into the emergency room and hoped they wouldn't have to wait long to see a doctor.

* * * * *

9:17 P.M.

"Come on, angel, let me take you home." Her husband was crouched in front of the chair he'd sat her in when they'd come inside the hospital. His concern for her was evident in his face. His blue eyes were serious and anxiety was practically rolling off him in waves.

"No, I'm fine," Laura Xander protested, even though she knew she wasn't. When was she going to get over this? When was this paralyzing fear of being out in public going to go away? It had been fifteen years since her assault, fourteen since she locked herself away in her apartment, and four since Jack had come back into her life.

That should be enough.

She should be over it by now.

Well, that wasn't quite true. Laura knew she could never get over what she'd been through, but surely things should have improved to the point where she could support her sister-in-law at the hospital without winding up an emotional wreck.

Sometimes she got so frustrated with herself that her recovery had been so slow. Everyone had been extremely patient with her. Jack, his entire family, her family. Their patience was part of the problem. They treated her with kid gloves. Always so careful never to push her too far or upset her too much. They didn't treat her like she was a real person. They treated her like she was a victim. And that made her feel like a victim.

"Baby, you're not fine." Jack rested his forearms on her thighs and leaned in close to kiss her forehead.

Laura just looked at him. She knew helplessness was shining from her eyes and she so hated to feel helpless.

Jack saw the helplessness there and immediately picked her up. "I'm taking you home," he announced.

For a moment, Laura just sank down into her husband's arms, wanting desperately to be back in their home, with their eighteen-month-old son, Zach. But then she roused herself. Hiding was not the answer. She knew that.

"Put me down, Jack." She pushed at him.

Reluctantly, he let her feet slide down to the ground but kept an arm around her waist. "You don't have anything to prove, Laura," he told her seriously.

Maybe. But she felt like she did. "Go and check on Sofia. I'll be fine; I just need to walk." Laura always felt better when she was moving.

Jack was unconvinced. "Laura," his voice held a hint of warning mixed with a heavy dose of concern.

"Jack!" she shot back. She hated when her husband got all bossy.

He held up his hands in surrender. "Okay, okay, I'll go check on Sofia, you walk, only don't go far and don't go outside on your own."

Laura rolled her eyes. Her husband was a protector, which sometimes thrust them into destructive cycle. The more Jack acted like her guard dog instead of her husband, the more helpless it made her feel. And the more helpless she felt, the more protective Jack got, and so on and so on in a never-ending circle.

She understood his protectiveness. They had been best friends their whole lives, dated in high school until he cheated on her, then when she was in college, she'd been abducted and held captive for four days. Jack, being who he was, blamed himself, as ridiculous as that is.

Especially for everything that had happened when they had been thrown back together four years ago. That had been as hard for him as it had been for her. And, in the end, it had cost him his partner and friend, Detective Rose Lace.

Laura still blamed herself for the death of Jack's partner.

However, guilt wasn't all she felt.

In the days and weeks following the carnage, she had nearly driven herself crazy trying to figure out the whys. Why had he hated her so much that he would go to such trouble to make her suffer?

She had become obsessed.

She had needed to know why. She had needed answers, only there was no one to give them to her. He was dead.

Trying to figure it out had nearly consumed her. She had thought about it every waking second. She had even dreamed about it. She had to know. She had to have a reason. She had to understand.

Her obsession had worried Jack. He could sense her slipping away from him—locking herself away in her mind just like she'd locked herself away in her apartment. He'd put a stop to it, told her therapist, pushed her into talking with him about it. And eventually, she had begun to let it go. What ifs still haunted her, and she still wished she could get answers, but she had been able to move on.

Thinking about all this right now, though, wasn't the best idea. It was hard enough just making an unplanned excursion without dredging up the mess of emotions her abduction produced.

Maybe, Jack and Ryan had been right. Maybe, she shouldn't

have come. Maybe, when Jack came back, she should let him take her home. Or, if he was planning on coming back here, maybe he could drop her off at his parents' house; they were babysitting Zach and Ryan and Sofia's kids. Maybe she could just spend the night there.

She was getting a headache.

She needed to sit.

Laura hummed to herself, sometimes concentrating on singing her favorite songs helped to distract her. She was just turning to head back to the waiting area when she walked straight into someone.

"Oh, sorry," she apologized. "I wasn't looking where I was going."

"That's okay." A teenage girl smiled at her. "Neither was I."

Laura immediately sensed that something was off with this girl. She had been a psych major in college and completed her degree online after her assault—it always embarrassed her that she was a trained psychologist and couldn't cure her own phobia. During her ten-year, self-imposed lockdown, she had worked as a phone counselor for teenagers in trouble. Now she worked as a counselor at the women's and children's center that Sofia had started.

"Are you okay?" The teenager was peering at her from concerned blue eyes.

"Yes." Laura tried to gather herself, aware of the fact that she was probably as pale as a ghost, and that she was shaky and most likely breathing too quickly.

"Are you sure?" The girl's gaze dipped to Laura's stomach. "Is there something wrong with your baby?"

Smiling to reassure the girl, she rested a hand on her swollen stomach. "No, the baby's fine. My sister-in-law is sick; that's why we're here. I'm Laura." She held out a hand.

The girl shook the offered hand. "I'm Alice."

"Are you sick, Alice?" Laura asked, wondering if that was why she was getting the feeling something wrong. "Is that why you're here?"

"Uh, no, I'm okay, it's my sister." The girl broke eye contact as she said that.

Laura's unease grew; her instincts were usually pretty spot on. She went with direct. "Is everything okay, Alice? Do you need help?"

Surprise and shock flitted through the teenager's eyes. "Why would you think I need help?"

She shrugged. "Just a feeling. I'm not usually wrong," she said gently.

Again, the girl diverted her gaze. "How far along are you?" she asked instead.

"Thirty-five weeks," Laura replied.

"Is this your first baby?"

"No, I have an eighteen-month-old son named Zach."

"Are you having a boy or a girl?"

"We don't know yet. My husband and I wanted to wait and be surprised." They'd done the same thing last time, and it made the birth all the more special waiting to find out if they were going to have a son or daughter.

"That's nice. I have a baby sister. Arianna is two months old; she just started to sleep through the night." Alice still wouldn't look her in the eye.

"It's a relief once they start to do that. Soon we're going to be back to those sleepless nights. Zach was pretty good, though. He slept well; I hope the new baby will, too." She'd played along with Alice's distractions for long enough. It was time to push the girl again. "Alice, what's wrong? You can trust me. I work with kids like you who need help. What's going on?"

Alice hesitated, her eyes slowly moving to meet Laura's. Her bottom lip trembled, and she opened her mouth to speak when a voice boomed behind them.

"There you are. I was worried, I couldn't find you anywhere."

Jack appeared at her side.

"I have to go." Alice was instantly nervous.

"Alice, wait," Laura called after the teenager. "If you change your mind, I'll be here, probably for a few hours at least."

The girl didn't stop, and Laura debated going after her, but Jack's hand on her arm stopped her.

"What was all that about?"

* * * * *

9:23 P.M.

"Why are you staring at me?" Annabelle Englewood asked her boyfriend. He'd been watching her since she arrived at the house they used to share fifteen minutes ago.

Used to share because she had moved out two weeks ago.

Why? Well, she wasn't entirely sure.

But she thought it was something she had to do.

For herself.

And Annabelle rarely did things for herself.

Xavier disagreed. Well, he didn't disagree that she rarely did things for herself, but he disagreed that this was something she had to do. He thought it was just another excuse.

Another excuse as to why she kept pushing him away.

"I'm watching you because I'm trying to figure out what you hope to achieve by this little stunt," Xavier replied calmly.

"I don't do stunts," she protested, offended.

"Okay, that's true," Xavier conceded, "but I don't buy that you really want to move out."

"Well, I am moving out," Annabelle replied.

"I can see that." Xavier gave her a small frown. "But that's not what I said. What I said was I don't think you really *want* to move out."

"I told you," she said quietly. She didn't want an argument; she hated arguments. They stressed her. "I have to do this."

"So you've said. Several times."

"I've never been on my own before. I lived with my parents until they were killed, and then I moved in with you. I feel like it's important that I know I can survive on my own."

In truth, Annabelle wasn't entirely sure that she wasn't making the biggest mistake of her life. She knew she was lucky to have Xavier. Not only was he good looking, but he was also sweet and smart and funny. He was so much more than she deserved.

And she guessed that was half the problem.

She didn't feel like she deserved Xavier.

Annabelle knew she wasn't pretty, despite Xavier's assurances that he thought she was the most beautiful woman he'd ever seen. He was biased. She was plain looking; there was nothing extraordinary in her face, and her hair was a common brown. Add to that her eyes were odd, such a pale blue that they appeared white, and she knew she was nothing much to look at.

It wasn't just in the looks department that Annabelle felt inadequate. She couldn't connect with people the way everyone else could. It wasn't that she had some kind of problem or condition that prevented her from interacting. Before her family was murdered, she'd worked as a preschool teacher. She had been part of a team and worked well with her colleagues, and she'd been good with both the children and their parents. But that was different. That was work. She hadn't been required to let anyone get close to her.

That was where she had her problems.

When she and Xavier had first gotten together, he had tried to involve her in every aspect of his life, including his circle of friends. It hadn't worked, though. She hadn't felt comfortable with them and had always kept her distance.

That distance had grown to include Xavier himself.

Ever since she had shot and killed Ricky Preston—the man who had destroyed her life—in self-defense, she had felt herself disconnecting. Annabelle had thought that when Ricky Preston was finally dead, everything would be better. That she would be able to finally move on.

"You don't really want to be on your own," Xavier said softly, all traces of irritation gone from his voice. Now he just sounded sad. "I don't want you to be on your own. I love you. I want you to stay."

Her internal struggle intensified.

Was she doing the right thing?

Did she even really know why it seemed so important that she leave Xavier's house? Even though she'd lived here for five years, she still thought of it as Xavier's house. When she'd first moved in, she hadn't ever thought she'd want to leave. So why did she feel like she had to now?

Was it just to test Xavier?

For some reason she couldn't quite articulate, even to herself, she kept needing him to prove that he wasn't going to leave her.

Annabelle was afraid that if she kept doing it, if she kept seeing how far she could push him before he gave up on her, then she was going to lose him.

But she didn't know how to stop doing it because she didn't know why she was doing it.

Maybe it was because he had walked out on her once with disastrous—almost deadly—consequences. She never spoke about that with Xavier because she knew he blamed himself for almost getting her killed.

Still, she couldn't shake the fear that one day he'd leave her forever.

And she didn't want him to. She loved Xavier. Really loved him. Before they'd met, she hadn't even believed that she would ever find anyone to love.

But she had.

And now she seemed intent on ruining it.

She was an idiot.

Tentatively, Xavier reached out to her, taking the stack of books from her hands and putting them down on a table. "Belle, stay, please."

"I ... I ..." she stammered. Why couldn't she just say okay? This was what she wanted, wasn't it? She wanted him to beg her not to leave. She needed him to fight for her.

Tilting her face up, he kissed her, slowly and deeply, and Annabelle felt herself melting into his arms. Xavier's arms were the one place she felt completely safe and at ease, despite the distance between them lately.

"Stay," he whispered as he broke the kiss.

Say it, she ordered herself. *Say yes. Stay. It's what you really want.* But instead, what came out was, "I don't know."

Sighing, Xavier released her and picked up the books he'd set on the table and all but threw them in the box at their feet. Then he went to the bookcase and began gathering the rest of her books, adding them to the box.

Annabelle just stood and watched him.

What was wrong with her?

How could she be so stupid?

She loved Xavier. She wanted to spend the rest of her life with him. All she had to do was lay her paranoia about him leaving her down and walk into his arms, tell him what was going on inside her head and stay here with him.

Instead, she just stood there and did nothing. She was such a coward. She always had been, and nothing had changed. Even killing her tormentor hadn't helped do away with her fears.

Picking up the box of books, Xavier headed for the door, pausing when he got there. "I hope you know what you're doing, Annabelle."

Watching him leave, Annabelle hoped so, too.

But she feared she was making the biggest mistake of her life.

* * * * *

9:32 P.M.

"What was all that about?" Jack repeated, turning Laura around to face him.

"Nothing," she replied distractedly.

Like he believed that. She was looking even worse than when he'd left her a few minutes ago to check on Sofia. He should have put his foot down, insisted that she stay at Ryan's house while they brought Sofia to the hospital. Or insisted that he drive her straight home.

No matter what Laura said, she was *not* ready for this yet.

She could cope with going out these days, which was a huge improvement from when he'd reconnected with her four years ago. But the places she was comfortable going to were limited. She went to work, she went to his parents' house, and her parents' house—if he pushed her. She could go to both of his brothers' houses and her friend Paige's. At a crunch, if she had time to prepare herself, she could make a trip to the supermarket, but she usually timed it for when it was the least busy.

But this—an unplanned trip to a busy hospital—was pretty much more than she could bear.

Jack knew it frustrated Laura that she wasn't all better by now. However, given the horrific nature of what she'd suffered, it was no wonder that she still struggled. No one could go through what she had and come out of it unscathed.

"Did that girl hurt you? Upset you?" he pushed, determined to find out what was going on. And if he found out that girl had done anything to distress Laura, then he would make sure he tracked her down and gave her a talking to, her parents as well. He was extremely protective of his wife.

Shaking her head, Laura pressed one hand to her head, the other to her stomach.

He narrowed his eyes. "Is something wrong with the baby?"

"What?" Laura lifted confused violet eyes to meet his, then followed his gaze to the hand she had on her pregnant belly. "Oh, no," she assured him, "nothing is wrong with the baby. Alice and I were just talking about babies."

"Alice was that girl?"

Laura nodded and closed her eyes, massaging her temple.

"You have a headache," he said grimly. Laura always got headaches when she was stressed. "Come and sit."

His wife made no protest when he took her arm and guided her back to the waiting area, pushing her gently down into a chair. Jack sat beside her and lifted her wrist.

She frowned at him. "Don't do that here," she admonished, snatching her hand back. "They'll think I'm sick."

He shrugged unapologetically. "That girl upset you somehow, and you were already pretty upset."

Laura rested her head on his shoulder. "She really didn't upset me. I was pacing—distracted—and I walked right into her, and I just got this ..." She paused as she searched for the right word. "... this feeling that something was wrong with her."

Laura wasn't usually wrong when she sensed something was up with someone. "Did you ask her about it?"

"Yeah, I think she was going to tell me when you showed up and scared her off."

"Sorry."

"Not your fault." Laura took his hand and entwined their fingers and almost infinitesimally moved closer. He knew her tells. When she was feeling overwhelmed, she sought physical contact with him to reassure herself. If they'd been at home, she would have climbed into his lap. She was reaching her limit.

"Want me to go and look for her?" Jack asked, hoping to keep her distracted and focused on the teenager and not on herself.

"No. Hopefully, she'll come and find me when she's ready. How's Sofia?"

"She's doing okay. They've started an IV, so hopefully, once she's rehydrated, she'll start to feel better." Wrapping an arm around his wife's shoulders, he stroked her long, straight, black hair. "Angel, Sofia won't mind that you went home. We're all well aware of your condition, and she's your friend. She loves you; she wouldn't want you to stay and torture yourself. Let me take you home."

She was debating—he could see it in her eyes. "No, Jack. I'm not going home."

"Laura ..." He was immediately exasperated. "Why are you being stubborn about this?"

Wearily, she lifted her head off his shoulder. "Don't, please. I don't want to fight with you."

Reluctantly, he relented, only because he knew what she really meant was she couldn't *handle* a fight with him right now. Hooking an arm under her knees, he pulled her sideways onto his lap, settling her against his chest.

"Jack, not here," she protested, but curled herself closer.

"Yes, here." He pressed her head down to lay on his shoulder. "Close your eyes and try to get some rest," he ordered sternly. If he couldn't convince her to let him take her home, he could at least make sure she slept.

Jack was extremely diligent in making sure Laura got enough sleep. When she didn't—when she got overtired—she had nightmares.

Nightmares had haunted her sleep every night for at least the first six months after he moved in with her. The bad dreams had nearly destroyed both of them. Lack of sleep had left them walking around in a fog. Seeing Laura suffering, forced to relive the horror she'd survived in her dreams each night, had nearly torn him apart. Jack had hoped his presence in her bed would help to ease the nightmares that had plagued her since the original attack, but it hadn't. His presence did make her feel safer, though; she kept assuring him.

After six months of watching Laura suffer each night, he had decided that neither of them could go on this way. So, he had spoken with her therapist and asked about putting her on sleeping pills, so she could, at least, start sleeping through the night. That seemed to help. They knocked Laura out enough that she no longer woke up screaming. And they had the added benefit that she slept deeply enough that, even if she dreamt, she didn't remember them when she awoke.

Laura had hated how the pills made her feel, leaving her groggy for much of the day, and after a few months, she'd weaned herself off them. Thankfully, by then, things seemed to have improved. She had been making progress with her therapist. She was more comfortable with him and their relationship, and so long as she stuck with her routine, she slept normally most nights. She still had the occasional nightmare, but Jack hoped as more time passed, the nightmares would continue to fade until they disappeared altogether.

"It's not even ten." She protested the idea of sleep. "And I'm not tired, and I can't sleep in front of all these—"

"Laura," he cut her off, "close your eyes and get some rest. If you don't, I'm going to pick you up and find a doctor and get them to give you something to make you sleep," he threatened. Laura didn't like him bossing her around, but this time he was putting his foot down.

"Okay …" Laura sank down against him. Her acceptance of his orders did not make Jack feel any better. "I have to get better, Jack," Laura whispered. "We're about to have two kids, and Zach will be in school in just a few years. I need to get better. Our kids deserve better; you deserve better."

Jack could feel tears seeping from her eyes and soaking through his sweater. Her tears broke his heart. How could she not know how much he loved her? How could she worry about disappointing him? He tightened his grip on her. "Baby, I am the luckiest guy in the world to have you as my wife. And Zach is the luckiest little boy in the world to have you as his mommy. This baby will be, too. You have a medical condition. You don't have any control over your agoraphobia, but you're learning to manage it. Your condition doesn't make anyone love you any less, it doesn't make me love you any less, and it won't make our kids love you any less. Honey, how can you not know that? What can I say to you to make you believe it?"

Shrugging, she just snuggled closer, burrowing into him and burying her face in his neck. "Just hold me."

"Always, angel." He kissed the top of her head. "Always."

Within mere minutes, Jack could feel Laura relax against him as sleep took hold. As he held his sleeping wife, he wondered how it was possible to worry so much about one person. Would he ever be able to stop worrying about Laura? If he couldn't, would it end up coming between them?

"She asleep?" Ryan suddenly appeared beside them.

"Yeah," Jack replied quietly. "She insisted she wasn't tired, but as soon as I convinced her to close her eyes, she was out like a light. How's Sofia?"

"She's good. She's asleep, too. The doctors have hooked her up to an IV. Once she's rehydrated and gets some rest, she should feel a lot better. How's Laura doing?"

Jack could feel concern crease his face. "She thinks she has to get better because Zach and the baby and I deserve better. She thinks we're all going to love her less because she has agoraphobia." How could he combat something like that? It was so completely untrue and unfounded.

"That's ridiculous," Ryan frowned.

"Yeah, it is," he agreed grimly. "I just don't know how to convince her of that."

"Sofia's going to be fine. She'll probably be released some time tomorrow morning. You should take Laura home. Let her get some proper rest. Maybe if she wasn't always so tired, she'd feel a little better about things. She still having nightmares?"

"No—at least, not very often—but she still has insomnia. She only sleeps maybe five hours a night."

"Then take her home, put her to bed; really, we'll be fine."

There was nothing Jack would love better than to take his wife home and make her sleep, but he knew she wasn't going to be able to relax until she knew that Alice was safe. "No, Laura met some girl. A teenager. She thinks the girl's in trouble and that she might be able to get her to open up."

"Laura is really good at what she does."

"Yeah, she is," Jack agreed. "Sometimes I think her work is the only thing that keeps her sane. It's her salvation."

"No, Jack, *it's* not," Ryan told him. "*You* are her salvation. You *and* Zach."

"Thanks." Jack shot his brother a brittle smile, wishing he believed that. "But I don't feel like her savior. I know everyone thinks that I'm always so good at knowing what to say and do with victims who are suffering, but it's different with Laura. When she cries in my arms and tells me that she doubts that we could love her because of what she's been through and what it did to her, I feel so helpless. So inadequate."

"It *is* different with Laura," Ryan gently reminded him. "She's your wife, you love her. And you give her exactly what she needs—your love."

"I do love her so much," Jack whispered, pressing a kiss to his sleeping wife's forehead. He wished his love was enough to help Laura heal. And he knew in a way it did, but both he and Laura were going to have to accept that she might never completely recover from all she'd been through.

"And that's why she gets up every morning, because she knows how much you love her. I'm going to go back to sit with Sofia; let me know when that kid comes back and tells Laura all her problems."

"When the kid comes back, not if?"

He shrugged. "People trust Laura. They open up to her. The kid will be back."

* * * * *

9:41 P.M.

"Angela, I don't want to stay here anymore," five-year-old Abigail tugged at her big sister's hand.

"Alice said we had to," Angela reminded her. Although she was wondering whether this was a good idea. They couldn't really change anything. Could they?

"Angela," Abby whimpered.

Her sister was getting scared, and if she were honest, she was, too. They never went anywhere. Never. And being here in a hospital on their own was overwhelming. "It's okay, Abby." Angela patted her sister's head. "Everything will be okay. We just have to do what Alice said."

"I want to go home." Abby was near tears.

"Really?" Angela shot her an incredulous look. "You really want to go back home?"

Abby hesitated. "No. Home is scary. I want Ariyel." The little girl began to cry.

Angela wrapped an arm around her sister. "It's okay, Abby." But Angela knew it wasn't okay. Nothing about their lives was okay. She may be only nine, but she knew what went on in her house. She knew what their father did to Ariyel and to Alice. Just as she knew that in a few years he would do it to her, too. And then to Abby and Arianna.

He needed to be stopped.

But how could they do it? They were only kids.

They needed Ariyel, but she was sick. And even when she wasn't, he kept her so drugged up that she barely knew who she was and what was happening around her.

Alice, however, thought they had a chance at saving themselves. She thought she could do it, but Angela wasn't so sure.

Still, she wanted to believe it could be true.

"Can't we go and find Ariyel?" Abby begged.

"No," Angela responded, her voice firm. Alice had trusted her with Abby and Arianna; she needed to stay strong for them. "We need to stay here. So he can't find us."

Tears were trickling down Abby's pale cheeks. Her blue eyes were red rimmed, and her pigtails were coming undone because she kept fiddling with them. Angela wasn't sure how long she'd be able to keep her little sister under control. Abby was an emotional child. She cried easily, she got scared easily, she was very serious for a five-year-old, and usually only Ariyel could calm the little girl down once she got upset.

To make matters worse, baby Arianna began to fuss. Arianna was only two months old and Angela had never looked after her on her own before. She wasn't completely comfortable being in charge of the baby. She knew how to change a diaper, but she'd only ever done it with Ariyel supervising. She'd only ever fed the baby with Ariyel close by, too.

But now it was all up to her.

She had to do her part.

"Come on, Abby, let's sing some songs while I feed Arianna, and then we can play a game."

* * * * *

9:46 P.M.

If she hadn't had an IV in her arm, Sofia would have gotten out of bed and gone for a walk around the hospital. She wasn't going to sleep, so lying in bed seemed like a waste.

Sofia hated hospitals.

Hated them.

With a passion.

FIVE

Too many bad memories. She knew what it felt like to think that you were dying and those months that she'd spent in and out of hospitals had been the worst days of her life.

Now she just wanted to be home with her husband and her kids. Her five-year-old daughter, Sophie, and two-year-old son, Ned, were the lights of her life. Although Sofia was technically Sophie's niece, the little girl was in every other way her daughter, and she loved Sophie just as much as she loved her and Ryan's biological son.

One day she was going to have to explain their whole complicated family history to Sophie. She was not looking forward to that. But the girl deserved to know who her biological parents were, once she was old enough to understand. For now, though, Sophie was just a happy, well-adjusted five-year-old, who loved going to kindergarten, ballet class, and playing with her friends.

Groaning, she rubbed at her head. She was exhausted, as most mothers of small children were. Her days were busy. Between work and the kids and household chores, she rarely had a spare couple of minutes to take care of herself, but she wouldn't have it any other way. She was living her dreams.

At least Ryan was getting some rest.

He was asleep in a chair beside her bed. His head was resting against the back of the seat, tilted at an angle that looked like it was going to give him a stiff neck if he stayed like that too long. One of his hands held hers, but his grip was limp.

She was glad he was sleeping.

Her husband was a worrier by nature.

And unfortunately, their lives and their friends' lives had been filled with plenty of things to worry about. She wanted to get out of here and back home as quickly as possible, because the longer she was here, the more her husband would worry.

With all the upheaval in her life in the five years since they had met, he had been her rock. He was always there for her, whatever she needed. He was the husband she had always dreamed of and the father to their children that she always wished she would have.

She was so lucky to have him.

Sofia looked up as the door to her room opened and a doctor bustled inside. She remembered the reddish-blond hair and dark blue eyes of Dr. Daniels; he'd treated her before. He'd been diligent, empathetic, and caring, and yet there had been something about him that had creeped her out a little.

"Good evening, Mrs. Xander." Dr. Daniels offered her a huge smile. Too big a smile, Sofia couldn't help but think.

She gestured at her sleeping husband. "Let's try to keep it down so we don't disturb him."

The doctor's smile deepened. "Sure. So, what brought you here tonight?" he asked as he picked up her wrist to check her pulse.

"She fainted," Ryan replied, lifting his head.

"Oh, did we wake you?" Although she wanted him to get some rest, Sofia was a little relieved that her husband was awake, and she didn't have to deal with the creepy doctor on her own.

"It's fine, I had a good power nap." Ryan took her other hand then focused back on the doctor. "She's had the flu, and she's been overdoing it, then tonight she just collapsed."

"Any chance you could be pregnant?" Dr. Daniels asked.

"No way." Sofia shook her head; she and Ryan weren't planning on having any more kids. Sophie and Ned were enough, so she was on the pill.

"As in it's physically impossible or because you use contraceptives?" the doctor asked.

It wasn't physically impossible, and she realized no contraceptive was infallible, so she supposed there *could* be a chance she was pregnant.

Dr. Daniels obviously concluded that from her expression. "We'll run a pregnancy test just to be sure. Other than the flu symptoms, have you noticed anything else off the last few weeks?"

"I don't think so, just sore throat, muscle aches, fever, cough, tiredness, and some vomiting and nausea," Sofia replied.

"All right, well it looks like you just got dehydrated; it can happen when you're vomiting and not replacing the liquids lost. You seem to be responding well to treatment, so providing you're stable in the morning, you can go home," Dr. Daniels told her.

"That's what the nurse said when I asked her." Ryan nodded.

Dr. Daniels didn't look pleased that Ryan had been talking to the nurses, but Ryan didn't seem to notice.

"When you go back home, you need to make sure you keep up with the fluids. You also need to make sure that you get plenty of rest. I know you have a little one at home, but maybe she can stay with relatives for a few days until you get your strength back."

"You remember that I have a daughter?" The knowledge that he'd remembered that from five years ago made her uncomfortable. He would have seen thousands of patients since then. Why had she stuck in his head?

The doctor shrugged disinterestedly. "Given who your family was and what happened to you, you were big news when you came through here. Well, I have other patients to check on, so I'll leave you to get some rest. I won't be on shift tomorrow morning. I finish in a couple of hours, but another doctor will discharge you, assuming your vitals are all good."

Watching him bustle out the door, Sofia wondered whether maybe she had misread the man.

Maybe he wasn't all that interested in her.

Maybe he wasn't really paying any more attention to her than he was any of his other patients.

Maybe he was just one of those people who seemed a little too intense.

"What's wrong?" Ryan was watching her closely.

"It's nothing." She didn't want to give Ryan another thing to worry about.

He gave her a half smile. "Do you think I believe that?"

She returned his smile with a half-smile of her own. "It's just Dr. Daniels, I don't know, there's just something about him that—"

"Creeps you out," Ryan finished for her.

She nodded. "I don't know why. It's not like he's done anything specific. It's just I don't like him for some reason."

"You should trust your instincts," Ryan told her. "You do have a stalker; it could be him."

"We didn't meet Dr. Daniels until I got stabbed, but I had a stalker long before that—years before," she reminded him. "I'm just tired and probably making way too much of it."

"Are you sure?"

"I'm sure," Sofia stated firmly.

* * * * *

9:56 P.M.

She was doing the right thing, wasn't she?

Alice really hoped that she was.

Even if she wasn't, it wasn't like she had many other options.

Or *any* other options.

This was it. Her one chance to save them all.

But she was scared. If she messed this up, she would probably never get another opportunity. They would all be trapped, stuck in that house—with that man—forever.

That was completely unacceptable.

Now was not the time to be scared. She had to suck it up and do what Ariyel would have done.

The others were counting on her. Alice was worried that Ariyel couldn't last much longer; the drugs were starting to make her sick. And the little girls were just that—little girls. They deserved a normal life. They all did.

If this was her one shot at freedom, then she had to make it

30

count.

Already she had set things in motion. Alice had hidden away the little girls where, hopefully, no one would find them. At least for a few hours. She'd lucked out that it had been nighttime when they'd brought Ariyel to the hospital. Things were quieter, so the chances of Angela, Abby, and Arianna being found immediately were slim. But come tomorrow morning, someone was bound to stumble upon them.

So she didn't have a second to waste.

With the little girls safe for the moment, it was time to move forward. And step two was to find someone to tell.

Initially, Alice had intended to talk to a doctor. You could trust doctors, right? So that had seemed like the perfect person to confess what had happened to her and her sisters.

But then she'd met that woman.

Laura.

She had just hidden the little girls away and was heading back down to the emergency room when they had literally walked into each other.

Laura was beautiful, and she reminded Alice of her mother. Laura's features were a little finer, and her eyes were an unusual violet color rather than blue like Alice's and her family's. But it wasn't the physical similarities that had Alice feeling like she could trust this woman. It was something else. Only she wasn't sure exactly what. She just felt like Laura would understand.

There was something in Laura's eyes. Something haunted. Laura had been through something terrible.

Instinctively, Alice knew that she could open up to her. That she could confess everything. She had been about to tell it all when that tall, blond guy had shown up. Scared, she had run. Worried that it was all pointless. That even if she told, no one could really help her.

No.

She couldn't think like that.

She couldn't get discouraged.

She was sure Laura could help her. The woman had said that she worked with kids who needed help. And she had known something was wrong even though Alice had never said a word.

Laura was the answer to her prayers.

She would tell her everything and trust that Laura could help her find a way to fix things.

What did she have to lose?

Things couldn't possibly get any worse.

They'd already pretty much hit rock bottom, so the only way from here was up.

This had to be the right thing to do. It had to work. Lives were at stake.

That day was a little over five years ago, but it was still as fresh in her memory as though it were yesterday.

Maegan, for she still thought of herself by her real name and not as Alice—the name Malachi had given her—had not been outside that house in all those years. Occasionally, Malachi would allow them a few minutes to play in the gardens, but only ever closely supervised, and always while he had his gun with him.

They hadn't gone to school. Malachi had taught them himself, and Maegan had been surprised to find that she actually missed school. She had missed her friends and her teachers. She had missed being a normal little girl.

She missed her parents, too—more than anything. And even her little brother.

She had thought that it was over. That she would never ever see them again. But now she had a chance. If she got this right, she'd be able to go home.

Home.

The word held a special meaning to her now that it never had before she'd been kidnapped. Back then, she'd taken it for granted. She would *never* do that again.

Glancing carefully up the corridor, she spotted Malachi deep in conversation with a doctor. She tiptoed cautiously toward Eliza's room. She only ever called her Ariyel when Malachi was around. When he wasn't, the girls always called each other by their real names.

Inside the room, Eliza was asleep in the bed. A tube looped across her pale face, delivering oxygen to her lungs. An IV hung beside her bed, the liquid inside dripping into Eliza through a tube in the back of her hand. A clip on her finger was attached to a machine that beeped and showed a range of numbers, but Maegan wasn't sure what all of that meant.

Crossing to the bed, Maegan gently took her sister's hand. For even though they weren't blood related, Maegan considered Eliza, Bethany, Hayley, and Arianna her sisters.

If Eliza hadn't gotten so sick, they wouldn't have had this opportunity. Her sister had been sick for days, but Malachi had done his best to treat her at home. Only when they'd checked on her this evening, they'd been unable to wake her. So Malachi had reluctantly bundled them all into the car and rushed Eliza to the hospital.

As thrilled as Maegan was to have this chance to escape and go home, she was extremely worried about Eliza. She loved her big sister so much. If it wasn't for Eliza, none of them would have survived the last five years.

"Eliza?" Maegan leaned close and whispered in her sister's ear.

Eliza didn't respond.

"Can you hear me?"

Again, there was no response.

Giving her shoulder a gentle shake, Maegan wasn't sure what was wrong with her, but she didn't want to do anything to make Eliza worse.

"Come on, Eliza, wake up, please," she half begged. This would be so much easier if her sister were there to help her. After all, this was really Eliza's plan. She'd come up with it years ago, only they'd never been able to make it work. "Eliza," she repeated desperately.

Just how sick was her sister?

Was she going to die?

What if this worked? What if Laura was able to help her, and she and her sisters were rescued, but Eliza didn't make it?

Would it all be worth it?

Would she trade freedom for her sister's life?

She was starting to panic. Her sister's pale face and limp hand, being around so many strangers after spending so long trapped in that house. It was a lot to deal with.

Doubts were starting to fill her mind.

She was crazy to think she could make this work.

Who was going to believe her?

She and her sisters all looked just like Malachi, and they all looked like each other. And Malachi was charming and a great talker. Even if Maegan was able to convince Laura that they were all kidnap victims, listening to Malachi spin things would likely convince her that Maegan was the crazy one.

Even though she and Eliza knew who they really were, Bethany had only been four when Malachi had kidnapped them. She only had a few hazy memories of her real identity and home and life before Malachi. And Hayley had only been a baby then. None of them even knew her full name, nor did they know Bethany's.

What if that meant that the police couldn't send them home?

What if they couldn't figure out the girls' real identities before Eliza was released and Malachi took them back home?

Then the little girls would go back to life with Malachi and without her and Eliza there to protect them.

That, she couldn't risk.

Maybe she should just give up.

Accept that she was never going to escape from Malachi's clutches. That she was destined to spend her life with her sisters in that house.

Even if it worked; even if the police were able to find out who Hayley and Bethany really were through DNA tests or something, and they all went home—to their real homes—that didn't help Arianna. The two-month-old baby really was Malachi's daughter.

But Malachi would be in jail, right?

Her and Eliza's statements and the DNA tests on the little girls would surely be enough to convict him and send him to jail. And once he was in jail, he could never hurt them again.

But what if it didn't work out that way?

What if Malachi was able to convince everyone that she was crazy? That the girls were all his and that she was just sick and delusional. Eliza was unconscious, so she couldn't back Maegan up. And Bethany and Hayley didn't remember their abductions. Malachi could easily whisk the children back to the house before the police could prove that he had kidnapped them all.

It was too big a risk.

She should just go and get the others and wait for Malachi to take them home.

Only that wasn't what Eliza would do.

Eliza would go for it.

She was a risk taker.

Maegan could feel tears pricking her eyes. She wanted to do the right thing, but she wasn't sure what it was.

Then she felt Eliza squeeze her hand. Startled, she glanced at her sister's face, but her eyes were still closed. Maybe she had imagined it. But then she felt it again.

She took a deep breath to calm her jangled nerves.

She could do this.

Eliza and the others were counting on her.

It was Malachi's fault that Eliza was here. He had made her sick with all those drugs he was always feeding her. Even if she survived this time, next time she might not. And how long before he started having to drug the rest of them to control them?

She was doing this.

She just had to trust that Bethany would do as she said and keep herself and the little girls hidden until they got help.

And she had to trust that her instincts were correct and that Laura really would help them.

"I'm going to end this, Eliza," she whispered. "I promise."

FIVE YEARS AGO

3:21 P.M.

They had been driving for hours.

Glancing down at her wrist to see the time, Eliza remembered that she never wore a watch. How could she have forgotten that? Right, because her head still felt like it was stuck on a carousel, spinning around and around and around with no end in sight.

Sighing to herself, she started to look for her phone, before remembering that she had dropped it and her bag on the ground when Malachi had drugged her. Sighing to herself again, she felt like her brain had turned to mush. It was useless.

Still, it had to be a good thing that her bag had been left behind. It meant she couldn't call for help, but Malachi wasn't likely to allow her to do that anyway. So the bag left by itself at the side of the road was probably the better option. Someone would find it. They had to. And once her family realized she was missing, and her things were found abandoned, surely the police would start looking for her.

They'd look for her, and they'd find her.

Something was wrong with her. She hadn't cried in hours; she wasn't scared anymore. Now she just felt numb. Maybe she'd moved to a place beyond fear. A place where nothing existed but making sure she continued to exist. Eliza knew she had to be ready to do whatever it took to escape.

A part of her brain recognized that she was probably in shock. And that was the reason why she felt completely empty. Another part of her brain knew that she didn't have time for shock. She had to focus. Had to keep a clear head. She was tough and strong,

37

and she could do this. She *had* to do this.

Glancing out the window, Eliza had no idea where she was. And no way of getting out of the car. Even if she could get herself out of the car, she couldn't leave those children behind. Eliza was almost positive that Malachi had kidnapped Bethany and Hayley, too, and as much as she wanted to get home to her family, she wouldn't leave without the little girls.

Suddenly, Malachi turned the car off the road into a gas station. She shook herself to try and wake up her brain; this could be her only chance at escape.

She got herself ready to scramble into the front seat and out of the car the second Malachi had his back turned. Once she was out of the car, she could scream for help. The gas station was busy, not *very* busy but she counted four other cars. People would come. They would call the police. And she and the children would be safe.

Eliza struggled to keep her face neutral. She could feel her heart thumping as Malachi turned off the engine and opened the door, climbing slowly out of the car.

Pausing before he closed the door, he turned to her with a creepy smile on his face. "Don't even think about going anywhere. You do anything, and I shoot every single person in this gas station." He carefully revealed his gun tucked inside his waistband.

Deflated, Eliza slumped back against the seat. There was no way she could risk the lives of every innocent person that was unfortunate enough to be buying gas when Malachi pulled in.

But she couldn't give up.

There had to be a way to take advantage of this opportunity. Because who knew when another one would present itself? However, try as she might, Eliza couldn't think of a way to get herself and the children help without alerting Malachi. And if he thought she was making a play for freedom, he would start shooting. She didn't doubt that one iota.

Staring aimlessly out of the window, she watched the people happily going about their lives with no idea that a monster was standing in their midst.

She watched as a dad staggered back to a car full of boys, his arms full of snacks. She saw an elderly couple standing together as they filled their car. She watched as a young girl of about ten stood beside the car next to Malachi's, tapping her foot impatiently as she watched her mother join the long line of people waiting to pay.

Malachi finished filling the car, and she watched him as he started toward the line. She wondered absently whether she had time to get both children out of the car and all of them hidden before Malachi noticed. But she saw him turn and wave to her, his hand tapping his waist where she knew the gun was hidden. Even if she did manage to get the three of them out and someplace safe, he would only kill everyone here.

Feeling helpless, Eliza clenched her hands together so tightly her knuckles turned white. She needed options. Something. Anything. She needed to feel like there was a way out. And right now, she didn't. Helplessness was slowly inching its way to fear. She couldn't let that happen. If she allowed herself to feel the terror that swam inside her, she wouldn't be able to function.

Just as Malachi was about to join the line, he turned and started walking quickly back toward the car. Surprised, Eliza wondered what had happened.

It soon became glaringly apparent.

On the way back to the car, Malachi snapped an arm around the little girl who had been impatiently waiting for her mother. Lifting the child off the ground, he spirited her toward his car.

Startled, the little girl didn't offer a protest.

Eliza looked around for the girl's mother, but the woman had gone to join the line and hadn't noticed that Malachi had snatched her child.

Just as Malachi was about to shove the stunned girl into his car, she let out a petrified shriek.

Everyone in the gas station turned to look at them.

Unflinchingly, Malachi threw the child through the driver's side door and across to the passenger seat. Then he jumped in and sped off, tires screeching.

As they hurtled out of the gas station, Eliza could see the girl's mother running after them. Even from inside the car, she could hear the woman's desperate screams.

The little girl began to cry.

Bethany began to cry.

Baby Hayley began to cry.

Malachi began to laugh.

Eliza rested her head against the window and let the tears she had desperately been holding back flood down her cheeks.

* * * * *

6:11 P.M.

She was scared.

She wanted her mother.

She wanted to go home.

Why had that man grabbed her?

Maegan knew she'd messed up by not screaming right away. Only she had been so surprised. She'd just been standing there waiting for her mom to finish filling up the car so they could go to Tiffany's sleepover. She'd been frustrated that it was taking so long. She was annoyed with her mother for not going to the gas station before she picked her up from school.

That could be the last time she'd ever see her mom.

And Maegan had been sulking and pouting like a spoiled little brat.

When that man had grabbed her, she'd been so shocked that she hadn't done anything. She'd just let him take her.

Her common sense had returned when she'd realized he intended to throw her into a car. So, she had screamed—as loud as she could. Maegan had hoped that someone would come running to rescue her. But they hadn't. The man had thrown her into his car and sped out of the parking lot before anyone could do anything to help her.

And now she was stuck in his car.

She wasn't alone.

There were two little kids in the back seat and a teenager, maybe five or six years older than herself.

What was creepy was that everyone in the car looked like her.

The man who had grabbed her and the girls in the back seat all had black hair and blue eyes. She wasn't sure about the baby's eye color, but the rest of them could have been her sisters and the man her father.

An uneasy feeling started in Maegan's stomach.

What was the main reason people kidnapped kids?

It was custody cases. She was sure it was, because she remembered her parents talking about it when her mother's sister split with her husband. Her uncle had been an alcoholic and had lost custody of his three kids, and Maegan remembered her parents discussing the possibility of him doing something stupid and grabbing her cousins and leaving the country.

But that wasn't the case here. Her parents were still married. So, what was the next most common reason? She wasn't sure. She didn't like to watch the news; it scared her, and she stayed away from any websites that mentioned anything scary. Whatever the reason was, it couldn't be good.

Before Maegan had time to ponder this more, the man suddenly pulled the car into a driveway. They had been driving for hours. The clock in the car now read six thirty. That meant it had been three hours since she'd been taken.

An electric gate opened, and the man drove through it. Before them was a huge, three-story, brown brick house. There were bars on all the windows, and the property looked to be fully enclosed with a tall, wire-topped, brick fence. It was an imposing building, and Maegan couldn't help but shiver when she looked at it.

Pulling the car into a garage, the man turned to all of them with a creepy smile. "We didn't get introduced earlier. I'm Malachi." He held out his hand for her to shake.

Maegan stared at his hand and made no move to touch it. She didn't want to touch this man. She didn't want to be anywhere near him. She wanted to be safe and sound in her own home.

He chuckled. "That's okay, Alice, we have plenty of time to get to know each other."

"My ... my name's not Alice." Maegan frowned in confusion. Maybe this man thought she was someone else and that was why he had grabbed her. Maybe once he realized she wasn't Alice, he would just let her go home.

"Of course, it is." Malachi gave her a reproachful frown. "Do you think I don't know my own daughter's name?"

"I'm not your daughter," Maegan protested. "My name is Maegan Masters. My parents are John and Susan Masters. I don't even know you."

"Any more talk like that, young lady, and I'll send you straight to your room without dinner," Malachi rebuked her.

Maegan wanted to protest again. To insist that she wasn't this man's daughter, but the look in his eyes stopped her. Was this man crazy? He must be if he thought she was his child.

"Come along, girls." Malachi opened his car door. Pausing before he climbed out, he pulled a gun from his waistband and held it up so they could see it. "Don't even think of trying anything stupid. Ariyel, would you please bring Abigail in with you?"

"My name's Eliza," the teenager in the back seat spoke. "And you said the baby's name was Hayley."

"I said no such thing." Malachi glared at her. "Now get the baby. Abigail," he added pointedly. "Hurry up, Angela." He opened the door and unbuckled the little girl's seat belt.

Reluctantly, all of them climbed from the car. The teenager, Eliza, hesitated, her gaze darting to the garage door like she was figuring out if she could make it there before Malachi fired his gun.

Before she knew what was happening, Malachi had wrapped an arm around her neck and was pressing something cold to her forehead.

It was the gun.

He was holding a gun to her head.

"I'd think very carefully before you try anything stupid, Ariyel," he cautioned the teenager.

"My name is Eliza," she repeated, tears in her eyes.

Maegan could feel tears welling up in her own eyes. She was so scared. But she didn't want to cry. Not again. She'd been crying practically since Malachi threw her into his car. And she didn't usually cry. She wasn't a baby anymore; she was ten years old.

Defeated, Eliza hung her head and headed for the door that presumably led into the house. Malachi nodded approvingly and then took her hand and the hand of the child he'd called Angela, although Maegan knew that wasn't her real name, and herded them inside.

Malachi closed the door behind them. The thunk echoed ominously with an air of finality. And Maegan wondered if she would ever leave this house again.

NOVEMBER 3RD
10:00 P.M.

10:06 P.M.

Running.

Laura was always running.

Behind her someone was laughing.

Even though she didn't turn around, he was suddenly in front of her.

The man who had destroyed her life.

He didn't speak, but he didn't need to.

The gun he held in his hand spoke volumes.

As he raised the gun, she screamed.

Laura knew who the bullet was going to hit.

Jack's old partner—Rose Lace.

But when she turned her head, it wasn't Rose standing beside her. It was Jack.

The boom of the gun echoed inside her head.

Mixing with her scream.

The bullet plowed into Jack's chest.

A bright red spot exploded on his shirt, growing steadily bigger.

With a gasp, she sprang awake.

Disoriented, Laura couldn't remember where she was, but she felt Jack's arms around her. Slowly things trickled back into her sluggish mind. They were at the hospital because Sofia had fainted. Jack had insisted that she get some rest. Laura had thought she wasn't tired, but the second she had closed her eyes she must have fallen asleep. And then she'd dreamed.

She could tell Jack knew the second she woke up because his voice whispered, "It's all right, Laura, I'm here. You're okay."

Shuddering, Laura just rested against her husband, trying to convince herself that it had only been a dream. That Jack was fine. That he hadn't been shot. That he wasn't dead. That he wasn't going to die on her.

"You had a nightmare," Jack stated grimly.

Not lifting her head from his shoulder, Laura nodded.

"It's been a couple of months since you had one. This is too stressful for you. I'm going to take you home." She could feel his muscles tightening, ready to stand up with her.

Too weary to protest, Laura thought maybe he was right. Maybe this was just too stressful for her right now. Maybe she should go home. Go to bed. Maybe they'd let Zach stay the night with his grandparents and she'd take a sleeping pill. She didn't like the way they made her feel the next day, but they did stop her from dreaming.

"Laura?" a timid voice spoke beside them.

Rousing herself, Laura lifted her head and forced open her heavy eyes. The headache she'd had before hadn't diminished with sleep; in fact, it was worse. However, her ordeal had forced her to learn to compartmentalize pain, so now she pushed it away.

"Hi, Alice." She mustered a smile for the teenager.

The girl's blue eyes narrowed in concern. "Are you all right? Is this a bad time?"

"No, its fine." With near Herculean effort, Laura pushed herself up off Jack's chest so she was sitting upright. "Did you want to talk?"

Her gaze darted to Jack. "I don't want to interrupt."

"You're not," she assured the girl. "Jack, let me up."

Somewhat reluctantly, Jack stood with her in his arms then set her on her feet, keeping an arm around her until he was sure she was steady enough on her feet to remain standing. "I'm going to go and see about getting you something for that headache. Come get me if you need me," Jack ordered. Taking hold of her chin, he tilted her face up and kissed her. "Don't go far, and stay where there's plenty of people."

"I will," she promised. She was too tired to move more than a few feet away from where she was right now, anyway. "I'm glad you came back." She smiled at Alice.

"Was that your husband?"

"Yes, that was Jack."

"He's worried about you." A wistful look flashed across the girl's face.

"Yeah, he is," Laura nodded. If Jack had his way, she'd probably be in a hospital bed right now.

"He's protective of you, too," Alice added.

"Mmhmm," she agreed. Laura always felt safe with Jack; she knew he would do anything to protect her.

"Should you be sitting down? You don't look so great." Alice was looking at her with concern.

"Just a little headache." She smiled reassuringly. "Let's go sit over here where it's a little quieter." She led the girl to a corner of the waiting room. Laura couldn't quite keep a small sigh from escaping her lips as she sank back down into a chair.

"Are you sure everything is okay with your baby?" Alice sat beside her.

Ignoring the thumping in her head, she replied, "The baby is fine. Really, it's just a headache. I get them when I'm stressed."

Understanding flooded Alice's eyes. "What are you stressed about?"

Laura hated this part of building trust and rapport. She was going to have to tell Alice what had happened to her if she wanted the girl to tell her what had happened to her. "I suffer from agoraphobia," she confessed. "I don't like to be out in public, and being around lots of people makes me really uncomfortable."

Another flash of understanding. "How did you know?" Alice asked. "How did you know that something was wrong? How did you know that I needed help?"

"Just a feeling," Laura replied.

"But you knew as soon as you saw me. How?"

Stifling a sigh, she may as well just get it over with. "Ever since I was kidnapped, I can just sense when someone has been through something terrible."

Her eyes grew wide like huge, blue saucers. "You were kidnapped?"

"Fifteen years ago, while I was in college. I was taken to the woods and tortured for four days before some hikers accidentally stumbled upon me, and I was rescued." Laura spoke the words dully, like they were nothing to do with her, like what had happened was really someone else's story.

Alice was looking at her in horror. Laura really hated how it changed the way people saw her once they knew what had happened to her. "Is that why you're agoraphobic?"

"Yes. They held me in the woods, chased me when they weren't hurting me, then at night they kept me in a hole in the ground. After the court case, I moved away from my family and stayed in my apartment for ten years."

Hope lit Alice's face. "The people who hurt you are in jail?"

"Two of them. At the time, I didn't know there was a third man involved. I thought it was all just random. But it turned out someone else was involved, too, and he hurt a lot of people to get to me again. One good thing came out of it, though. Jack came back into my life, and he helped me get my life back."

"What happened to that man? He's not in jail? Did he get away?" Panic flared in the girl's eyes.

"He's dead. He came after me. He shot Jack's partner. He was going to rape me and then kill me. I killed him first," she explained emotionlessly.

"Your husband is a cop?"

"Yes." That answer seemed to please the girl. "Okay, I told you my horror story; it's your turn, Alice."

The teenager hesitated for barely a second. "My name isn't really Alice," she confessed.

"Did you make up the name so I wouldn't know who you really were if you decided not to talk to me?"

"No." The girl's voice dropped to a whisper. "*He* calls me Alice."

"Who's he?" Laura asked. She had a bad feeling about this. She was sensing that Alice, or whoever the girl really was, was in a lot more trouble than she'd first thought.

Alice's eyes darted nervously around the emergency room waiting area. She lifted a hand to her mouth and began to chew on one of her fingernails.

"What's your real name?" Laura asked instead, giving the girl some time to ready herself to tell her story. Laura knew the feeling.

"Maegan," the teenager replied softly.

"Maegan what?"

"I'd rather not say, in case ..." she trailed off.

"In case what, honey?" Laura prompted.

"In case you can't help me in time."

"What do you need me to do for you? I can't help you unless you tell me, Maegan."

Maegan's blue eyes filled with tears and words came tumbling out of her mouth as tears tumbled down her cheeks. "He kidnapped me. Five years ago. He grabbed me while I was at a gas station with my mom. Not just me. He kidnapped three other girls, too. He took us to this house. He kept us locked up there all this time. He's crazy. Completely insane. He thinks that we're his daughters. His real daughters died. In a fire, I think. So he took us to replace them. Only, I think he really believes that we're them," Maegan finished with a sob.

For a moment, Laura didn't know what to say. She put her arms around the teenager and held her while she cried. She hadn't been expecting to hear that Maegan had been abducted. She'd been expecting a story of abuse, maybe sexual or physical, perhaps problems with a boyfriend, or maybe a date rape.

"Maegan?" Gently, she sat the girl back up, keeping hold of her shoulders for added reassurance. "What's the name of the man who did this to you?"

She sniffled. "His name is Malachi. I don't know his last name."

"When we first met, you said you were here because your sister was sick; is that true?"

"Yes, we brought my older sister, Ariyel, here tonight."

"Is Ariyel her real name?"

She hesitated slightly. "No, it's not."

"What's her real name?" Laura prompted when the girl didn't offer up a response.

"I don't know if I should say."

"Why not? We can't find your families if we don't know your names." Laura was wondering why the girl was holding back. "Before, you said you didn't want to tell me your surname in case we couldn't help you in time. What is it you're afraid of?"

"Malachi is crazy, but smart. And charming, too, in a creepy sort of way." Maegan shuddered. "I'm scared that he's going to be able to convince the police that we really are his kids and that I'm just crazy. You need proof, proof that we're really missing kids, but I don't know the real names of my little sisters, and Ariyel is still unconscious, so she can't back me up. If you don't get proof of who we really are before Ariyel gets released, then he'll leave with us."

"But if we know who *you* are, then we'll have proof he kidnapped someone. Your sisters will be put into foster care until we figure out who they really are." Laura attempted to reason with the teenager.

Maegan didn't look convinced. "Malachi is so smart, I can't risk it. What if he panics and takes the little girls back to his house and leaves me and Ariyel behind? They're just little kids and he'd have them all to himself; they'd have no protection."

The girl wasn't thinking logically. She was only a teenager and scared. She'd been kidnapped and locked away from the world for five years. For the moment, Laura was just going to have to go with it. She'd convince her to give up her name and the other missing kids later. "How many little sisters do you have?"

"Three."

Laura was confused. "You said that Malachi kidnapped you and three other girls, but you also said that Ariyel was your older sister. That only leaves two other kids."

"Angela and Abby were the other two kids he kidnapped. Angela was only four and Abby was just a baby, that's why we only know their first names and not their surnames."

Laura didn't have to ask if Angela and Abby were the girls' actual names; she knew they weren't. They were the names Malachi had given them. "The baby, Arianna. You mentioned her earlier. Is she Ariyel's daughter? Ariyel and Malachi's?"

Maegan gave a minute nod.

"He forced himself on her?" Laura asked gently, wondering whether Malachi had done the same to Maegan.

Another tiny nod. "Ariyel was eighteen when Malachi kidnapped us. She fought him. All the time. It made him so mad. She was always trying to figure out a way for us to escape. She nearly managed it one time. But Malachi stopped us. I'd never seen him so angry. He took Ariyel away. He did something to her—brainwashed her or something. She was different after that. And he drugs her. Most of the time, she's so out of it, she really does think she's Ariyel."

"Do you know what's wrong with her?"

"No."

"What about your little sisters; where are they?" Laura scanned the waiting area, but she couldn't see a group of three little girls.

"I hid them," Maegan replied. "Malachi won't leave here without them."

"Where?"

"I can't tell you." Maegan's gaze met hers squarely, her blue eyes full of grim determination. "Not until I'm sure that you can help us."

"All right." Laura stood, ignoring the thumping in her head and the swirling of nausea in her stomach. "Let's go find my husband and tell him your story."

* * * * *

10:14 P.M.

Malachi stood and watched the sleeping woman.

He seethed with hatred toward her for all she'd put him through. And yet, at the same time, he loved her deeply.

She was his daughter, after all.

Ariyel was his oldest daughter, and the one who had always caused him the most trouble.

The others were fairly docile. Although, Ariyel's bad influence appeared to be beginning to rub off on Alice. He would have to put that girl in her place. Let her know that he was the one in charge.

He'd done it with Ariyel when her behavior had become unmanageable. And it had worked like a charm. After that, he'd never had another problem with her.

Until tonight.

Well, granted, it wasn't really her fault.

She couldn't help being sick.

But still, having to bring her to the hospital was an inconvenience he didn't need right now.

It was risky to take the girls out in public.

That's why he never did.

He couldn't protect them out here.

At home, they were safe. Safe from anyone who might want to

hurt them.

And there were a lot of bad people in the world who would love nothing more than to destroy beautiful young women.

Malachi was proud of his daughters.

They were very beautiful.

They all had silky black hair, just like his. And his bright, piercing blue eyes. They were smart, too.

It was his job to protect them.

And he took it very seriously.

There was nothing that Malachi wouldn't do to protect his family. He would lie. He would cheat. He would steal. He would kill.

In a second.

Killing didn't bother him.

All that bothered him was keeping his family safe.

No one was going to get in between him and his daughters.

No one.

He would take out anyone who even considered it.

But the longer they remained at the hospital, the greater the chances that someone could figure things out.

Maybe he shouldn't have listened to Alice and brought Ariyel here. Usually, he didn't let the kids dictate what he did, but Alice had been in a complete panic when she couldn't wake Ariyel up.

When one of his daughters was sick, he typically treated them himself. But this had been different. Ariyel had been unconscious, completely unresponsive, her pulse had been weak, and her blood pressure low.

Malachi had been concerned. Had he been feeding her too many sedatives? He crushed them up and put them in her food every day. He had to keep her drugged to keep her under control. She was a little spitfire.

But what if he'd overdone it? Unintentionally given her an overdose.

As much as Ariyel could drive him crazy, he didn't want her to die.

He couldn't imagine his life without her.

Crossing to the bed, he carefully lifted one of her limp hands. "Ariyel?"

She didn't respond either to his grip on her hand or his voice.

A tinge of real concern gripped him.

The doctors didn't know what was wrong with her yet, but they'd taken blood. No doubt they would detect the sedatives in her system. He would have to come up with a convincing lie.

He could claim post-partum depression.

But that may lead to questions about the baby's father.

He could claim grief. Say that his wife had just died and that Ariyel was grieving her mother.

But that may lead to doctors wanting to question the other girls.

He could claim he hadn't known that Ariyel was taking anything.

But that may make him look like a bad father.

And what would Ariyel say when she woke up?

The doctors would no doubt question her about why she had been taking sedatives and if she had purposefully swallowed too many.

If they suspected she was suicidal, they would want to commit her.

Without her daily dose of tranquilizers, he couldn't guarantee that she wouldn't tell everything to the first person who asked. Sure, it hadn't just been the drugs that had gotten her under control. He had put a lot of time and effort into breaking her down and building her back up again to be his daughter. But the drugs were key to keeping her in check.

It would be a disaster if some psychiatrist got their hands on her.

Or what if what was wrong with Ariyel had nothing to do with the drugs?

What if it were something more serious?

What if it were something terminal?

What if Ariyel was dying?

How could he live without her?

She was his oldest child. He loved her despite her problems.

And she was so good with her little sisters. If it weren't for her, Alice, Angela, Abigail, and Arianna wouldn't be such good sweet children. Alice really looked up to her, wanted to be just like her when she got older.

Which was both a good and a bad thing.

He couldn't handle anther Ariyel.

Her teenage years had had her defying him at every turn. Constructing fanciful delusions. Attempting at every turn to leave the safety of their home and live in the outside world.

Still, if Alice turned out to be like Ariyel, then she would receive the same treatment that her big sister had.

But Alice was the least of his concerns.

How would he deal with Abby without Ariyel?

The five-year-old was such an emotional little girl, and she clung to Ariyel, who was the only one who could calm her down most of the time.

Then he would be stuck having to deal with an infant without her help, too.

No. He simply wouldn't allow anything to be wrong with Ariyel.

Once the doctors stabilized her, he would whisk her and the little girls back home.

She would get better, and their lives would go back to the way it had been before.

He wasn't losing his daughters.

He quite simply wouldn't.

Nothing was going to get in the way this time.

Nothing.

* * * * *

10:28 P.M.

While Maegan went to the bathroom, Laura went to find Jack. She found him at the nurses' station, chatting away with one of the nurses.

For a moment, she just stood and watched him. His blue eyes were twinkling, his dimples were showing, and he was waving his hands about as he spoke. He needed a haircut. His blond hair had grown too long and fell down into his eyes. Sure, Jack was hot, but she couldn't have cared less about his looks. His heart was why she loved him. He was so dedicated to her and had been so patient with her, helping her carry her baggage as though it were his own. And she had a lot of baggage.

Laura knew how lucky she was to have Jack in her life, and she wished so much that she could get better so he didn't have to keep dealing with her problems.

Jack caught sight of her and immediately finished off his conversation and hurried to her side. Once he reached her, he gave her an appraising glance and obviously didn't like what he saw. Immediately, he grabbed her elbow and eased her down into a chair. "You need to sit," he informed her.

"I'm all right, Jack," Laura murmured tiredly. Her head was still pounding, and now that Maegan was gone, she didn't seem to have the strength to lock away the pain.

"Mark is working tonight. I asked him to come down and check you out." Jack was crouching in front of her, his face a picture of earnest concern.

"I don't need a doctor," she protested. "And, even if I did, we're in the emergency room; there are doctors everywhere. Your brother doesn't have to stop what he's doing to come down here and see me." Jack's youngest brother worked as a trauma surgeon in this hospital, and Laura was sure he had much more important things to do than seeing her.

He tucked her hair behind her ear. "Yeah, but if we get one of the ER doctors to look at you, then you have to get admitted and wait your turn. This way, Mark can look you over right away and give you something for that headache," Jack explained.

"I don't know, Jack."

"Laura, it's not a request. Mark is coming down to check you out," Jack stated firmly.

"Okay," she agreed, mainly because arguing about it took up more energy than she had right now.

"You know it doesn't make me feel better when you let me boss you around," Jack informed her.

"Sorry." Laura took her husband's hand and tugged him toward her. He stood and took the chair beside her and she leaned against him, resting her head on his shoulder and closing her eyes.

"How did it go with that girl?" Jack asked, his fingers tracing absently up and down her arm. "Did she tell you what was going on with her?"

"Yes, and she needs help, Jack. Serious help. *Your* kind of help," she added.

"What's wrong with her?"

"She says she was kidnapped five years ago, along with three other girls. She says the man who took her calls them his daughters and gave them new names. She said her real name is Maegan, but she wouldn't tell me her last name or the real names of the other girls because she's scared we won't be able to help her before this man, Malachi, takes them home," Laura summarized.

Jack blew a low whistle. "Well that's quite a story. You believe her?"

Laura didn't even need to consider this. "Yes. She's scared. She says this Malachi is crazy, but that he can be very convincing. She's scared he'll convince us she's unbalanced."

"Is there a chance she is?" Jack asked.

"No, I don't think she's delusional."

"I'll call Xavier and ask him to come over so we can interview Maegan."

"Thanks, Jack." Laura snuggled closer.

"Just doing my job."

"I know, but you always go well beyond what's required with your job. I really love you." Her headache and stress were making her emotional, and Laura could feel herself getting teary.

He pressed his lips to the top of her head. "I love you, too, angel. There's Mark."

"Hi, guys," Jack's brother greeted them a moment later.

"Thanks for coming down here," Jack told him.

"No problem."

"All right, I'm going to go and call Xavier and ask him to come down here so we can talk to the girl." Carefully, Jack eased her off his chest, keeping an arm around her until he was convinced that she wasn't going to keel over. "Love you and I'll be right back." Jack gave her a quick kiss on the lips.

"Hey, Laura," Mark dropped into the seat beside her.

"Hi, Mark." She attempted to muster a smile. "Sorry Jack made you come down here; I'm fine."

"Let's look you over and make sure of that." Mark lifted her wrist and focused his gaze on his watch. "Everything going okay with your pregnancy?"

"Fine." Laura wanted to find a quiet, dark place and curl up in a bed and sleep for about a week.

"Jack said you've been suffering from headaches," Mark stated as he shined a light in her eyes.

"Yep."

"When you get them, do you ever get nauseous?" Mark strapped a blood pressure cuff on her arm. Her brother-in-law didn't bother asking her to pull up her sleeve because he knew she always wore long clothing to cover her scars. Laura didn't even like Jack to see her naked. Scratch that, she didn't even like to see herself naked. Her scars were a constant, inescapable reminder of what she'd been through.

"Sometimes."

"Any sensitivity to light or sound?"

Mark was starting to worry her with his questions. Was he suggesting something was wrong with her? Something other than a simple headache? "Sometimes the light bothers me."

"How long do they usually last?"

She shrugged. "Several hours, sometimes a day or two. Why?"

"Deep breath," he instructed as he positioned a stethoscope on her back, ignoring her question. "Do you usually know when you're going to get a headache?"

"Most of the time I can feel it coming on."

"I think you're getting migraines," he told her as he put the stethoscope around his neck and turned to study her.

"I don't get migraines," she protested. "I never had them as a kid."

"I know." Mark smiled at her. "We grew up together, remember? Migraines can be associated with post-traumatic stress disorder and can be brought on by psychological stress. Do you find you tend to get headaches when you're stressed and fatigued?"

"Yeah, I do."

"Then I think we can probably give you a diagnosis of migraines. How bad is the pain right now? Do you think you need to take something for it?"

She shook her head. "I don't want to take anything that might harm the baby."

Mark shook his head. "You're in pain, *that's* not good for the baby. I'll get you some paracetamol; that's perfectly safe. A lot of women experience a decrease in migraines during pregnancy. It seems you're one of the unlucky ones. Once the baby's born, there are preventative medications that you can take when you feel a migraine coming on. But there are other things you can do, like you can try to get yourself on a schedule of eating and sleeping regularly." He shot her a pointed stare. "I know you struggle with that, but it'll be good for you. Are you still seeing your therapist?"

"No," she answered in a small voice. Laura knew that she probably still needed counseling, but she wanted to believe that she had moved beyond that stage.

"Maybe you should consider going back," Mark said gently. "You still don't sleep much, do you? How are the nightmares, are you still having them?"

"Not so much anymore."

"More when you're stressed?"

"Yeah, Jack usually tries to make me stick to a routine and go to bed the same time each night, but I don't usually sleep more than four or five hours a night." That was probably the hardest thing. The lack of sleep made everything else so much more difficult.

"You don't eat much, either." Mark's blond brows narrowed. "You need to work on that. And you shouldn't have come tonight, should you? This is too much for you right now. Why do you keep putting yourself in situations you know are going to stress you out?"

Laura shrugged. "Because I want to get better," she replied.

"Do you really think pushing yourself to the point where you make yourself physically ill is the way to do that? You just have to give yourself time."

"How much time?" She wished someone could give her a definitive answer to that. How long would it take her to get better? It would make it so much easier to struggle through each day if she knew exactly when it was going to end.

"I'm sorry, honey, I can't answer that for you. No one can. Why are you in such a hurry? What you went through was horrific—you have to know that you're not going to get over it in a minute."

"It's been way more than a minute; it's been fifteen years."

"There's no time frame for this kind of thing." Mark took her hand and squeezed it. "It takes your mind longer than your body to heal. Laura, I wish I could snap my fingers and make everything better for you, but I can't. If you want the headaches to ease, though, you can try and avoid your triggers, which I'm guessing are stress. Why don't you let Jack take you home, and you can try and get some sleep?"

Rubbing at her eyes, sleep sounded fantastic right about now, but she couldn't leave yet. Maegan needed her. "I can't. There was this girl and—"

He cut her off with a sigh. "Yeah, yeah, Jack filled me in. If you won't go home, then I'm going to get you something for your headache, and then I'm going to see if they can set you up with a bed in Sofia's room. You need rest, Laura," Mark told her seriously. "You can't keep running on fumes indefinitely. So, consider yourself out for the night. If that girl needs to talk, she comes and sees you in your room."

Laura knew arguing with Mark was pointless; he'd already made up his mind. So, she merely nodded her assent, and Mark waved Jack back over.

Her husband jogged to them and immediately sat beside her, tugging her into his lap. "So?" he looked to his brother.

"I think she's getting migraines."

"There're things she can take for that, right? That can prevent her from getting them?"

"There are preventative medications," Mark agreed. "But some aren't suitable to take while she's pregnant. Still, she's at thirty-five weeks so she doesn't have much longer to go, and then she can see a doctor who will hopefully prescribe something that helps."

"Okay, we'll set something up as soon as the baby's born. Is there anything she can do to ease the headaches right now?"

"She can try to avoid her triggers, which I'd guess are stress.

And, Jack, she needs to rest. I'm serious." Mark looked deadly serious. "She's pushing herself too hard, and she's going to make herself really sick if she doesn't start easing up. I'm going to try and get a bed for her in Sofia's room and you need to make sure she stays in it. Seriously, she's done for the night. If that girl wants her, she goes and sees her there."

"Stop talking about me like I'm not here." Laura hated when people did that.

They ignored her. "I'll make sure she stays in bed," Jack said. "Xavier's coming over because we need to interview this Maegan girl, but I'll get Ryan to keep an eye on her."

"No one needs to keep an eye on me," Laura objected.

Again, the brothers paid her no mind. "And you're going to have to make sure she starts getting more rest," Mark continued. "I know you're about to have a toddler and a newborn, but you're going to have to make it a priority. Jack, you're going to have to be firm with her. I know she's stubborn, but it's really important to her health."

"I'll talk to Sofia about making sure her schedule at the women's shelter gives her time during the day to take a nap."

"I'm not taking naps during the day; I have work to do. And when I'm at home, we have a toddler and housework and cooking." Laura knew she was fighting a losing battle. If Jack wanted her to spend more time sleeping, he was going to be on her about it until she complied.

"Okay, I have to go back to work, but if she gets any worse, then get someone to admit her; otherwise, keep her in bed, make her sleep, and then take her home in the morning. And maybe see if Mom and Dad can keep Zach another day or two so she can take it easy. I'll come back down to check on her in a couple of hours," Mark informed them.

Laura groaned and gave up trying to include herself in the conversation. She *was* really tired. And Sofia's hospital room would be quieter than the waiting area, which was a bonus.

Maybe after she took the painkillers, her headache would go away, and she'd actually be able to grab a little sleep.

Now that Jack and Xavier were going to take over helping Maegan, she could take a step back and leave the teenager in their capable hands. She'd still talk to the girl if Maegan needed her, but she'd probably be busy with the cops for a while.

She was so tired.

She just needed a little sleep.

To recharge her batteries so she could help Maegan and her sisters.

Closing her eyes, Laura was asleep before she even realized it.

* * * * *

10:39 P.M.

Dr. Bruce Daniels watched as a tall, blond man carried a black-haired lady into Sofia's hospital room.

Bruce knew that the man was Sofia's brother-in-law, Jack, and the woman was his wife, Laura. He knew every member of Sofia's family, including the children and all her friends.

He also knew their history.

He knew about Laura's assault when she was just twenty-years-old. And he knew that she suffered from agoraphobia. He was surprised to see her here tonight.

Bruce liked Sofia's sister-in-law; he felt sorry for her. If the men who hurt her weren't already dead or in jail, he'd be tempted to take care of them himself.

He wondered what was wrong with Laura. Was she simply asleep? Apparently, she didn't sleep much; she suffered from insomnia and nightmares. Or maybe she was unconscious. Perhaps there was something wrong with her baby. Bruce sincerely hoped there wasn't. She deserved some happiness.

He should go and check in with her.

If nothing else, it would give him an excuse to go and see Sofia again.

Sofia was his life.

The center of his universe.

It killed him that he couldn't be around her all the time.

But he knew he couldn't.

If he wasn't careful, they'd figure things out.

And then he'd never get to see her again.

It was a pure fluke that he'd gotten to see her tonight. He had been surprised—and thrilled—when he'd seen Ryan carrying her into the emergency room. Bruce had quickly claimed her as a patient.

It had been a couple of years since they'd been in the same room, but he still got that wonderful feeling of peace and tranquility when he was around her.

There had been a time when he had been so consumed by his feelings for her that he couldn't resist making attempts to be around her all the time. He had visited her house regularly and left her gifts and letters so she would know how much she meant to him. But he'd realized he couldn't do that all the time.

And besides, he was so pleased that Sofia's life was going so well these days that he felt like he could safely take a step back. She deserved some happiness after the despicable family she'd had to endure for most of her life. He was glad they had all been killed. Now, with her family out of the way, she was free to be happy. And happy, she was. She had a husband who adored her, two beautiful children, extended family who were infinitely better for her than her biological one, and wonderful friends.

Well, except for that one friend.

Detective Paige Hood.

Sofia's husband's partner.

She was one that needed watching.

A few years ago, she and Ryan had had an affair. She had denied it, but he knew it was true. Fueled by fury that Sofia's husband and friend would betray her, he'd unleashed his anger on Paige and attacked her. In fact, he had intended to kill her, but he'd been interrupted by Ryan, and Paige had survived. Still, his assault had served as a warning for the woman, and she had since kept her hands on her own husband and stayed away from Sofia's.

He still kept a close eye on the woman, ready to swoop in once again if she in any way threatened Sofia's happiness.

In fact, he kept tabs on all Sofia's family and friends.

It wasn't hard.

He'd bought a house across the street from Sofia and Ryan's so he could watch over her.

He needed to watch over her.

After all, she was all he had in the entire world.

Without her, he would be completely alone.

He often ached with the need to be close to her again. To be able to touch her and talk to her. But he kept his distance.

The last few times he had visited her, he had scared her—unintentionally, of course. Bruce would never intentionally do *anything* to hurt or scare Sofia. However, his timing had been a little off. She had even shot at him. She missed, but it had been a wake-up call that she wasn't ready to know him yet. So, he had assured her that he meant her no harm, told her that he loved her, and then kept his distance.

Luck had given him the opportunity to treat her once before in the hospital, and those few days where he had been able to see her regularly—talk to her, even touch her—had been the best of his life.

And now, here she was again.

He had to be careful, though.

Bruce had gotten the sense that Sofia might have known who he really was.

And he wasn't quite ready for her to know yet.

Perhaps he should keep his distance.

Let another doctor take care of her.

Go back to watching her from afar.

Only, he knew he wouldn't. Or couldn't.

He *needed* to be around her. He *needed* a connection with her.

Determinedly, he set out for Sofia's room, forcing himself to look casual instead of goofily enamored.

"Everything okay in here?"

Inside the room, Laura lay on a bed, her eyes closed. Sofia was still in her bed, and Mark, Ryan, and Jack Xander were all hovering around the beds. Bruce knew Mark Xander. As well as being one of Sofia's brothers-in-law, he was a surgeon here at the hospital.

"Hi, Bruce. My sister-in-law, Laura, has a migraine. She just needs to sleep it off for a while," Mark explained, keeping his voice quiet so as not to wake the sleeping woman.

"Do you want me to check her out?" he offered, anything to spend as much time around Sofia as he could.

"No, that's okay, I already did. She's stable, but I have to go back upstairs. She really just needs rest, and my brother, Ryan, is going to keep an eye on her, but if there are any problems, he'll let you know."

"Sure." Bruce nodded agreeably. "I'm happy to help if she needs it. No problems with her pregnancy?" He knew there weren't, but thought it seemed appropriate to ask.

"No, none," Mark replied.

"Is this her first child?"

"Second."

"You should also know she's agoraphobic," Jack Xander added as he pulled a blanket up to cover his wife.

Pretending he didn't know that already, he nodded thoughtfully. "Okay, so she's likely to be stressed when she wakes up then. I'm on for another few hours, but I'll let the next shift know when they come on." He turned to Ryan. "Call me if she needs me. You're doing okay, Mrs. Xander?" he asked Sofia.

"Fine, thank you," she nodded, a little curtly, but Bruce

assumed it was just because she worried about Laura.

Fighting the urge to go to Sofia and pick up her wrist to check her pulse or take her blood pressure or anything that involved touching her, he nodded at the group and hurried out the door.

As he went to the desk to grab another patient chart, Bruce decided it was almost time. He'd waited long enough. Soon, he would reveal himself to Sofia, and then the two of them could be together forever.

* * * * *

10:46 P.M.

Detective Xavier Montague was heading toward the hospital room where his partner, Jack, had told him to meet him when he saw someone familiar leaving the room.

Dr. Bruce Daniels.

Xavier vividly remembered the man.

Back when he'd been investigating a killer who wiped out entire families leaving one member alive, Dr. Daniels had been a suspect. The man had had connections to most of the families, and there was just something about him that left Xavier feeling on edge. He couldn't quite put his finger on it. Although it had turned out that Bruce Daniels hadn't committed the murders, Xavier still didn't like the guy.

That investigation had also led him to Annabelle.

He loved Belle with all his heart, but she kept insisting on pushing him away. He had thought, hoped, that with her tormentor finally out of the picture, she'd be able to move on. And she had. In a way. Only her moving forward seemed to not include him. While he truly loved Annabelle and wanted to spend the rest of his life with her, he wasn't sure how much more of her pushing him away he could take.

Right now, he was just going to focus on work.

His girlfriend may not need him, but there were four kids here who most certainly did.

Striding into the hospital room, his gaze immediately fell on Laura, and his eyes narrowed in concern. Her face was pale, and her dark hair accentuated her lack of color. Her eyes were closed, and she appeared to be asleep. At least Xavier hoped she was merely asleep and not unconscious.

"I thought Sofia was the sick one, what's wrong with Laura?" he asked.

"Running on fumes finally caught up with her. Mark thinks she's getting migraines and it's important that she start taking better care of herself. Like actually eat and sleep." Jack's face and tone were a mixture of concern and frustration. "I don't know how I'm going to manage to make her do that, though, since we're about to have a new baby."

Xavier felt a stab of jealousy. It wasn't that he begrudged any of his friends their children, but he really thought he would have had kids of his own by now. He was thirty-seven years old; he'd been with Annabelle for the last five years, and their relationship was in the worst shape it had ever been. Kids did not look to be in his future.

"She's just asleep though, right?" he gestured at Laura. "She's not unconscious?"

"She's asleep," Mark assured him, carefully picking up Laura's wrist and checking her pulse. She didn't stir, and a moment later he set her hand back down. "And she's still stable. I better be going. Call me if you need me; otherwise, I'll see you in a couple of hours."

Mark moved toward the door, but Xavier stopped him. "What do you know about Bruce Daniels?"

"Not a lot, why?" Mark asked.

"He was a suspect for a while in an old case of mine," Xavier informed them.

"He creeps me out," Sofia shuddered.

"Me too," he agreed.

"Did you have anything concrete against him?" Jack asked.

"There were some allegations that he'd been making kids who were brought in to the emergency room sicker so he could swoop in and save them. Nothing was ever proven. He ended up treating several of our victims, including Annabelle, and he just seemed a little too interested in them."

"That's how Sofia feels," Ryan added.

"I just have a bad feeling about him; I can't explain it." Xavier knew the man was bad news and wished he had the time to put into proving it.

"I suggested to Sofia that he could be her stalker," Ryan told them. "But she said she didn't think so."

"Are you sure?" Xavier asked.

Sofia's pale face went thoughtful as she considered this. "No. I'm not sure. He could be, I guess."

"We should get Paige to talk to the doctor, and see if she thinks he's the man who attacked her," Jack suggested.

Ryan's flinch would have been imperceptible had Xavier not been looking for it. Ryan was extremely protective of his partner. Xavier knew the two had always been close, and Ryan blamed himself for the attack on Paige four years ago.

"I hate to put her through that," Ryan said, "but yeah, we should. She's not safe so long as the stalker is out there and neither is Sofia and neither are the rest of us since this guy is unpredictable. But, in the meantime, Dr. Daniels doesn't come near Sofia or Laura."

"Sorry, Sofia," Xavier said. "I haven't even asked; how are you doing?"

She offered up a weak smile. "I'm okay, just tired."

"Hopefully you can get some sleep."

"Ryan, that reminds me. Laura had nightmares earlier, so she may have more. She might wake up in a panic," Jack told his brother.

"No problem. If she does, I'll handle it." Ryan looked completely unfazed.

"Thanks, text me when she wakes up or if you can't calm her down. Xavier, you ready?" Jack looked to him.

"Yep, ready when you are."

"I'm ready." But Jack hesitated, pressing a tender kiss to Laura's forehead.

"I'll stay with her, Jack," Ryan said gently. "And she would want you to go and help this girl."

He roused himself. "Yeah I know. I just don't like leaving her when she's so stressed. All right, let's go before I change my mind."

However, once they left the room, Xavier could tell Jack's mind was still firmly back inside with his wife. They'd been partners for four years now, and Xavier considered both Jack and Laura to be amongst his closest friends. He also considered Jack's brother Ryan and his wife Sofia, and Ryan's partner Paige and her husband Elias, to be good friends, too. He had hoped that his transfer to work out of a different precinct and their new group of friends would make Annabelle more comfortable.

But it hadn't.

Annabelle seemed to like all of them, especially Laura, but that was no surprise since Laura exuded sincere empathy that put people at ease. But, she hadn't connected with them in the way he'd hoped. She was still closed off. Still distant. Still living on her own even as they lived together.

Not that they were living together anymore.

Xavier couldn't understand why Annabelle was pushing him away.

He loved her, but that hurt.

A lot.

"Jack, you're not focused," he told his partner, deliberately focusing himself.

"Yes, I am." His blue eyes narrowed defensively.

"No, you're still thinking about Laura. She's going to be okay. She's improving, I know slower than she wants, but she's still getting better. And she's asleep now anyway so even if you were there with her you couldn't do anything for her. And Ryan is with her. She'll be fine."

"I know," Jack sighed. "I just can't stop worrying about her."

"I know the feeling."

"I'm sorry. Any luck convincing Annabelle to stay home or she still insisting on moving into her own place?"

"She's still moving."

"You want Laura to try talking to her?" Jack offered.

"Thanks, but I think this is something Annabelle has to work through on her own. Besides, Laura has enough going on right now. Look, I'll make you a deal; you stop worrying about Laura, and I'll stop worrying about Annabelle."

"Deal." Jack offered up a half smile.

They shook on it, but Xavier knew neither of them was going to be able to follow through.

"There's Maegan." Jack pointed to a teenage girl standing by the door. Maegan appeared to be around fifteen, with long black hair and large blue eyes that were currently staring, seemingly unseeingly, at the busy emergency room.

"Maegan?" Xavier asked as they approached.

Startled, the girl's eyes grew wary as they settled on him and Jack. "Where's Laura?"

"She's sleeping," Jack replied.

"I knew she wasn't okay," Maegan exclaimed.

"She *is* okay," Jack assured the teenager. "My brother checked her out, and he said she's stable."

"Your brother is a doctor?" the girl asked.

"Yes, a surgeon. Laura is just really tired, and she needs some rest." Jack sounded like he was trying to convince himself as much as Maegan.

"And you're a cop, right?"

"Yes, and we can help you, Maegan, but you need to work with us."

The look she shot them was doubtful. "Who's that?" She nodded her head at him.

"I'm Jack's partner, Xavier," he introduced himself.

"Why don't we go and talk someplace more private," Jack suggested.

Maegan hesitated, clearly still undecided about whether or not she trusted them. Then she exhaled slowly. "Okay, I trust Laura, and she obviously trusts you since she married you and has kids with you, so I guess that has to be enough. Besides, I have to trust *someone*. It may as well be you guys."

With that ringing endorsement, Maegan followed them to a small office. They all took seats, Maegan choosing the one on its own farthest away from them.

"All right, Maegan, tell us what happened to you," Xavier said.

"Didn't Laura already tell you?" she asked.

"Yes, but we need to hear it from you," Jack told her gently.

For the next ten minutes, Jack led Maegan through the day she'd been abducted and the events that followed. He asked her questions and prodded her gently for as much information as the girl could offer.

While Jack questioned her, Xavier watched her closely for any signs that she was lying or delusional. Laura had told Jack that Maegan had been scared that the man who kidnapped her would paint her as mentally ill. They'd get a psych evaluation done if needed, but for the moment, he and Jack just had to be confident that the girl was telling the truth so they could begin investigating.

"You're asking me so many questions." Maegan's eyes were shining brightly with unshed tears. "Don't you believe me?"

"We believe you, honey," Jack reassured her, and instantly the girl relaxed a hair. Jack possessed an innate ability to soothe and put at ease even the most traumatized of victims. "But, if we're going to prove that Malachi did what you say he did so that you and your sisters can go home, then we need to know everything you can tell us. Now, you told Laura that you don't know Malachi's last name?"

Maegan nodded.

"But you told her that he's insane, that he thinks you're his daughters who died in a fire?"

Another nod.

Getting information out of Maegan wasn't easy. The teenager was scared. And if what she'd told them was true then she had every right to be afraid. Xavier was wondering whether, given the girl's traumatized state, Laura would have better luck at getting information.

Jack wasn't fazed by Maegan's unwillingness to talk and continued with his questions. "Do you know anything about the fire or Malachi's real daughters?"

"No," Maegan answered in a small voice. "I think they died a little before he kidnapped us, which would make it around six years ago. I've never seen any pictures of them. Malachi must have gotten rid of them. But I guess they looked like us, since we all look like Malachi with the black hair and blue eyes. His kids must have looked like him, too. He calls us Ariyel, Alice, Angela, and Abigail, so those must have been their names. I was ten when he took me; Abby was just a baby; Angela was four; Ariyel was eighteen, but I think he thought she was only sixteen. That must have been his daughters' ages when they died."

He was surprised by the sudden flow of information. "What about Malachi's wife? His children's mother? Do you know anything about her? Is she still around?" Xavier asked.

"I don't know," Maegan replied. "He never talks about her, but she must exist. I mean, someone had to have his children."

"Honey, we need something if we're going to arrest Malachi," Jack told her gently. "We need something to go on. If you tell us your real name, we can prove that he kidnapped you."

She shook her head. "What if you confront him with my

abduction, and he just claims he doesn't know me? He could tell you that he's never seen me before. How would you prove otherwise?"

The girl was so terrified that she was inventing extremely unlikely scenarios. "If you give us the names of the other girls, we can prove he took all of you," Xavier attempted to reason with her.

"I don't know their full names, only their first names. You won't be able to find out who they are in time," Maegan protested.

"Tell us where they are so we can talk to them. If we have your statement, and their statements, we can arrest Malachi. In fact, we have enough to arrest him right now," Jack told her. "We have your statement. We can take him down to the station now."

"What would happen to us? Would we go into foster care?"

"You could go straight home with your family. The others, yes, they'd have to go into foster care until we find out who they are."

Maegan seemed to consider this. "But even if you arrest him, Malachi could get out on bail and find out where the others are and take them back. Then they'd be alone with him without Ariyel or me to protect them. Or he might not even get charges filed against him. You don't know my whole name, so you can't prove that I was even kidnapped. Malachi will convince you I'm just crazy."

Xavier wanted to grab the girl and shake some sense into her. But Jack remained calm. "I'll give you a couple of hours to get used to the idea that you are going to tell us who you really are and who your sisters are. Xavier and I will talk to Malachi here, but you are to stay out of sight. Seriously, I don't want you anywhere near Malachi."

"Okay." Maegan looked relieved. "Can I go and see Laura?"

"She needs to get some sleep at the moment, but yes, when she wakes up I'll take you to see her," Jack replied.

"Thank you," Maegan smiled.

"Maegan," Jack waited until the girl was looking him in the eye, "I need to know why you're doing this now. This isn't necessarily going to be easy, and I need to know you're prepared for whatever happens. So, why now?"

"Because this is the first chance we've had. I told you, he hasn't let us leave that house in five years. This plan, it isn't mine. It's Ariyel's. She thought it up years ago. Only when she tried it, it didn't work. But this time it *is* going to work. I'll do whatever I have to, to make sure of it."

The fierce determination in the teenager's voice had Xavier almost believing that it would.

However, the glint in her eyes left him wondering whether there was a possibility that she was insane after all.

* * * * *

10:53 P.M.

Malachi knew that if she'd been awake, Ariyel would be thrilled that he had caved and brought her here.

He remembered her attempt to manipulate him into bringing her to the hospital. Because she thought that once she was here she could escape from him.

Only he had outsmarted her then and he would outsmart her now.

He was *never* letting those girls go.

They were his.

And yet tonight he had brought her here.

How could he have been so stupid?

This was a mistake.

A *big* mistake.

He had to leave. Now.

He'd round up the kids and then take Ariyel and get out of here. It might look a little suspicious if he carried his unconscious daughter out of here before she'd been discharged, but there was nothing he could do about that. Besides, he'd left fake contact information so no one would be able to find them.

Leaving Ariyel's room, he scanned the waiting area in search of Alice and the little girls.

He couldn't see them anywhere.

A slice of panic shot through him, but he shoved it down. They were probably just in the bathroom. He headed for the ladies' room and was at the door when he realized he couldn't go inside. Malachi was about to barge inside anyway when the door opened, and an elderly lady walked out.

"Excuse me, was there a teenager in there with two little girls and a baby?" he asked.

"No, there was no one else in there," the lady replied before walking off.

Where else could they be?

Maybe Alice had taken them outside for some fresh air.

Hurrying out the doors, he scanned the area in front of the emergency room. A few people hovered about, but no signs of his girls.

They weren't outside.

They weren't in the bathroom.

They weren't in the waiting area.

They were gone.

* * * * *

10:57 P.M.

"Why aren't you asleep?"

Giving up the pretense that she was sleeping, which she was only doing for Ryan's benefit anyway, Sofia opened her eyes and gazed at her husband. "Every time I doze off, something startles me awake. I don't know what. I just have this feeling that something bad is going to happen."

Ryan perched on the side of her bed and took her hand. "Nothing bad is going to happen, Sofia," he soothed. "Everyone we love is safe and sound." She must have looked doubtful, because he continued. "You're just tired and sick and worried. If you'd just close your eyes and try to actually sleep, I'm sure you'll feel a lot better."

Despite her husband's assurances, Sofia just couldn't shake the feeling of foreboding that had been weighing down on her since they'd gotten to the hospital.

Was she being silly?

Was it really just stress and being sick and exhausted that had her feeling all apprehensive?

What Ryan said made sense. Not only was she sick, but she *was* worried about Laura, Paige, and Annabelle. Right now, Laura was topping her list.

Her sister-in-law was tossing and turning restlessly in her bed. "She shouldn't have come. You and Jack shouldn't have let her come." Sofia shot Ryan a reproachful frown.

"How could we have stopped her?"

"Well, since you're both cops, and you and Jack are both a good foot taller than her, and even being eight months pregnant, you and your brother can bench press double her size, so it couldn't be all that hard to make her stay home."

He chuckled. "Yeah, but Laura's stubbornness makes up for her small size."

She rolled her eyes, then sobered. "Do you think she's really doing okay?"

"I think that she wants to keep challenging herself shows she is. And tonight, hopefully, helping this Maegan girl will keep her distracted and help her hold it together. She really attracts people in need. It's like they can sense that she understands, like somehow they know she's been through something horrible."

"Laura hates that," Sofia mused. While Laura loved helping

people, she hated that people could read her so easily. "She wishes she knew how to hide it like she can hide all her physical scars."

"It's what makes her so good at what she does, though. Think of how many women and kids she's helped at your women's shelter. Think how many people's lives she's improved because she can truly get what they're going through."

"I know," she agreed quietly. "Sometimes it seems like it's too high a price to have had to pay to help others."

Beside them, Laura gave a small moan and began to whimper.

"Ryan, wake her up, she's having a nightmare."

Ryan was already moving toward Laura as Sofia said it. Grabbing her shoulders, he gave her a shake. "Laura. Wake up. Laura, you're dreaming. Come on, wake up."

With a sob, Laura bolted upright, her fists swinging wildly.

Keeping hold of her with one hand, with his other hand, Ryan pinned her fists against his chest. "It's all right, Laura. You're safe. It was just a nightmare."

"Ryan?" Laura's voice was shaky, and she was trembling all over.

"Yeah, honey, I'm here. You're safe," Ryan assured her again. "You're in the hospital, remember?" he added in response to her disoriented gaze.

Laura nodded, then shuddered violently and rested against Ryan, his arms immediately wrapping around her and holding her. "Where's Jack?" Laura asked.

"He and Xavier are interviewing Maegan. You fell asleep while Jack and Mark were still talking, and they brought you here, into Sofia's room, to rest while they talked to the girl. You want me to go and find him for you?"

"No, Maegan needs help." Laura was still breathing hard and lifted one thumb to her mouth to suck on.

Sofia knew that Laura had had the habit of thumb sucking since she was a kid. Her parents had worked hard to break the habit and had eventually succeeded, but Laura had picked it up again after her kidnapping.

She fought a surge of what she knew was unwarranted jealousy as she watched Ryan comfort Laura. It wasn't that she thought anything romantic was going to happen between them; she knew her husband loved her and that Laura was completely in love with Jack. Besides, Ryan and Laura were like brother and sister. Her jealousy stemmed more from the fact that Laura knew Ryan in a way that Sofia never could.

Because they'd grown up together, they were comfortable with each other. They'd spent summer holidays together, gone trick or treating together, waited for Santa Claus together, ridden their bikes together, played together, gone to school together, lied to their parents together, snuck out to parties together. Their whole childhood and adolescence had been spent together, and Sofia knew that, for most of that time, Ryan had had a crush on Laura. She knew it was stupid to be jealous that Laura and Ryan were such good friends, but sometimes it was how she felt.

"You all right?" Ryan was holding Laura at arm's length and studying her face.

"Yeah," Laura replied, but Sofia could hear the exhaustion in her tone.

"Yeah, you really look it. You know it was a bad idea to come here tonight, don't you?" Ryan asked.

She rubbed wearily at her eyes. "I already got lectures from both your brothers," Laura told him.

Ryan's smile softened. "You're still shaking. I'll go grab you another blanket. And here," he reached for the paper cup of water and painkillers on the small bedside table, "Mark left these for you."

"That's okay, I don't really need them," Laura protested.

"Do you still have a headache?"

Laura looked like she was debating whether or not to lie, but then gave in and nodded, "Yeah."

"Then you take them." Ryan passed her the cup and set the

pills in her hand. He pressed on Laura's shoulders until she rested back against the bed. "You should close your eyes and try to go back to sleep. Both of you should." Ryan shot her a pointed frown.

"No, I don't want to dream again," Laura said immediately. "I'm sorry I keep disturbing you, Sofia. You're sick; you should be resting. Jack and Mark shouldn't have brought me in here," Laura apologized.

"Of course, they should," Sofia reprimanded her sister-in-law. "And I wasn't sleeping, anyway." She didn't tell Laura about her bad feeling; she didn't want to add to her stress. "Why don't we chat for a while, help to calm each other a little."

"Yeah, okay," Laura agreed, her violet eyes all watery.

"All right, I'll grab you another blanket, and then I'll be right outside the door. Laura, when I see Jack I'll tell him to come and see you, and I'm telling him you had another nightmare," he warned. "Sofia, I'm not planning on going far, but if Jack and Xavier need help, and I do, make sure that doctor doesn't come near you or Laura," Ryan ordered.

Sofia was more than happy to not have Dr. Daniels near her ever again. Ryan grabbed another blanket, spread it over Laura, then sat on the edge of Sofia's bed and gave her a kiss. At the door, he paused. "I would tell you two to let me know if you need anything, but I don't like my chances of either of you actually doing that." Ryan shot them both irritated frowns.

Once he was gone, Sofia turned to Laura, who was looking lost. If she wasn't hooked up to an IV, she would have moved to Laura's bed; instead, she said, "Come sit over here."

Laura obliged, bringing the blankets with her and joined her on the bed. "I'm really sorry, Sofia. You should be asleep. You fainted earlier tonight."

"I'm fine; I was just dehydrated. As soon as they started giving me fluids, I started feeling a lot better. Right now, I'm more concerned about you."

"I'm okay." Laura's gaze dipped, and she began to fiddle with the blanket.

"Why did you come here tonight?"

"Because you were sick."

"And you thought that by torturing yourself you could make me better?" Sofia asked gently.

"No," Laura replied in a small voice.

"Honey, look at me." Sofia waited until Laura's violet eyes slowly rose to meet hers. "What is going on with you?"

Laura just shrugged fitfully.

"Come on, Laura," Sofia coaxed. "Something's been off with you for a few weeks now. If I hadn't been sick I would have pinned you down and figured out what it was before now. Now, what's wrong?"

"I don't know." Laura gave another shrug.

"Yes, you do," Sofia contradicted. Not only was Laura a trained psychologist, but she was also extremely insightful. Sofia would bet anything that Laura knew exactly what had been bothering her.

"Pregnancy hormones are just making me emotional, I guess. I don't remember being so sensitive last time."

She wasn't buying Laura's excuse, but Sofia couldn't help but smile. That was *not* how she remembered Laura's previous pregnancy. "You were an emotional wreck when you were pregnant with Zach," Sofia reminded her. "You cried about everything those last few months. Now stop giving me excuses, and tell me what's wrong with you."

With a sigh, Laura sank back against the mattress and closed her eyes. "I don't know why, but I've been thinking about Matilda a lot lately."

Matilda Warren had been Laura's best friend in college. They and a couple of other girls had been roommates. Matilda had been murdered because she had been unlucky enough to be at home the day Laura was abducted.

"She died because of me, and I never even grieved her properly," Laura said miserably.

"Of course, you didn't. You'd just been through hell, and you were attempting to deal with that," Sofia reminded her. After she had lived through Isabella's murderous rampage, it had been months before she'd been able to even attempt to deal with anything else.

"And then so many people got hurt just because someone wanted to get to me. Including Rose." Laura's voice broke.

Sofia and Rose had become good friends in the year they'd known each other and even though four years had passed since she'd died, Sofia still missed her. Knowing where Laura was heading with this, she nipped it in the bud immediately, "You know Jack doesn't blame you," she told Laura sternly. "No one does. You are not responsible for that man's actions. You were his victim."

"I know. Jack's told me a million times that I shouldn't blame myself, but how do I do that? It *was* because of me that all those people got hurt. All because I didn't see him for who he really was."

"How could you have known? Being a psychology student didn't make you psychic," Sofia pointed out.

"I should have seen it. I should have seen that he was unstable," Laura protested. "He hurt so many people."

"Honey, he hurt you, too," Sofia reminded her.

She shrugged like that didn't matter. "I worry that I could get it wrong again. What if I miss something or I say or do the wrong thing, and someone else ends up getting hurt?" Laura finally opened her eyes to stare dismally up at Sofia.

"You can't save everyone," Sofia said gently. "If you put yourself under that kind of pressure, it's going to crush you."

"Working at the women's center isn't the same as working my old job. When I was a phone counselor, I never saw anyone, so I didn't feel as connected—as involved. But now ... now, everything seems so personal."

Sofia had thought that working at their center was good for Laura, but maybe she'd been wrong. Maybe it was too much for her. "Honey, if you need a break, that's fine …"

"No, I don't need a break. I like my job. I'm scared I'm going to mess things up with Maegan," Laura continued. "What kind of life is she going to have once she goes back home to her family? Being away from your family and suffering a trauma, it changes the relationship."

Sofia knew that Laura still struggled with her own family relationships. She was more comfortable with Jack's family than her own. "Having people around who love her will help her," Sofia assured her. "Think how much you improved once you had Jack back."

"Yeah, but even having him there some days was so hard. There were times when I didn't even have the energy—physically or mentally—to get out of bed. I remember days where Jack would lie in bed with me all day, watching movies or reading, because I just couldn't get up. And then, there were days when he pushed me to talk and made me get up even when I didn't want to. I wouldn't have made it through without him, but it was still hard. I had to fight for every inch of progress that I made."

"But you got through it, and Maegan will, too. How could she not with you to help her?"

Laura offered up a small smile. "I really appreciate that you named your women's center after Matilda."

Laura's friend had been intending to graduate with a degree in social work, so it had seemed only fitting that they name the place after both her and Rose. And thus, the Matilda Rose Women's and Children Center was formed. "You're welcome, but it isn't *my* center, it's *our* center. You and Paige and Annabelle and I all needed something to focus on. We all needed a purpose. I'm just grateful that the center has been able to help so many people in need as well as all of us."

"It's really been a lifesaver," Laura agreed. "Oh, who was the doctor that Ryan was talking about earlier? The one who he didn't want to come near us?"

Sensing Laura needed the distraction, Sofia began to explain about Dr. Daniels and Ryan's theory that he could be her stalker. Part of her didn't want to think the doctor was her stalker, and the other part desperately hoped that he was.

She didn't want to live in fear anymore, constantly wondering whether her stalker was going to break into her home again. Or even worse, whether he was going to make another attempt on Paige's life or go after someone else that she loved.

She needed him caught.

FOUR YEARS AGO

2:35 P.M.

"How long has it been?"

"Almost a year," Eliza replied.

"A year?" Maegan looked up at her with sad blue eyes.

Eliza hated the sad look in the little girls' eyes. Maegan, Bethany, Hayley—the poor little things—were always so miserable.

Not just them.

She was miserable, too.

For almost a year, this house had been their home. Malachi occasionally let them out in the yard, but even that was a rarity. Their days were spent locked inside this place.

During the day, they studied. A lot. Malachi tutored them from eight in the morning until six at night. Apparently, despite being insane, he truly valued education.

And Malachi *was* insane.

He thought that they were his daughters. Ariyel, Alice, Angela, and Abigail had been killed in a fire. And after that, he'd lost touch with reality and kidnapped them all as replacements.

Eliza wasn't going to do this anymore.

She wasn't going to keep living in this house.

Spending her days studying and caring for the little girls, cooking, and cleaning. It wasn't that she minded looking after the girls. After spending the last year together, she loved those children like they really were her sisters. And despite where they were, she had enjoyed seeing some of their milestones. Like Bethany learning to read. And Hayley had taken her first steps just a month ago and was so close to saying her first word.

She would do anything to protect them.

She was about to risk everything in an attempt to save them all.

What she was planning was risky.

Very risky.

Risky enough that there was a chance she might die.

But she had to do it. There were no other choices. She wasn't spending the rest of her life here as Malachi's prisoner. And she wasn't going to let those children remain trapped in this house.

This wasn't the first time she had attempted an escape.

It was practically all she'd done since Malachi had brought her here.

So far, nothing had worked out, but this one had to be foolproof.

"Now, you know what to do, right?" she checked with Maegan.

Eliza knew she was putting a lot of pressure on a little girl who was only eleven years old, but there was no other choice. She needed Maegan's help. They were only going to have one shot at this.

"I know what to do," Maegan stated firmly. "You can count on me. I won't let you down. I know what's riding on this."

"Are you sure you can handle it?" Eliza asked.

"I'm sure. Are you having second thoughts, Eliza?"

"No."

Maybe. Yes, she thought to herself.

Was she crazy to try this?

What if she did die? How would Maegan and Bethany and Hayley cope? What would happen to them? More importantly, what would Malachi do to them when she wasn't here to protect them?

But what other choice did she have?

"Let's do it." Eliza stood and headed for the stairs. It was Saturday, and Malachi was working in the garden. There were no lessons today, so it seemed the perfect time to do it. She had put Hayley down for her nap and instructed Bethany to stay with her. The girls were obedient, and she had no doubt that Bethany would do as she was told. She didn't want them to see this. No need to traumatize them further.

"I'm coming with you," Maegan said immediately.

"No, I don't want you to see this, sweetie," Eliza told the girl.

"You can't do it alone," Maegan protested.

"I can, and I will." She made her tone stern. "Go and check on the little ones and stay with them."

Maegan's blue eyes were fierce, and she opened her mouth as if to argue, but then snapped it shut. "I love you, Eliza." She threw her thin arms around Eliza's waist, gave her a quick hug, and then ran up the stairs.

Eliza, too, kept walking up the stairs, only at a much slower pace. She wasn't looking forward to this. It was going to be painful, but if it worked out, she could go home. She missed her family so much. And George, too. Did he ever think about her? Did he even remember her? Had he moved on? Was he dating someone else now, or was he hoping that one day she would be found?

When she reached the third floor, Eliza went to her bedroom and opened the window. There were bars on all the lower floor windows, but Malachi hadn't thought it necessary to put them in up here.

Looking down at the ground below, Eliza's stomach began to churn. She didn't like heights.

But she wasn't backing out.

Before she could change her mind, she jumped.

* * * * *

8:52 A.M.

Pain.

That was the first conscious thought Eliza had.

So much pain.

Her body burned with it.

Why did she hurt so badly?

She couldn't remember.

In fact, she couldn't remember much of anything right now.

She didn't even remember where she was.

Was she at home? Sick, maybe?

Was she in the hospital? Maybe she'd been in an accident.

Eliza was going to open her eyes and try to get some answers, but a sickening wave of pain so intense she nearly wished she were dead flooded through her.

Sleep was tugging at her mind, and she wanted nothing more than to give in to it. Indeed, she was about to let it wash her away into peaceful blackness when she heard a voice.

"Nice try, Eliza."

The malevolent tone was enough to momentarily block the pain and somehow her eyes struggled open.

A face hovered above her. The face was familiar, but she couldn't place it. Pale skin, blue eyes, curly black hair. She should know who this is.

She was too tired to try and figure it out. Her temporary reprieve from the pain was over; it was back worse than ever. She couldn't think. She couldn't focus. All she could do was fade toward unconsciousness.

Sometime later, Eliza awoke again.

The pain was still there, but her mind was a little clearer. She remembered Malachi abducting her. She remembered him taking the other children. She remembered being locked up in his house. She remembered her plan. She remembered throwing herself out the window in the hope it would force Malachi to take her to the hospital and give them a chance to be around other people and tell them what had happened to them.

She must be in the hospital.

Hope flooded through her, working as effectively as a morphine drip, and her eyes snapped open.

She expected to see a hospital room, doctors, nurses, and other patients. But she saw none of it.

She was in her room at Malachi's house.

Turning her head hurt, but she did it anyway when she heard cackling laughter.

Malachi was there.

Grinning at her.

"Nice try, Eliza."

He'd said that before. Malachi never used her real name. He always called her Ariyel. The glint in his eyes was different, too. Less crazy and more calculating.

"I know what you were planning, and it didn't work," Malachi continued. "I didn't take you to the hospital. You're still right here, and you are not going anywhere. Ever."

Eliza opened her mouth to speak, but her throat was dry, and she was tired and in so much pain that all that came out was a squawk.

Chuckling again, Malachi held a cup of water with a straw to her lips. Despite how much she hated him, Eliza knew she needed the water and sipped a little of it. The cool, fresh feel of it in her mouth cleared away the feeling of cottonmouth, and she tried once again to speak.

"I'm injured." Her voice was weak, insubstantial, reminding her just how powerless she was when it came to Malachi. "I need a hospital."

"You underestimate me, Eliza," Malachi said with fake disappointment. "I can take care of you just as well as any hospital. I am your father."

"You know you're not." She could feel herself starting to pass out again and felt a twinge of fear stronger than the pain. Her injuries were obviously serious, and she needed proper medical attention. If Malachi refused to take her to the hospital, then she really might die.

Seemingly reading her mind, he said, "You're not going to die. You have head injuries but you're obviously not impaired, so they aren't too serious. You have a broken leg and a broken arm, but no neck or spinal injuries, and no internal bleeding. I borrowed some medical supplies, reset your breaks, gave you morphine and sedatives so you wouldn't be in too much pain."

Malachi was truly insane. How could he think it was okay not to take her to a hospital? He couldn't really have known whether she was bleeding internally. Nor could he have known the extent of her head injuries.

A sharp prick in her arm refocused her attention. And she turned her head to see Malachi with a syringe in his hand.

"Just some morphine, unless you'd rather I not give you any more?"

Eliza knew she needed the drug; she was in too much pain to do without it. She gave her head a shake. The medication was already taking effect, dragging her back toward unconsciousness. She was almost out cold when she felt a firm grip on her arm. Forcing her eyes back open, she looked up into Malachi's deadly serious face.

"Just so you know, Eliza, I'll never let you go. I'd rather see you dead first."

NOVEMBER 3RD
11:00 P.M.

11:01 P.M.

"So, all we know is that two kids and a baby are hiding somewhere in the hospital?" Paige Hood asked Jack as they systematically walked the hospital's corridors. Her partner, Ryan, had called her and asked her to come and help with this— apparently unofficial—case that they had stumbled upon while at the hospital with Ryan's wife, Sofia.

"Yep, that's it," Jack agreed.

"And there's no chance of getting this girl to just tell us where the kids are?"

"Nope, she wouldn't budge. Xavier and I tried to convince her to let us take them somewhere safe, but she wouldn't. Even Laura couldn't get her to give it up."

If Laura couldn't get the girl to tell where her little sisters were, then no one could. Laura was amazing at getting people to open up. Paige herself had talked to Laura numerous times, telling her things that she hadn't confessed to anyone else.

"How do we know these kids are even here?" Paige asked.

"We don't."

"This could be a wild goose chase."

"It could be," Jack acknowledged.

"You talked to this Maegan. Do you think what she told you is true?"

Jack hesitated. "Laura thinks it is, and I trust her judgment."

"But?" Paige prompted, sensing there was more to it than that.

"Xavier has some doubts," Jack told her.

"He does? Why?"

"Something about a look in her eyes as she was talking to us earlier."

"What kind of look?"

"Maegan told Laura that she was scared that the man who kidnapped her would try to convince us she was insane if we confronted him. Xavier's concerned that she may actually be unbalanced and that this whole thing is just all in her head."

"If she were a kidnap victim, why would he leave her alone in a busy hospital?" Paige asked.

"If she were crazy, why would her loving father Malachi leave her alone with two young children and a baby?" Jack countered.

"All right," Paige conceded, "either scenario could be true. Someone needs to talk to this Malachi and see if that helps us figure out what's really going on."

"Yeah, I plan to talk to him later. I wanted to see if I could find these kids first. Not only might it help us find out the truth, but I don't like the idea of three little girls alone in the hospital."

"Whatever the truth, whether the girls are kidnap victims or Maegan is crazy, they aren't safe in that house. Hey, Jack, what if these kids don't even exist?"

He considered it. "You think Maegan made them up?"

"Well, no one has seen them, and she won't tell you their real names or her full name. If she's unstable, maybe she just made them up, or maybe they're like her imaginary sisters," Paige suggested.

"Maybe," Jack nodded. "But right now, we have to assume they're here and I want them found."

"I don't know where you could hide three kids in a hospital; there are too many people about. Plus, there are thousands of rooms. We can't possibly search them all quickly. We should be working on getting Maegan to give them up."

"We will," Jack assured her. "For the moment, let's just check out a few places, and then we'll go back down to the emergency room."

"Okay," she agreed. Paige could feel Jack's eyes on her as they walked the hospital halls. He had been looking at her that way since she had come to help him look for the missing girls. "Why are you looking at me like that?" she finally asked when she could take no more of it.

"Because I'm concerned about you," Jack replied evenly.

"Well, there's no reason to be," Paige snapped at him.

"Ryan's worried ..."

She stopped in her tracks to glare up at Jack. "I don't care what Ryan is worried about."

"He worries because he cares about you. We all do," he added.

She sighed. "Which would be great if there was actually something to worry about. But there's not. So it's just annoying."

Jack grinned at her.

"What?" she growled.

"When you're angry, I almost believe that you're actually okay."

Paige sighed again. She and Jack had been friends for a long time. At one time, they'd even been more than friends. She'd met Jack through her friend Rose, when Jack had become Rose's new partner. They'd dated briefly—for a month or two—but neither of them had been all that into the relationship. They had quickly realized they were better friends than anything else. She and Elias had started dating shortly after, and Jack had continued to date sporadically until Laura came back into his life.

She was glad things had worked out well for both of them, but the downside to the fact that they'd dated and were still friends was that Jack worried about her, even when it wasn't necessary. The fact that she and his brother had become partners and were really good friends didn't help.

"Jack," she groaned.

"All right, all right," he held up his hands in surrender. "If you change your mind and you want to talk, I'm here and Ryan's here and Laura and Sofia and Xavier. Whatever you need."

"There's nothing to talk about," she said adamantly, even though some of the conviction had gone out of her voice.

She had turned to start walking again when Jack caught hold of her arm and held her in place. "Paige, I'm serious."

Her frustration fading away, she softened. "Yeah, I know you are. Thanks, Jack. Seriously though, I'll be okay. Even if it doesn't ever work out."

Despite her constant attempts to convince everyone that she would be fine if an adoption never worked out, she wasn't so sure she would be. Not long after her attack, when Elias had finally garnered up enough courage to tell her that her lifesaving surgery had left her unable to have children, her therapist had told her that she would go through a grieving process. At the time, she hadn't understood how she could grieve for something that never even existed. But now she understood.

It was true. She had grieved for the children she'd never be able to have.

But now she was ready to have a family with her husband. She really wanted an adoption to work out, but so far, they'd been disappointed twice, and she had a bad feeling about this third one.

Jack shook his head at her. "I knew you weren't okay."

Ignoring that, she wasn't going to debate that with Jack all night. And debate it all night, he would. And then Ryan would jump in and Laura and Sofia and Xavier. She'd never win against all of them. "So, does Laura know we dated for a while?" she asked.

Raising an eyebrow at her to indicate that he knew she was attempting an avoid and distract, he responded, "Yeah, she does. She thinks it's funny; she can't see us as a couple at all."

Paige chuckled. She really liked Laura; they'd gotten to know each other well over the last few years, and Paige considered her and Sofia amongst her best friends. Thinking of her friends always made her think of Rose. She and Rose had been friends for years, and even though it had been four years since Rose had been murdered, the shaft of pain and loss that shot through Paige every time she thought of her hadn't diminished.

"You know, Rose had a crush on you when you two first became partners," she said softly.

Pain flooded Jack's blue eyes. "She did? I never knew that."

"She thought you were hot, but bossy." Paige attempted a smile even as she could feel her eyes fill with tears. "I still miss her, Jack."

"I know, honey. Me too."

"Sometimes I still go to call her and then I remember that I can't." Tears spilled down her cheeks, and Paige brushed them quickly away, embarrassed.

"Me too," Jack put his arms around her.

Paige allowed Jack to hold her while she cried. Sometimes life was so unfair. It was unfair that her best friend had been killed. It was unfair that now she couldn't have kids just because some insane stalker was delusional and believed she had had an affair with her partner. And it was unfair that she had to live her life under the constant cloud of knowing that the stalker could come back and attempt to kill her again at any time.

"Paige, go home, and try to get some rest."

Tugging herself free from Jack's arms, she brushed at her wet cheeks. "No, I'm okay, Jack. I like to keep busy."

Even though he didn't make a sound, Paige could practically hear his inward groan. At least he didn't offer another protest and they quickly searched for several minutes before heading back down to the emergency room.

Paige gave her own inward groan when she spotted her partner. She didn't really want to see Ryan tonight. He was going to pepper her with questions she didn't want to answer. Her hope that he wouldn't spot her just yet was short lived when he looked over, his blue eyes narrowing directly at her. If she'd been able to come up with a legitimate excuse to disappear, she'd have done it. Now her only hope was that Ryan would just let it go and focus on these missing kids.

"You've been avoiding me. Why? What's wrong?" Ryan pounced on her as soon as she and Jack reached him and Xavier.

"Nothing is wrong, and I haven't been avoiding you," she protested immediately, even though she knew she had. She hadn't answered Ryan's call earlier, but she'd listened to his message and come down here like he had asked her to. When she'd gotten here and spotted Jack, she had immediately offered to go with him to search for the kids so she could delay seeing Ryan for as long as possible.

"Jack, did she talk to you?" He ignored her and turned his attention to his brother.

"Jack," Paige shot him a warning glance. She didn't want him telling Ryan anything they talked about.

"Look, I'm not getting in the middle of whatever is going on between you two. And, Ryan, even if she did talk to me, I wouldn't tell you what she said. Paige and I are friends. Anything she tells me is confidential unless she says otherwise."

Ryan's scowl included both of them, but he let it go. For now. Paige knew he'd be back at her soon. Other than her husband, Ryan was her best friend as well as her partner, but over the last four years, she'd thought a lot about whether or not they should remain partners.

As much as she couldn't imagine working with anyone else, perhaps it would be for the best. Ryan had found her beaten, covered in blood, and struggling to breathe after her attack. Maybe it would be better to start from scratch with someone who hadn't seen her like that. Which was unfair, she knew. Ryan had saved her life that day. If he hadn't turned up when he had, she'd be dead.

Paige knew that Ryan and Sofia blamed themselves for her attack, but it was one hundred percent her own fault. She had been tired and distracted that day, and that was how the stalker had managed to sneak up on her without her noticing. She loved her friends, but she didn't love that they worried about her. She was doing okay now—she didn't need or want them worrying about her all the time. But she knew as long as the stalker remained at large it was inevitable that she would continue to be a source of worry for her friends.

"Maegan said she didn't know Malachi's last name, so we can't do a background check on him," Xavier announced, breaking the tension by focusing them back on the case.

Paige shot him a grateful smile. She liked Xavier, considered him a good friend. She and Ryan had met Xavier shortly before she was attacked when their two cases had suddenly morphed into one. Now Xavier was Jack's partner—because Rose was dead. Paige gave herself a mental shake. She wasn't going to start thinking about Rose again. If she did, she'd wind up all emotional and then everyone would be pestering her all night about whether or not she was okay.

"Do we even know that Malachi is his name?" she asked, forcing herself to focus.

"You think the name's a fake?" Xavier asked.

She shrugged. "Maybe. Supposedly, he's given the girls other names. Maybe he gave himself one, too," she suggested.

"Maybe," Jack nodded. "But Maegan said the names he gave them were his daughter's names, so I think Malachi is his real name."

"Let's assume for the moment it is," Ryan continued. "We know what he looks like, we could attempt to ID him through his driver's license."

"That could take a while," Jack protested.

"Malachi isn't that common a name," Ryan reminded him. "We know approximate age. If one of his daughters was sixteen when she died, and that was approximately five to six years ago, he has to be at least mid-thirties, probably no older than mid-forties. We can eliminate everyone too old and too young. We know he has blue eyes, and we can get an approximate height. I think it's worth a try."

"Okay, I guess it's worth a try," Jack agreed.

"And we have the daughters' names," Paige added. "We know approximately when the fire was, so we should be able to find something on it. Even aside from anything official, four girls killed in a fire would have made the news. If we look it up, we may be able to get an address and an ID on this Malachi."

"Plus, we know Maegan's name—first, at least—and when and how she was abducted. We should try and find her case file. That might help us identify her, which might help us to identify Malachi, or at least prove who's telling the truth."

"All right, you guys work on that," Jack said. "I'm going to go and talk to him, see what he has—"

"Detectives?"

A woman in her fifties approached them. She was short and too skinny, wearing scrubs, and her hair was pulled back in a messy brown ponytail. Her brown eyes looked small behind a pair of oversized glasses.

"Dr. Roma, do you have the results of Ariyel's blood work?" Jack asked, having spoken with the doctor earlier.

"Drug overdose," Dr. Roma replied.

"What drug?" Paige asked. If these girls were really kidnap victims who hadn't been allowed to leave the house they'd been taken to in five years, it seemed unlikely that they would have access to illegal drugs. Unless, of course, this Malachi was a drug dealer, which was theoretically a possibility.

"Barbiturates," the doctor answered.

"Sedatives?" Paige clarified.

"Yes," Dr. Roma confirmed.

"Is she going to be okay?" Paige wondered if the girl had attempted suicide.

"She's going to be fine," the doctor smiled reassuringly. "At least physically." She turned to Jack. "You said you believed she was a kidnap victim?"

"We believe she and three other girls were abducted five years ago by the man who brought her here tonight. What can you tell us about him?"

"Not much. He said he was her father. I didn't see any other girls; it was just him and Ariyel. He said he went into her room after dinner to ask her something and found her passed out and unresponsive, so he rushed her here," Dr. Roma explained.

"He didn't say anything else?" Jack pushed.

"Nope, I asked him a few background medical questions like did she have any known medical conditions or allergies. He said no, then mentioned that she'd been complaining of headaches recently. That was it. I ordered some tests and moved on to other patients. When I came back to check on Ariyel, the man was gone, and you were there," she said.

"Did he give a surname?" Xavier asked.

"Smith," the doctor answered.

"I'm going to guess that was a fake," Ryan noted wryly.

"We're going to need to know when she's conscious so we can speak with her," Jack informed Dr. Roma, who was already looking distractedly around the emergency room. She, no doubt, had several patients awaiting her.

"Sure, I'll make sure someone lets you know when she wakes up. If you need anything else, I'm around all night." Dr. Roma gave them a quick smile and then headed off.

"Okay, I'm going to go and find Malachi, see what he has to say about this," Jack announced once the doctor was gone.

"Before you do, Jack, you may want to check on Laura. She had more nightmares earlier," Ryan told his brother.

"This is ridiculous," Jack muttered. "I might call Mom or Dad to come and get her and take her back to their place. I shouldn't have let her stay here this long."

As Jack headed for Sofia and Laura's hospital room, Paige decided she better make her own quick getaway, or she was going to be stuck alone with Ryan who would no doubt be jumping into digging for answers to his questions.

"I'm going to go to the bathroom and then check on Maegan," she announced, and without waiting for a response, turned and all but fled to the bathroom.

Paige thought she heard Ryan call her name, but she ignored him and thankfully he didn't follow her. Inside the bathroom, she splashed some cold water on her face. The cold felt fresh against her skin and helped to calm her a little.

Then her phone rang.

* * * * *

11:19 P.M.

The first thing Jack saw as he opened the door to Sofia's hospital room was his wife in a bed with an oxygen mask on her face. "What happened?" he demanded, quickening his stride as he headed for the bed.

Laura's eyes opened, and she pulled a hand out from under the blankets to tug the mask from her face. "Nothing. I'm fine."

"She had a panic attack," Sofia informed him.

He just managed to catch a growl before it escaped. This was ridiculous. He knew Laura wasn't coping. He should have insisted on driving her home and not taken no for an answer.

"It was nothing," Laura muttered.

Perching on the bed beside her, Jack pulled the oxygen mask from her hand and placed it back over her mouth and nose. "What happened?" he repeated, this time directing the question to Sofia.

"She went to go to the bathroom, walked out the door, saw all the people and had a panic attack. The nurse who found her is a friend of Mark's. She called him, and he came down and saw her," Sofia explained.

It had been a while since Laura's agoraphobia had caused her to have a panic attack. She'd had them frequently when they'd first gotten back together, but over time, they'd faded. This ridiculous desire to push herself was going to wind up with her going backward instead of forward. And now she was having nightmares again after months without a single one. Jack was about to open his mouth and unleash his frustration on Laura when she looked up at him with teary eyes.

"Jack, don't," she whispered.

"What am I going to do with you?" he said instead, kissing her on the forehead. "Ryan told me you had another nightmare earlier. I don't want you to leave this room until we sort out what's going on with Maegan and I take you home. Mark say she was okay?" Jack asked Sofia.

"Yeah, he just reiterated that she needs rest," Sofia replied.

"Okay, both of you should be asleep, I don't want to see either of you out of bed again tonight. I don't want to, but I really have to go and talk to this Malachi man, so please, please, Laura, just stay in bed and try to sleep. Promise me." He didn't want to worry about her all night. He was going to anyway, but if he at least knew she was in bed asleep, he'd worry less. A *little* less.

"I promise," Laura agreed.

He didn't want to, but Jack doubted the sincerity of her promise. If Maegan came in here and asked Laura for help, then his wife would more than likely do whatever Maegan asked her to. If Laura weren't eight months pregnant, he'd be tempted to get someone to sedate her so she had no choice but to rest.

Laura must have read something in his expression because she pulled the oxygen mask from her face again and said, "Jack, please don't be angry with me."

"I'm not angry with you, angel," he promised, easing her off the pillows and holding her close against his chest. "I'm concerned about you."

"I'll stay here, in bed, and try to sleep, I promise. Even if I have nightmares," she added. "Really, Jack, I promise. I don't want you to worry about me anymore."

"I know you don't, angel, but I can't help it." Jack felt Laura sigh, but she didn't say anything. He knew that she hated that what she'd been through changed how people saw her.

"I'm not a helpless victim, Jack. I kept myself alive for four days while Frank and Francis Garrett tortured me. And I shot Axel Christenson when he tried to rape and murder me. I know I messed up before by hiding, but I'm not doing that anymore."

"I know, angel, I know," he soothed. Jack was worried that Laura's sudden intense drive to prove she wasn't hiding anymore was going to wind up causing her more pain and anguish.

She took a deep breath, "I'm okay, Jack. Go and help Maegan. Sofia and I will stay here and sleep."

Reluctantly, he stood. "All right, I'm going. I love you." He pressed a quick kiss to Laura's lips, laid her back against the pillows and replaced the oxygen mask. "Remember, you two, don't let that Dr. Daniels come in here," he reminded them.

"We won't," Laura assured him. She caught his hand as he turned to leave. "I love you, too."

Outside the room, he shrugged off his concerns. Laura was safe and sound for the moment. There was no point in obsessing over her emotional well-being right now. In the morning, once they'd sorted out this issue with Maegan and Malachi, and Laura had gotten a proper night's sleep, they'd talk about her going back to see her therapist.

It didn't take him long to locate Malachi.

The man was standing in a corner of the waiting area, his gaze circling the room over and over again. Standing ramrod straight, his hands clenched into fists at his sides, he looked on edge.

"Malachi?" Jack asked as he approached.

Immediately, the man schooled his features to calm, cool, and collected. "You're not a doctor."

"No, I'm not," Jack agreed. "I'm Detective Xander. We need to talk." He gestured toward a door just down the corridor a little.

When he'd explained to the head of the ER what was going on, the man had offered him a couple of offices to do his interviews in.

For a moment, it looked like Malachi was going to refuse, but then he smiled and nodded. "Sure thing," he agreed and followed along as Jack led him to the office.

"Who was that woman you were with earlier?" Malachi asked, taking a seat at the table and looking much too comfortable for Jack's liking.

"Which woman?" Obviously, the man had pegged them as cops and been watching them.

"About your age, pretty, curly brown hair, big brown eyes." Malachi's eyes went dark with lust as he explained.

"That's a colleague of mine," Jack replied, not liking at all that this man was lusting after Paige.

"I'd be happy to talk to her," Malachi suggested.

No way was Jack letting this sleazy man around Paige. Not that he was going to tell her that; she would think that was extremely overprotective. She'd probably be right. But that was just too bad. Jack did feel protective of Paige.

Even though they'd both known from the beginning that it wasn't going to work out between them, Jack didn't regret dating Paige. They had decided to remain friends once they'd broken up and he'd been pleased when she and Ryan became partners.

Despite Paige's protestations that she was fine, Jack knew she wasn't. She'd been on an emotional roller coaster the last few years. Knowing that the man who had tried to kill her—who had nearly succeeded in killing her—was still out there, had taken its toll. As unobtrusively as they could, all of them had been attempting to ensure that Paige was on her own as little as possible. No one wanted to risk the stalker getting to her again.

He'd already lost Rose; he didn't want to lose anyone else that he cared about.

Losing Rose had been hard. Really hard. And just like Paige, he was still grieving. There were lots of times that something funny would happen and he'd want to text Rose and tell her. Or when he needed to talk, he'd go to call her and ask for her opinion. And there were so many things in his life he'd missed out on having her there for. His wedding, the birth of his son, the impending birth of his second child. Not to mention all the things Rose had missed out on: falling in love, getting married, having kids of her own.

Jack tried not to talk about Rose too much since he knew Laura blamed herself for her death. Which was completely untrue—as he'd told her many times—not that it made much difference. He understood the feeling of blaming yourself for something that you knew intellectually wasn't your fault, but he didn't like seeing it in the woman he loved.

As much as Laura had issues to work through these last few years, he had, as well. The depression he experienced following being held hostage in a bank robbery had grown steadily between then and the three years until Laura came back into his life. But having Laura, who so badly needed him to be strong, had been the push he needed to work through his own feelings of helplessness, inadequacy, and failure.

His family, his friends, and his job were all important to him and he didn't like anyone threatening any of them.

"Detective Hood is otherwise occupied at the moment," Jack informed him.

"Too bad." Malachi looked disappointed. "So, did something happen here at the hospital? Is that why you wanted to talk to me?"

"Did you see something happen?" he asked, wanting to get a read on the man.

He shook his head. "No, I just didn't know what else you'd want to talk to me about. Unless you're not here about some sort of crime. I mean, I just assumed, since you said you were a detective, but are you here about a family member?" Malachi feigned confusion.

"Actually, I am, but one of your family members." Jack watched the man closely to see how he'd react.

"Ariyel?" Malachi asked. "I thought she was still unconscious?"

"No, not Ariyel. Maegan."

The confusion didn't leave his face. "Is that some sort of trick? I don't know anyone called Maegan."

In his gut, Jack believed that Maegan was telling them the truth. Laura wasn't usually wrong about people. If she believed in Maegan, then he did, too. "Oh." It was his turn to feign surprise. "She identified herself as your daughter. Long black hair, blue eyes, skinny, about fifteen," he listed.

"You mean Alice?"

"She said her name was Maegan. She also told us a very interesting story."

Seemingly unfazed, Malachi's brow creased in concerned understanding. He nodded slowly. "Sometimes Alice has a very overactive imagination. She's not quite well, you know. In the head," he added.

Exactly what Maegan had predicted Malachi would claim. "She seemed quite sane."

"It's sad, isn't it? She's often quite convincing; sometimes if I didn't know better, she'd almost convince me." His blue eyes crinkled sadly.

"She says she's not your daughter. She says that you kidnapped her—her and three other girls. She says that was five years ago. She says that you haven't let her and the others out of your house in all that time." As he spoke, Jack watched for signs of stress, but Malachi showed none. Only disappointment.

"Poor little thing. It just breaks my heart when she gets like that. I'll have to call her doctor in the morning, try and get her an appointment as soon as possible. Perhaps her medication needs changing."

"So, Maegan—I'm sorry, *Alice*—is really your daughter? This story she told us about you grabbing her at a gas station five years ago is all just … lies?"

"Delusions," Malachi corrected.

"Are just delusions?" Jack played along. "You never abducted her? You never abducted Ariyel? You never abducted two other little girls?

He chuckled grimly. "I can assure you, Detective, Alice is my daughter. I can show you photographs of her as a baby, if you'd like." He pulled his wallet from his pocket, opened it, and showed him some photos of a smiling, dark haired, blue-eyed toddler. The little girl could have been Maegan, or she could have been anyone.

"Maybe we could talk to your two younger daughters, let them clear things up. What were their names again?" Jack asked, knowing the names Maegan had given them and wanting to see if Malachi offered up the same names.

"What two other daughters?" Malachi looked baffled. "I only have two daughters, Alice and Ariyel."

"So, Angela and Abby are just figments of Alice's imagination?"

"I guess so."

"And she's currently under the care of a psychiatrist?"

"Yes, she is, for over a year now."

"Is she on any medication?" Thinking of the fact that Ariyel had been drugged, or drugged herself, with sedatives.

"Yes, she is."

"Would you be willing to let us do a blood test on her to confirm that, clear everything up?" That could be the simplest way to prove who was lying. Not that Jack had any real doubts, but proof meant that they could put Maegan's fears to bed and get more answers and information out of her.

"Sure, whatever." But for the first time uncertainty flashed through his blue eyes.

"Did you know that Ariyel suffered a drug overdose?"

His eyes grew wide—too wide—fake wide. "Is that why you're

talking to me? Do you think that Alice tried to kill her sister? She would *never* do that. Ever. Let's go and find her and clear all of this up right now. If Ariyel suffered a drug overdose, it would have been an accident. I didn't kidnap anyone, and I haven't done anything wrong. And neither did my daughter. I'm sorry Alice caused you so much trouble. I'll talk to her."

In principle, Malachi seemed sincere and convincing. He was calm, cool, and in control. Everything he said sounded believable. But Jack didn't believe him one iota.

* * * * *

11:29 P.M.

Ryan was distracted.

Xavier was talking to him, but he hadn't heard a word the other man had said. It wasn't that he didn't care about Maegan and her sisters. If the girls were kidnap victims, then he hoped that they could help them go back to their real families.

He just had a lot on his mind. He hated it when Sofia was sick, although it was an inevitable part of having young kids who picked up every germ going around, it brought back a lot of bad memories for both of them. At least she was looking better, so that was a load off his mind.

He just wished that things would go as smoothly for Paige.

She was avoiding him, despite her protestations that she wasn't, which meant that something was wrong. And she was talking to Jack about whatever was going on. Ryan knew that Jack and Paige were good friends, but she usually talked to him about what was going on with her, not with his brother.

As if on cue, Paige walked out of the bathroom, heading straight for the door. She looked like she was in a daze. That couldn't be good. He was about to tell Xavier he was going to go and check on his partner, but Xavier spoke first.

"Go to her, she doesn't look good."

Following Paige out into the parking lot, he found her off to the side staring blankly into space.

"Paige?" he said softly as he approached.

She turned to him in slow motion, her brown eyes watery, and Ryan's concerns stepped up a notch.

"What happened? What's wrong?"

Instead of answering, his partner just turned away and resumed her sightless staring.

He sensed this wasn't the time to be tough and push her too hard. "It's cold out and you're not wearing a jacket," he said gently, shrugging out of his and slipping it onto Paige's shaking shoulders.

"It should have been me." Paige's voice trembled.

Confused, he asked, "What should have?"

"That night. It should have been me who stayed with Laura, not Rose."

He frowned. "What? So you could have died?"

She shrugged indifferently. "I feel like I'm half dead already. It would have been better for me to die than Rose." Paige's hands gripped the lapels of his jacket and pulled it tighter around herself, like a protective shield. She shuddered violently; the movement seemed to send the tears brimming in her eyes tumbling out. "I miss Rose so much."

"You're still grieving," he reminded her. So much had happened so close together for Paige, being nearly killed, the threat of the stalker still being out there, finding out she couldn't have kids, losing Rose—it had all been too much; no wonder she hadn't been able to deal with it.

"It's been four years." Paige brushed at the tears still trickling down her cheeks.

"You never stop grieving someone you love," Ryan reminded her. He was positive that this had been what Paige and Jack had been talking about earlier. They had been the closest with Rose and he knew that they both still missed her a lot.

"Do you still miss Katrina?"

"Yeah, I do," he admitted. Not that he thought about Katrina that much anymore. Katrina had been his fiancée; she'd committed suicide eight years ago. At first, he'd thought about her a lot, but over time, and especially once he'd met Sofia and they'd fallen in love, gotten married and had kids, Katrina had bit by bit faded from his mind. But she'd never completely leave it. From time to time something would remind him of her, and he still wished he knew why she'd taken her own life. Katrina was a part of him, and that part of him would always love her.

For a long time after her death, Ryan had blamed himself. A part of him still did. She had been his fiancée; he should have noticed that she was suicidal. He should have been able to say or do something to help her. Yet, he hadn't. While he still wished things had turned out differently, he had to accept that what Katrina had done was not his fault. Accepting that was a process. A long process.

"Now tell me why you feel like a part of you is already dead," he prompted Paige.

Paige didn't reply, just turned away from him and seemed to shrink further inside herself.

Fearing she was about to flee, Ryan grabbed hold of her shoulder and turned her back around to face him. "Because you can't have kids?" he asked gently.

Fresh tears welled up in her eyes and she nodded.

"It'll happen, Paige. An adoption will work out; you just have to be patient."

At that, Paige began to cry and all but collapsed against him. Wrapping his arms around her, Ryan held her as she wept. She didn't need to tell him that this latest adoption had fallen through.

"I can't do it again, Ryan," Paige said through her tears.

"Do what, honey?"

"I can't have another adoption fall through ... I'm not doing it again."

"I'm so sorry, Paige." Ryan wished there was something he could do to help her. "It's going to work out, you just have to keep having faith." She shook her head against his chest. "It will, I promise."

"You can't promise me that."

While Ryan knew that was true, he still wanted to reassure her and make her feel better. "What about other options? What about surrogacy?"

"No, I have to accept that Elias and I are never going to be parents," Paige's muffled voice insisted.

Letting it go for now, she needed time to process this latest disappointment before she could consider taking another avenue to become a parent.

She pulled herself out of his arms. "I'm sorry," Paige sniffed as she wiped at her eyes.

"About what?"

"Crying all over you."

"That's what friends are for, Paige," he rebuked gently.

Her gaze dipped. "I'm sorry I haven't been a very good friend lately."

"What are you talking about?"

"I avoid you sometimes," she whispered, still refusing to look at him. "And sometimes I even think about asking for a new partner."

"What?" Panic sliced through him. He did *not* want a new partner.

"I don't really, Ryan." She finally looked up at him. "But I don't like that you saw me beaten nearly to death. Knowing that it happened because I was distracted. I don't know how you can trust me to have your back after seeing me like that."

"That's ridiculous, Paige," he admonished. "We've been in dangerous situations in the past four years since that happened, and I always trust you to have my back. You *do* always have my back. Now, tell me why you avoid me."

She shrugged fitfully. "I get jealous sometimes. Because you and Sofia are so happy with Sophie and Ned. I'm sorry. I love your kids, and I'm so glad that you have such a fabulous family. I'm sorry." Her pale cheeks heated a little with embarrassment.

"Would you please stop apologizing to me?"

"Sorry," she said the word before she realized it, and a small smile lit her lips. "I can't help it," she said as way of explanation.

He smiled back, pleased that she seemed a little more in control of her emotions. "Come on, let's go back inside. You're still cold, and Jack's probably finished talking to Malachi by now."

"Ryan," Paige grabbed hold of his arm and held him in place as he moved to head for the door. "You're a really good friend. Thanks."

Paige gave him a hug, and as he hugged her back, Ryan prayed that somehow something would work out and Paige would get a chance to be the awesome mother he knew she'd be.

* * * * *

11:36 P.M.

Fuming.

He was completely fuming.

Bruce had just spent the last ten minutes or so watching Detective Paige Hood throw herself all over Sofia's husband.

Even now as he watched, Paige once again shoved herself into Ryan's arms.

Carefully, he studied the other man's face and body language to see if he was reciprocating Paige's blatant attempts to seduce him. If Bruce thought that Ryan was in any way going to cause Sofia pain, he would do something about it.

Paige had the ability like no one else on earth to get his blood boiling.

He hated the woman.

Really hated her.

It seemed he had made a mistake by not taking her out before now. He'd thought she had learned her lesson. He'd thought she had learned to be content with her own husband. Obviously, he'd been wrong.

Bruce had seen her earlier with Jack Xander.

Once again, she'd used the crying jag to elicit sympathy.

He'd been too far away to hear what they were talking about, but he'd seen her start to cry and then barge her way into Jack's arms.

It seems Paige couldn't stop with just one man.

She had her husband, and now she was after both Ryan and Jack. And who knew how many other men.

Bruce wasn't about to let her go on seducing married men.

He would put a stop to it.

Put a stop to *her*.

He wouldn't allow her to go on causing pain to the people she claimed to be friends with. He felt guilty that he hadn't stopped her before now. He had known that she was bad news. He had known that she had tried to have an affair with Ryan before. When his attempt to take her out had been thwarted, he should have gone back at her right away. He shouldn't have waited so long.

But he wouldn't wait a single day longer.

He was going to take her out.

Permanently.

And he was going to do it tonight.

* * * * *

11:40 P.M.

"Everything okay?" Xavier asked Paige and Ryan as they came

back inside. Paige's eyes were red-rimmed. She'd clearly been crying, but she looked like she was holding it together. Given Paige's history, it didn't take a genius to figure out that the latest adoption had fallen through. Xavier felt so bad for her and wished there was something he could do to help her.

"Everything's fine," Paige assured him with only a hint of a wobble in her voice.

Obviously, it wasn't. Xavier caught Ryan's eye and arched a brow, wanting confirmation of that. Ryan gave a discreet half nod, and Xavier let it go. However, he made a mental note to check in with Paige later.

"Jack, you talk to Malachi?" Ryan asked.

"Yes." Jack gestured to the office where they'd interviewed Maegan earlier. "Let's talk in there. It's quieter."

He, Ryan, and Paige trailed after Jack, taking seats in the small room and then looking expectantly at his partner.

"So, Maegan was right," Jack announced. "Malachi claimed she was crazy. Said that she's delusional, that she sees a psychiatrist, and is on medication."

"Did he give you a doctor's name and permission to do a blood test on Maegan?" Xavier asked. With both of these pieces of information, they could clear this up immediately.

"Both," Jack nodded. "Although he was adamant that her name was Alice and not Maegan. And he was adamant that she was his daughter. He showed me some pictures of a toddler that could have been Maegan, but there's no way to be sure."

"What did he say about the other kids?" Paige asked.

"Said they don't exist," Jack replied. "He claimed to only have two daughters, Alice and Ariyel."

"So, we could have been searching the hospital for children that aren't even here?" she asked.

"Possibly," Jack acknowledged.

"What was his demeanor like?" Ryan asked.

"Calm and totally in control. He was appropriately shocked,

concerned, apologetic," Jack explained.

"So, both Maegan—or Alice—depending on what her real name is, and Malachi tell a convincing story," Xavier mused.

"And both are completely contradictory, so one of them is lying," Jack added. "Any progress in IDing Malachi?"

Paige's pale cheeks pinked in embarrassment.

"We got a little distracted," Ryan replied.

"Everything okay?" Jack's blue eyes were glued to Paige.

"Yes," Paige answered firmly, holding Jack's gaze.

"Ryan?"

"Sorry, Jack. Paige and I are friends, and anything we talk about is confidential unless she tells me otherwise," Ryan parroted back what Jack had told him earlier in response to the same question. Jack rolled his eyes at his brother, who grinned back at him.

Some of the tension eased from Paige's face at her partner's attempt to lighten the mood. "We need confirmation from someone else in order to confirm Maegan's story," she said. "We either need to talk to Ariyel or to the other little girls—if they even exist."

"I agree," Xavier nodded, glad the case was helping to distract Paige. She always did better when she kept busy, but he doubted she could keep it up forever if they never found the stalker. Living with the knowledge that someone wanted her dead had taken its toll on her, and she'd never be able to move on so long as the stalker remained at large. "We can't prove a kidnapping at the moment. Even if we do a blood test on Maegan and she comes back clean. It still doesn't prove kidnapping. Malachi could claim that she's been pretending to take her medication."

"He'd probably say that Maegan used the drugs she was supposed to be taking to drug Ariyel," Jack added.

"What do we think on the overdose?" Xavier asked. "Let's count out the little girls. Even if they exist, I don't think they'd be capable of drugging Ariyel, so that leaves her, Maegan, or

Malachi."

"Depends if the overdose was accidental or intentional," Paige mused thoughtfully.

"I don't think it was Malachi," Jack replied. "If he wanted to kill her, he wouldn't have brought her here."

"What if it was an accident?" Ryan pressed. "He's trying to keep her under control and accidentally gives her too much, then he can't wake her up and panics, bringing her here."

"If they really are kidnap victims, then Maegan could have done it on purpose," Paige put forward. "She wants an excuse for Malachi to take them out of the house so she can get help, only she's too scared to hurt herself, so she thinks she can overdose Ariyel and get Malachi to bring them here."

"If she did, that could have her up on charges of attempted murder," Ryan noted.

"What about Ariyel?" Jack asked. "Do we think it was a suicide attempt? Could have been if she's a kidnap victim. She just decided she'd had enough."

"While you guys were talking, I started doing a little research into the fire—" Xavier began.

"Don't even think about starting up with the apologies again," Ryan interrupted to order Paige, who had opened her mouth presumably to apologize for not helping.

"I'm glad you talked to Ryan, Paige," he assured her.

"Ryan called me to come here and help, not hinder." Paige wasn't about to be placated.

"You're not a hindrance," Ryan assured her.

Paige didn't look convinced, but turned her attention back to him and asked, "Did you find anything?"

"So far, no. I've started trolling the internet for fires where four sisters were killed, since we don't know if the mother was also killed or not. Plenty of hits came up, but so far nothing that looks like it could be related. And we don't even know where this happened. We're assuming he lived around here, but there's no guarantee of that. He could have lived anywhere."

"So, right now," Ryan said, "we have two completely different and yet convincingly told stories. Who are we believing?"

"Maegan," Jack replied immediately.

"Because of Laura?" Xavier agreed that Laura was fabulous at reading people, but *everyone* got things wrong once in a while.

"Not just because of Laura." Jack looked unfazed by the challenge. "When we were talking to Maegan, the only look in her eyes was fear that we couldn't help her. When I talked to Malachi, he was in control the whole time except for a brief moment of panic when I asked about letting us do a blood test on Maegan."

"You still have doubts about her, Xavier?" Paige asked.

He wasn't sure. Maegan seemed genuinely afraid, but if she were truly suffering from some sort of psychiatric disorder, then her fear could be genuine and yet unfounded. "I don't know yet. I need more information."

"Since Ariyel is still unconscious, let's take another go at Maegan," Jack suggested.

"Ryan and I will keep trying to ID Malachi, and then we'll have a go at him ..."

"No," Jack interjected firmly.

"What?" Paige looked at him with irritated surprise.

"You're not to go near him."

"What? Why?" Paige's indignation was growing.

"He was watching you, Paige. He asked about you. I don't trust him, and I don't want you going near him." Jack was in full bossy mode.

"You don't decide what I do and don't do in the course of an investigation," Paige objected.

"Unofficial investigation," Jack corrected.

"Whatever," Paige growled.

"We don't know if this guy is dangerous ..."

"You know, believe it or not, Jack, I've been in dangerous situations before. It kind of goes with the job."

"I know that, Paige. But would you please just keep your distance from him until we know more?" Jack gentled his voice and this time phrased it as a question instead of an order.

"Jack," she groaned.

"Please, Paige. I'm already worrying about Laura. I don't want to be worrying about you, as well."

Jack's honesty seemed to do the trick. Paige rolled her eyes but nodded. "Fine, I'll stay away from him. Ryan and I will go and try to ID Malachi." Paige stood and strode for the door. "I'm going to the bathroom. Don't worry, Jack, if I see Malachi I'll run in the other direction and hide."

"I think she's mad at me," Jack said dryly when the door swung closed behind Paige.

"She'll get over it," Ryan said. Then shot his brother a look before Jack could say more. "Yes, Jack, I'll go follow her, and I won't let her out of my sight."

"Think Malachi will run?" Xavier asked Jack once they were alone.

"Maybe. The only time he really lost his control was when I told him he couldn't see or speak with Maegan. He didn't like that. Told me I couldn't stop him from talking to his own daughter. I told him that since we're investigating whether she's a kidnap victim, he can't for the time being. If he feels backed into a corner, then yes, I think he might try to disappear. I asked hospital security to keep an eye on him and let me know if he makes a move."

"Let's hope Maegan decides to be a little more forthcoming with information so we can actually do something to sort this mess out."

* * * * *

11:48 P.M.

Maegan was fretting.

She was so scared that she was making a mistake.

If this didn't work out, if the police couldn't help her and her sisters and Malachi took them back home with him, then Maegan knew without a hint of a doubt that the consequences would be severe.

Malachi would be furious.

And he would take those frustrations out on her and the others.

Mostly her.

She was okay with that, especially if it kept him away from Angela and Abby for a while longer.

She hadn't seen any of the cops in a while.

Where were they?

Why weren't they doing something?

She'd done as they asked and remained in this office, anxiously pacing up and down, getting more and more worked up as each second ticked by.

But they hadn't come back.

Had they given up on her already?

Then the door opened and she spun toward it, trying to gauge from the looks on their faces what was going on.

"Maegan, let's take a seat. We need to ask you some more questions," Jack announced as he entered the room, his partner behind him.

"More questions?" she demanded incredulously. "Why aren't you helping me? Why won't you do something?"

"We're trying, honey." Jack took her elbow and eased her down into a chair. "But you're not giving us much to work with."

She fought down her frustrations. What Jack had said was true. She hadn't given them much to work with, but she needed them to take it and *do* something.

"We've been working on trying to identify Malachi; hopefully, that will help," Xavier told her.

She studied the man. He had doubts about her, Maegan could tell. It was in his eyes—they didn't trust her. Why he didn't, she didn't have a clue. While she wanted him to believe her, she didn't really care. Jack believed her because of Laura, and for now, that was enough to make sure someone did something to help her.

"Are you sure you don't have any idea what Malachi's surname could be?" Xavier asked her.

"I already told you I don't," Maegan snapped. If this man thought she was lying, then why was he here?

"Maegan." Jack's voice was calm and soothing and diverted her attention away from Xavier. "I talked to Malachi."

For a moment, everything seemed to freeze. Her heart, her lungs, her body, her mind—nothing seemed to work. She couldn't breathe, couldn't move, couldn't speak, couldn't think. The two men in the room seemed to freeze right along with her.

Maegan had known, of course, that Jack was going to talk to Malachi.

It was inevitable.

But knowing that he had made all of this feel so real.

Malachi would lie. She knew he would.

So it would come down to either him or her. Jack and his friends couldn't believe them both.

Who would it be?

Malachi or her?

"Maegan?" Jack's hand rested on her shoulder. The touch brought her snapping back into the moment. "Are you all right?"

She jerked a nod. "What did he say?" she asked breathlessly.

"Exactly what you said he'd say," Jack replied gently.

"He said I was crazy." Maegan had known he would and yet hearing it confirmed still made her heart thump painfully in her chest. If Jack and the others believed him, then she'd risked everything for nothing.

"Yes, he did," Jack confirmed. "He said that you're delusional and that you're under the care of a psychiatrist. He says that you really are his daughter, and that he only has two daughters. He denied that the younger girls even exist."

Her fear changed into frustration. Hadn't Malachi ruined her life enough already, without painting her as crazy? And, if the cops were asking her more questions, then they must have decided to side with Malachi. "You believe him?" she demanded.

"No, Maegan." Jack eyes met hers directly, not breaking contact to emphasize his words.

"Why?"

"Because when I look in your eyes, I see true fear."

"Maybe I'm just crazy and my fears are unfounded." She raised a challenging brow.

"Maybe," Jack agreed, "but I don't think so. Now Malachi said that you're on medication, and we can do a blood test to prove that you aren't on anything."

"What's the point? Malachi will come up with a reason why my blood tests turn up negative." Maegan shrugged restlessly; she was feeling hopeless. Why was she even bothering to do this? It was never going to work.

Jack leaned in closer until she had no choice but to meet his gaze. "Don't give up, Maegan," he told her.

She fought against the urge to give in and accept her fate. "Okay."

"Good girl. Now, Malachi also said that the younger girls don't exist. Why would he say that?"

"So you're not looking for them. He probably thinks Ariyel and I are a lost cause, but if you don't have the little girls, then he can find them first and he doesn't lose all of us."

Maegan was sure that Jack was going to begin pressuring her again to give the girls up. If he did, she may even give in and give up where she'd stashed them. She couldn't keep them safe. She was finally coming to realize that.

Instead of mentioning the children, Jack said, "Ariyel suffered a drug overdose. Do you know anything about that?"

Pure outrage shot through her, as sharp and fast as an arrow. She jumped to her feet. "You think *I* drugged her?"

"I didn't say that, Maegan," Jack said in an overly patient tone.

"But you thought it," she growled.

"I didn't say that, either." Jack looked like he was starting to get frustrated with her. Well, that was just too darn bad because she was pretty frustrated herself.

"Even if you didn't think it, *he* certainly did." She threw a glare in Xavier's direction. "You think I'm a liar. You don't believe anything I've told you."

"I have some doubts," Xavier acknowledged calmly.

His admission took some of the wind out of her sails, and she sagged back down into her chair. Tears were brimming in her eyes now, and she angrily brushed them away. "Why don't you believe me?"

"I guess I just don't get why you won't tell us everything," Xavier replied. "If you were a real victim needing help, I'd imagine that you'd be wanting to give us all the information you can, so we can help you."

Maegan wished she had a clever comeback for that, but she didn't. Bottom line—she wasn't trying to be difficult; she was just scared. Despite her best efforts, her tears began to spill out, trickling down her cheeks leaving wet trails in their wake. "I *do* need help, I'm just afraid," she cried. "You don't know what my life has been like the last five years. I've prayed every day for a chance to get away from Malachi, and now I have one, and I'm scared I'm going to mess it up. Malachi's already saying things that have you doubting me. If this doesn't work and I go back to that house with him, he's going to be angry. Really angry. And he's going to take it out on me and the others. I promise you that everything I've told you is true. Malachi did kidnap me. And I would *never* do anything to hurt Ariyel."

"Do you think it's possible that Ariyel would intentionally give herself a drug overdose?" Xavier asked, some of the doubt erased from his eyes.

"Yes," Maegan answered without hesitation. "I don't know if she did or not, but she's tried it before. Not with drugs. But a few years ago, she tried to force Malachi to take us to the hospital by jumping out of a third-story window. She was badly hurt, but he wouldn't bring her here. He treated her at the house."

Seeing Ariyel's broken and bloody body had been terrifying. Not only because she had been afraid that Ariyel might die but because she had finally realized that Malachi intended to never let them go.

Jack passed her a tissue. "Ariyel loves you," Jack stated the obvious. "She'd do anything to help you, no matter the cost to herself. Maegan," his blue eyes met hers and held her gaze, "you opened up to Laura, told her your story, because you wanted to do the same for her. I know you're scared. I've talked to Malachi, and I get where you're coming from, but you started this, and we want to help you finish it, so please, give us the information we need to end this for all of you."

She wavered. She was tired, physically and emotionally. The last five years had aged her and the last few hours had drained her. Maybe she should just do it. Tell them everything. Let them deal with it all. And she really did want to see her parents. When this was over, she could finally go home.

Home.

The word sounded almost magical to her.

The thought of being wrapped up in her mother's arms again after all these years was almost too good to be true.

As if reading her mind, Jack spoke again. "Once we know who you are, Maegan, you can go home. And we can find out who the other girls are, find their families. You can all go home."

She wanted to tell him, she really did. And still, she hesitated.

"What's Ariyel's real name?" he pressed.

Taking a deep breath, it was now or never. "Eliza," she replied in a small voice.

"How did Malachi get his hands on her?" Jack asked gently.

"She was walking home from college. He pretended his car had broken down and asked to borrow her cell phone. He had the two little girls in the car and that made Eliza feel safe, so she gave him her phone, and then when her back was turned, he grabbed her. He knocked her out with something. Eliza thought it was chloroform." The words came tumbling out in a rush.

"Was this before or after he took you?"

"Before. Eliza said she woke up in the car and they were driving around. After a while, he went to the gas station and grabbed me while my mom went to pay. I ... I was angry with her. My mom. I was complaining that she hadn't filled the car up before she picked me up from school because I was going to a sleepover at a friend's house." Tears ran anew down her still wet cheeks.

"It's okay, honey," Jack soothed. "Parents are used to their kids complaining. Your mom knows you love her."

Maegan nodded distractedly. She wished she believed that. But she didn't.

"Okay, honey, now tell us the names of the other girls," Jack continued.

"Detectives?" The door swung open before Maegan could speak. The doctor she had seen with Eliza earlier was standing there. "You wanted to know as soon as Ariyel was awake."

"Thanks, Dr. Roma." Xavier nodded at the woman who nodded back and disappeared. "Well, hopefully we'll get this all cleared up right now," Xavier addressed her. "Ariyel or Eliza—whatever her name really is—will either confirm your story or Malachi's."

That could be a nightmare, Maegan thought to herself. Malachi had messed with Eliza's head. There were no guarantees that her sister would back her up. "She may tell you that she really is Malachi's daughter, Ariyel," Maegan warned. "He's brainwashed her. Sometimes she doesn't know who she really is."

Xavier arched a brow. "Isn't that a little convenient?" he demanded.

She growled in frustration. She had thought she was making progress with the cops, but now it seemed like she was back where she started. "I told Laura that from the beginning," she snapped. "I can get through to her." Maegan strode toward the door.

Jack moved to block her path. "You can't talk to Eliza right now."

"What do you mean?" she demanded.

"We need to talk to her alone first. I told Malachi he wasn't to speak with her, either. Once Xavier and I have taken her statement, then you can see her," Jack explained.

"You're treating me the same as you're treating Malachi? As a suspect?" She was incredulous. "You really do think I might have hurt her."

"No, I don't," Jack rebuked firmly. "But we need to talk to her without anyone in the room to bias what she tells us."

She sighed. There was obviously nothing she could say to change his mind, so there didn't seem much point in arguing. "Can I go and see Laura?"

"Not right now," Jack replied.

"What? Why not?" This was unbelievable. They weren't letting her do anything. They thought she was crazy, that she was a risk to those around her, that she was dangerous. "I'm not going to hurt her," she protested, offended. She'd thought Jack believed her, but she'd obviously been wrong. Now he didn't want her near his wife. His betrayal stung more than she'd have thought.

"Calm down," Jack grabbed hold of her arm. "I don't think you're going to hurt her. Laura's asleep. She had a panic attack earlier and she's resting right now."

Some of her anger melted away. The concern in Jack's eyes when he spoke about his wife was genuine and convinced her he was telling the truth. "Because of her agoraphobia?"

"Yes. When she's feeling up to it, you can go and visit her in her room," he promised.

"All right," she agreed since it seemed she had no choice in the matter.

"Okay, stay put, we'll be back soon," Jack informed her.

"What if Malachi tries to come and talk to me?" She couldn't stop fear from inching into her voice.

"Security is watching him, and if you stay in here, he won't know where you are," he reassured her.

Once alone, she began to pace.

Maybe it had been a mistake to tell Jack and Xavier so much.

Jack was good. *Really* good. His voice was so calm, so soothing, virtually hypnotic, and he was so sincere. When he spoke to her, he had her believing that in that instant she was the most important person on the planet. He'd made her feel safe, so she'd given up more information than she'd intended. If that doctor hadn't come in when she had, then Maegan probably would have given up her little sisters, too.

It hurt that they thought she might be insane.

She just wanted this to be over. And she prayed that, by the end of the night, it would be.

Exhausted, angry, scared, Maegan dropped down to the floor, hugged her knees to her chest, and cried.

* * * * *

11:57 P.M.

The young woman in the bed looked frail. That was the only word Jack could think of to describe her. Eliza, for Jack was positive that Maegan had told them the truth, had skin so pale it was basically colorless. There wasn't an ounce of flesh on her face. Her eyes appeared sunken and were underscored by black circles which made it look like she'd been beaten. The hands that rested on top of the covers were as thin as a newborn's.

Jack was pleased that Maegan had caved and given them some information on Eliza's abduction. Now she just needed to give up the younger girls so they could reunite the children with their families and arrest Malachi.

Right now, Maegan was angry with them, mainly because she knew Xavier had doubts about her. But she was going to have to get over that if they were going to help her. Hopefully, she could set her frustrations aside and do what needed to be done.

With Maegan tucked safely away, Laura resting, and Ryan keeping an eye on Paige, Jack was finding it easier to focus. And he had the feeling he was going to need to in order to interview Eliza.

So as not to spook the girl, while Jack approached the bed, Xavier hung back. There were an awful lot of unknowns about her: she may or may not be a kidnap victim; she may or may not have attempted suicide; someone may or may not have tried to kill her; she may or may not have been brainwashed. They had decided not to double team her.

Jack was right beside her before she realized he was there. Her eyes fluttered open, dazed and disoriented at first, then they flashed with fear when they settled on him.

"It's okay, honey," he soothed, sitting beside the bed.

"Who are you?" her voice was faint, and she shrunk back into the bed, moving as far away from him as physically possible.

"My name is Jack. I'm a police officer," he told her.

If it was possible, she seemed to shrink even farther away.

"Everything's all right. We just need to ask you some questions about you and your sister," he said gently. Her scared eyes just stared back at him. "Maegan came to us looking for help." He studied Eliza's face for any reactions to what he was saying.

"Maegan?" Eliza repeated, her pale face confused.

"Alice said her real name is Maegan. She also said that the man who brought you here isn't really your father, but his name is

Malachi and that he kidnapped her. She said he kidnapped you, too."

Eliza didn't say anything, but her large blue eyes were haunted.

"Maegan says that Malachi calls you Ariyel, but that your real name is Eliza."

Eliza's terrified eyes darted around the room, settling on Xavier for the first time. At once, some of the tension in her face eased and a little of the fear trickled out of her eyes.

Sensing that Eliza would be more receptive to Xavier, Jack stood and gestured for his partner to come and take his place. "This is my partner, Xavier," he said as Xavier sat beside the bed, and Eliza immediately relaxed.

"Did Malachi hurt you?" Xavier asked softly.

Eliza shook her head, inching a little closer to Xavier.

"Are you sure? If he hurt you, we can help you, Eliza."

"Ariyel," she corrected quietly. "My name is Ariyel."

"Maegan says your real name is Eliza. That Ariyel is just the name that Malachi gave you when he kidnapped you," Xavier pressed on.

"My sister's name is Alice," she protested.

"Do you have any other sisters?" Xavier let the kidnapping go for the moment since Eliza obviously wasn't ready to discuss that yet.

She nodded.

"What are their names?" Jack asked. If Eliza backed up Maegan about the little girls, then it would be proof that Malachi had lied about that. It would also bolster Maegan's claims that they were all kidnap victims, even if Eliza wouldn't admit it. Maegan had told them that Malachi had brainwashed Eliza, and from the young woman's haunted eyes, Jack believed it.

"Angela, Abigail, and Arianna."

Jack didn't want to confront her on Arianna's true parentage yet. She was clearly extremely emotionally vulnerable. Instead, he asked, "Do you know where you are?"

Her eyes skimmed the room. "The hospital?"

"Do you know how you got here?" Xavier asked.

She gave a slow shake of her head.

"You suffered a drug overdose," Xavier informed her.

Disbelief had her eyes widening, making them seem even larger in her thin face.

"Maegan thought you might have done it on purpose."

"Why?" Eliza kept her gaze fixed on Xavier, which seemed to help her to remain calm.

"To get help for all of you."

"But we don't need help," she protested.

"Maegan thinks you do," Jack pushed. He didn't want to push too hard, but if they could get Eliza to fill in the gaps, then they could arrest Malachi and send these girls home.

"I already told you my sister's name is Alice. And I didn't try to kill myself. No one hurt us. Our father didn't do anything to us." Eliza was becoming agitated.

"So, no one kidnapped you?" Xavier asked, but Jack could hear in his voice that he now believed Maegan. Eliza's terror was written all over her face and could be heard in her voice.

"No."

"And your name is Ariyel, not Eliza?"

"Right."

"And Maegan's name is really Alice?"

"Yes."

"Then do you know why Maegan would lie to us? Why she would tell us that Malachi hurt her, that he hurt you, that both of you and your little sisters need help?"

"I ... I ... I don't ... I'm not ..." Eliza stammered. Tears brimmed in her eyes now and her distress was growing. They probably weren't going to get much more time with her before a doctor came in and requested they leave her alone.

Deciding it was time to push, he asked, "Eliza, are you Arianna's mother?" Jack asked.

Pure panic flushed across her face, and she began to pull at the wires and tubes still attached to her body. Xavier grabbed hold of her arms, stilling them, and keeping her in the bed before she could fling herself out.

"Did Malachi force himself on you, Eliza?" Jack pressed, not wanting to upset the girl, but they needed to know.

Still caught in her desperate attempt to escape, Eliza didn't respond. When it seemed to dawn on her that she wasn't going anywhere, she burst into hysterical sobs. Getting any answers out of her was going to be even harder than extracting answers from Maegan.

Whatever Malachi had done to Eliza's head wasn't going to be undone overnight.

THREE YEARS AGO

4:26 P.M.

Eliza was getting desperate.

She didn't know what else to try.

Not that that meant she was going to give up.

She would *never* stop trying to escape from Malachi. No matter how long he kept her here. And she knew that would be forever. Malachi had told her that he'd never let her go, that he'd rather see her dead first, and she believed him.

That knowledge only further fueled her desire to find a way to escape.

Over the last two years she'd tried numerous things.

One day she'd set a fire in one of the upstairs bedrooms hoping that the fire would bring firefighters who would find them and rescue them. Making sure the children were safely downstairs, right by the front door, she had gone to the room farthest away and lit the match. However, as soon as the fire took hold of the curtains, a sprinkler system appeared, and the water quickly extinguished the flames. When Malachi had arrived home, he'd been so furious he'd hit her across the face so hard she'd seen stars.

Another time she had tried to dig a hole under one of the fences on the property. It hadn't been easy. They weren't allowed outside much, and when they were, Malachi usually kept a pretty close eye on them. But she had worked away at it, bit by bit, for several weeks. She had intended to make the hole big enough for Maegan to fit through, so she could take Hayley and Bethany with her and get them someplace safe. Eliza had intended to remain behind. Malachi had found the hole before it was big enough to fit the baby.

She'd tried cutting the electricity, but when the electrician came, Malachi locked her and the others in the basement.

She'd tried flooding the house, but when he'd had workers come to fix it, he'd locked them in the attic.

Then, of course, there was the disastrous time she'd thrown herself out the window in the hope that Malachi would take her to the hospital. That had been a year ago, and it had taken months for her to recover. The arm and leg that had been broken in the fall still ached at the end of a long day.

After each failed attempt came the punishment.

It got worse each time as Malachi became more and more frustrated that she wouldn't accept her fate.

He hadn't punished her for the flooding scam yet, but she knew it was coming and she knew it would be bad. How bad, she didn't know, but she was expecting a lot worse than all the other times.

Not that his punishments would stop her.

Eliza didn't know what to try next, but something would occur to her. One of these days she'd find something that worked.

She was aware of his presence behind her before he spoke. She always knew when he was coming.

"Let's go," Malachi grabbed her arm and began to drag her toward the basement stairs.

Eliza knew better than to resist and allowed him to take her to the basement. It was time to face the consequences for her last attempt at freedom.

"I've had enough of dealing with you and your stupid games," Malachi's voice growled in her ear. The feel of his warm breath on her skin made her shiver. "I'm not putting up with it anymore. You are never leaving this house. If you can't accept that, then I'll *make* you accept it."

"I'll never stop trying to get away from you," Eliza told him defiantly. She wasn't afraid of Malachi anymore. Her fear had died a long time ago. He'd hurt her too many times, and now the only focus in her life was trying to save herself and her little sisters.

"Oh, I think you will," Malachi singsonged.

Something in his voice had the hairs on the back of her neck standing up. Whatever he had planned was going to be worse than bad.

Releasing her, he went to a corner of the basement and opened a door. "You, in here," he gestured to her and reluctantly Eliza crossed to him. Malachi stood outside a small room that had been painted black. The room had no windows and only the one door. "You will not come out until you're ready to obey every word I say."

"I'll never obey you," Eliza snapped.

"You will. You won't come out of this room until you learn to be obedient. You won't have water or food or light until you learn to obey. Nor will you have clothing."

She gaped at him, in shock. Malachi couldn't really be meaning to lock her inside a room and leave her there—naked and in the dark—until she agreed to do whatever he said. It would never work. There was nothing he could do that would make her obey him.

She was going to defy him. She refused to do it, but he approached her with a pair of scissors. "I said clothes off!" he roared, snipping the scissors at her. Eliza flung her arms up in self-defense as he rushed her. But Malachi managed to cut a hole in the sleeve of her sweater, and the sharp blades sliced into the flesh of her arm.

"Okay, okay," she surrendered. Her arm burned from the cut, and she could feel blood dripping down it. Despite the fact that Malachi had seen her naked numerous times, her cheeks flamed red with embarrassment as she climbed out of her clothes.

"Now, in!" he screamed, shoving her violently inside the room. She stumbled and fell to her knees, then scrambled immediately to her feet but before she could get to the door, it slammed closed with a horrifying air of finality. With the door shut, the room was completely dark. Not an ounce of light slid through the cracks around the doorframe. She couldn't even see her hand when she held it right in front of her face. It was quiet, too. Scarily quiet. So quiet that the quiet seemed to take on a life of its own and produce its own sound.

Even though she knew it was pointless, Eliza spent the next few hours feeling around every inch of the room, hoping to locate a weakness.

She found none.

Eventually, she was forced to give up.

Curling up in a corner of the small, dark room, Eliza buried her head in her hands and cried.

This was so unfair.

All she wanted was to go home to her family, but instead, she ended up trapped in this horrible room.

Eliza didn't know how long she lived in the cold, dark space. Without any clues, she had no way to keep track of the time. It could have been hours, days, weeks, months. Logically, she knew it couldn't have been all that long because her body couldn't survive without water for more than a couple of days, but it felt like she'd been here forever.

At first, she talked aloud to herself, reciting stories and poems, and giving herself pep talks.

Then she lost the will to speak out loud, and she curled up in a ball on the ground and retreated inside herself, making up stories of how she would be saved.

Then she lost the will to do even that. She just laid there. Doing nothing. Not even thinking. No longer hungry or thirsty or cold. The darkness of the room was so all encompassing that it reached its tentacles inside her, filling her with darkness.

And then one day, the door opened.

The light that flooded the room blinded her. Eliza squeezed

her eyes shut. The pain was unbearable.

Someone knelt beside her, but her eyes still weren't cooperating, and all she could do was squint through them and make out a big blurry shape.

"Are you ready yet?"

The darkness may have squashed her, but it hadn't broken her yet. Wearily, she lifted her head from the floor and shook it.

"Maybe you need a few more days." Malachi took hold of her neck, tilted her head back and poured some water into her mouth. He poured so quickly that she choked. Desperately, she swallowed as much of it as she could. Her body needed it. She was so parched, already badly dehydrated.

Then Malachi was gone. The door closed and locked behind him. The darkness was back.

The water had invigorated her a little, and for a while, Eliza felt her spirit returning.

But this time it didn't take as long for the darkness to claim her.

And this time, it claimed her completely.

Crushed her.

Her resolve, her strength, her spirit, all drained out of her until they became as weak as her body.

More time passed. All she did was lay on the floor in a huddle. Most of the time she wasn't sure if she was awake or asleep.

Cold.

Hungry.

Thirsty.

Dark.

Cold.

Hungry.

Thirsty.

Dark.

That was all her life had become.

Malachi returned.

And this time when he asked her if she was ready to give in, she nodded. She was too weak. Her body needed food and water. And she was cold. Her naked body shivered almost constantly. Most importantly, she wanted out of the dark.

"On your knees," he commanded.

Wobbly and worriedly light-headed, with her eyes still clenched shut against the light, Eliza only just managed to comply.

"You want water and food, you ask for it."

"Please." Her voice nothing but a faint croak.

"Ask properly," Malachi reprimanded. "Say, 'please, sir, may I have some water?'"

"Please, sir, may I have some water?" Eliza parroted back.

"Very good," Malachi praised. "Here you go." She heard him setting some things down beside her.

Eliza had thought that once she gave Malachi what he wanted, he would let her out of this hell. But he didn't. Once he'd set down what he'd brought for her, he left after closing the door once more and plunging her into blackness.

Feeling around, Eliza found that he'd left her a bottle of water, some soup, and a blanket. She ate greedily, her body crying out for sustenance, but she was careful with the water. She didn't know when Malachi would return. The blanket felt wonderful when she wrapped it around her shoulders, and she snuggled down into it and slept the best sleep she'd had since she'd been locked up here.

Malachi's visits became more regular.

She played by the rules. Asked as he wanted her to. And she earned clothes, more food, and plenty of water.

It got easier each time to do what Malachi wanted.

The darkness had invaded her mind, made it sluggish and tired, compliant. When he visited her now, he talked to her about his family. About Ariyel. The more Malachi talked about Ariyel, the more she came to believe that she really was her.

She understood.

Malachi was in charge of her. Without him, she had nothing. He had what he wanted—her obedience.

NOVEMBER 4TH
12:00 A.M.

12:00 A.M.

Five-year-old Abigail woke up with a start.

Where was she?

She wasn't home in her own bed.

Not that she slept in her own bed very often. Her room was scary. It was too quiet and big. And she didn't like the pictures on her walls.

It wasn't just her room that scared her; the whole house was scary. Because of *him*. He was scary. Scary and mean.

Most nights she crept into Ariyel's room to sleep in her bed. But right now, she wasn't in Ariyel's bed, either.

She was lying on a hard floor.

She opened her mouth to scream for her sister when a hand rested on her shoulder.

"It's okay, Abby," Angela's voice soothed. "We're at the hospital, remember? Ariyel got sick and we came here, then Alice told us to hide."

Abby remembered. She remembered how still Ariyel had been in the car. She remembered how serious Alice had been when she'd told them they needed to stay quiet and hidden no matter what. She remembered singing songs and telling stories with Angela while they waited for Alice to come back and get them.

But she didn't want to wait anymore.

She wanted Ariyel. Now.

Ariyel always made her feel safe.

Abby didn't have a mommy, but Ariyel was like her mommy.

Well, she had a mommy; she just didn't remember her. Ariyel had told her that Malachi wasn't really their daddy. He had taken them from their real families. Only Abby had been a baby then, so she didn't remember it.

And Abby wasn't even her real name. Her real name was Hayley. Angela's real name was Bethany, Alice's real name was Maegan, and Ariyel's real name was Eliza. But they weren't supposed to use their real names because it made Malachi angry.

None of them wanted to make Malachi angry.

He got even scarier when he was angry.

He hurt Ariyel all the time. He hurt Alice, too. And even at five, Abby knew that one day he'd hurt her, Angela, and Arianna, as well.

That's why they always did whatever they had to so Malachi didn't lose his temper.

The older girls wanted to go back to their homes. Their real homes. But Abby didn't remember her real home. She didn't remember her mommy and daddy. She didn't want to live with Malachi, but she didn't want to leave Ariyel.

She loved Ariyel.

And if leaving Malachi meant leaving Ariyel, then she didn't want to do it.

But that's why they were here.

That's why Alice had made them hide. She was going to tell someone that Malachi had taken them, that he wasn't their father. Then they were all going to go home.

Abby was scared.

What if her real home was just as scary as Malachi's?

What if her real mommy and daddy were as scary as Malachi?

What if she never got to see Ariyel or the rest of her sisters ever again?

"Abby? What's wrong?" Angela set the baby down and pulled Abby into her lap.

"I want Ariyel," she whimpered, crying. She was five years old;

'too big to cry,' Malachi always said. But she cried a lot. She knew it made Malachi mad, but she couldn't help it.

"I know you do. I do, too, but we have to do what Alice said so we can go home," Angela reminded her.

"I don't want to go home," she pouted.

"Sure, you do. Your home will be wonderful, not at all like our house. I know you're scared, because you don't remember. I'm a little scared, too," Angela admitted. "I was only four when Malachi took me. I hardly remember my family, but what I do remember is really wonderful."

"But Ariyel won't be there."

"No, she won't, but I'm sure you'll be able to visit her whenever you want. You'll be able to visit all of us. And when you go home, you'll be able to go to school and make friends, and your mommy will do all the things for you that Ariyel does. And your daddy will tickle you and give you piggyback rides and read you stories, and do all the things that daddies are supposed to do. And you know how you love ballerinas? Well, maybe you'll be able to take dance classes and learn how to dance just like a ballerina."

"Really?" Abby thought all of those things sounded wonderful, but she still didn't want to leave Ariyel. "How much longer do we have to stay here?"

"I don't know, but hopefully not much longer."

Abby wanted Ariyel, but if she couldn't have her sister, then she at least wanted to feel like her sister was close by. Whenever Abby was scared or sad, Ariyel would tell her stories. "Angela, can you tell me a story?"

"Sure." Angela picked up Arianna and Abby moved over to make room on Angela's lap for the baby. "Which one?"

"Hansel and Gretel," Abby replied immediately. That was her favorite. Ariyel always used a funny voice for the witch, so it wasn't too scary. Settling back, she listened to Angela tell the story and hoped that they could see Ariyel again soon.

* * * * *

12:06 A.M.

This was quickly going from bad to worse.

The cops were in talking to Ariyel.

That girl was going to be the death of him.

Breaking her down hadn't been easy. Malachi had locked her in the blackout room for two solid days before returning the first time. She'd refused to do as she was told. After giving her some water so she didn't dehydrate, he'd left her for another three days. That time when he came back, her spirit had been extinguished and she'd done as he'd ordered.

In total, she'd spent nearly a month in that room.

Over time, she had stopped resisting. She had learned that he was her master. She had learned to be obedient, become completely compliant, let him do whatever he wanted to her.

The first time he took her, she had fought so hard she had kneed him in the groin so badly he could barely walk for a week. After that, he had restrained her, but still she fought, and it was never all that pleasurable. But her learned obedience had changed her, she started just lying there and letting him do what he wanted to her. It was never about pleasing them. It was always about pleasing himself, so he liked his women to do as they were told. And Ariyel had come to learn that lesson perfectly.

She had learned to be a good daughter.

But was she still a good daughter?

What was she telling the police?

Was she backing up that brat, Alice, and saying he had abducted them?

Was she backing him up and saying they really were his daughters?

Had she admitted the little girls existed?

Perhaps it had been a mistake to lie about them, but he'd panicked. That police officer had caught him off guard. He'd spotted the cops earlier; his internal radar had pegged them immediately. But he hadn't thought they were there for him. He hadn't known Alice had it in her to try to get help.

Too bad it hadn't been that pretty woman who had interviewed him. She was hot. Detective Hood, the other detective had said her name was. If she'd been the one to talk to him, things would have turned out differently. He would have been able to manipulate her a lot easier than he could a man. Women were a lot more pliable, especially with his mixture of good looks and charm.

The police obviously believed Alice's story since they wouldn't let him see either her or Ariyel.

Even if Ariyel backed him up, the police wouldn't let it go.

They would search this entire hospital and find the little ones. That would be proof he'd lied. The little ones would almost definitely affirm Alice's story. And given enough time, Ariyel would, too.

The police would find out the girls' real identities. Then they'd send them back to their old families. And he'd have nothing.

Losing Arianna would hurt the most.

He could always find more pretty girls, but Arianna was his daughter. His *blood* daughter. The police had no right to take his baby from him, but they would. They would take all his girls and then they would throw him in prison.

He couldn't accept that.

He *wouldn't* accept that.

They could take his girls, but they couldn't take his freedom.

He didn't want to do it, but he was going to have to cut his losses and run.

The police already had Alice and Ariyel. It was only a matter of time before they had Angela, Abby, and Arianna. He could try to find the little ones, but chances were, he wouldn't be able to do it in time. And every second he stayed here gave the police more time to find out the truth about his girls and how he got them.

This was killing him, but he knew it was what had to be done.

He would disappear. He'd have to. There was a chance the girls could locate his house. So he'd have to leave it.

Leaving the house would be almost harder than leaving his girls.

That house meant a lot to him.

It was where it all started.

Where *everything* started.

He had been born in that house. Lived there his entire life. It had shaped him into the man he was now.

Malachi couldn't imagine that house not being a part of his life.

If there were any way he could remain there, he would.

Maybe he could give it a little time. Stay at the house and see how things played out. In reality, it wouldn't be all that likely that the girls could ever find the place.

He wasn't sure yet, but if there was a way to not have to leave, then he would find it.

Now, though, he needed to get out of here.

Before he could leave, he'd have to create a little diversion.

The cops had told hospital security to keep an eye on him, so he'd have to do something about that so he could slip away.

He already had a plan.

Taking a deep breath, he said a silent goodbye to his girls—hoping it would only be a temporary separation. He could always return to get them at a later date.

There were two little boys playing with a ball in a corner just a few yards from where he was currently sitting.

He could take advantage of that.

Children had little accidents all the time. He should know, he had several daughters. They weren't usually good at paying attention to their surroundings. Sometimes they broke things.

No one would think twice if the little boys' ball were to break a window.

Malachi didn't want to get too close, and he was only going to get one shot at this. When the guard's head was turned, he carefully eased a ball of elastic bands from his pocket. Abby was obsessed these days with finding any and all elastic bands around the house and adding them to the ball. He had confiscated it in the car on their ride here. At the time, he hadn't known that that simple act was going to end up saving him.

When the little boy facing the window went to toss the ball to his friend, Malachi rolled the elastic band ball toward the children. The boy who had his hands up to catch the ball his friend had thrown to him, noticed something coming toward him and transferred his attention away from the ball.

Just as Malachi had predicted, the ball connected with the glass, shattering it into a million tiny glass shards. While everyone's attention snapped immediately to the children and the broken window, Malachi headed for the door, without running. He didn't want to draw attention to himself.

Outside, the cold night air invigorated him.

Leaving his car behind, on the odd chance the police had already linked it to him and had him followed, Malachi ran.

* * * * *

12:12 A.M.

"He's gone," Ryan told his partner as he walked back into the office where they had set themselves up. They'd been busy working when they'd heard the shattering of glass. He'd gone to see what had happened, finding two young boys and their very embarrassed mother apologizing profusely for her sons accidentally breaking a window while their dad was being treated for a suspected heart attack.

"Malachi?" Paige asked.

"Yes, the guard got distracted when some kids broke a window, and when he looked back at where Malachi had been sitting, he was gone," he explained.

Paige shot to her feet. "We should go and look for him."

Ryan blocked the door. "Jack didn't want you near Malachi. You stay here and I'll go and look for him." He didn't necessarily agree with his brother on this one. They all knew Paige was more than capable of taking care of herself, but he also understood that Jack was just being overprotective. Wondering whether Dr. Bruce Daniels could be Sofia and Paige's stalker had them all remembering the eight long days Paige had spent in a coma following her attack. Right now, he was happy to go with better safe than sorry where his partner was concerned.

She glowered at him. "One, Jack is not the boss of me. Two, I was nice and did as he asked and haven't gone near the man. Three, I'm sure he'd rather we went after Malachi than let him get away. And four, I am not letting you go after him alone. Jack's not the boss of you either, Ryan," she added.

He knew that, yet his big brother had been bossy all throughout their childhood and adolescence that sometimes he was so used to Jack bossing him around that he went along with it. But Paige was right, they couldn't let Malachi just walk out of here. "All right, let's go."

Outside, they both shivered. Neither of them had grabbed their coats. "He can't have gone far." Paige scanned the parking lot. "Ryan, over there."

Following his partner's pointed finger, he saw what had caught her attention. A man was running, dodging between cars as he went. Without a word, they both pulled out their guns and took off after him. The man they were chasing disappeared as they got closer, so they split up.

He was weaving his way slowly through the parked cars. That Malachi had run seemed like proof he was guilty. And if he was guilty of abducting four girls, holding them prisoner for five years, and impregnating one of them, then he was capable of anything.

Up ahead, he saw a shadow dart behind a truck. Cautiously, he followed. The figure had gone by the time he rounded the truck, but he became aware of a presence behind him at the same time he heard Paige shout his name.

"Malachi, don't!" Her gaze was directed to someone behind him, and her gun was pointed in the same direction. "Put the gun down."

"You've already got the girls; I've got nothing to lose," Malachi replied.

"Ryan, duck!" Paige shouted a split second before a gunshot pierced the night air.

Ryan felt the bullet go whizzing by as he took his partner's command seriously and dropped to the ground. Paige fired off a shot, and he heard footsteps pounding behind him. Before he had a chance to climb to his feet, he heard the revving of an engine. Headlights glowed, their beam falling on Paige.

He immediately knew that something was wrong.

The car was moving too quickly.

Heading straight for Paige.

His partner was still staring in the direction Malachi had fled, preparing to run after him.

The car roared, and Paige turned, finally registering that it wasn't stopping.

Ryan launched himself off the ground and at his partner, tackling her to the ground just as the car rocketed past. If he hadn't pushed her out of the way, the car would have plowed right into her. If she hadn't been killed outright, she'd have been left fighting for her life.

Images of Paige lying so badly beaten she was barely recognizable were seared into his mind. The guilt he felt over her attack hadn't diminished in the four years since it had happened. He'd apologized several times. In fact, an apology had been the first words he'd spoken to her when she'd finally woken up. She'd been conscious less than an hour at the time, so weak she couldn't lift her head off the pillows, and her voice was so faint that he'd had to hold his ear practically right over her mouth to hear her. She'd told him not to blame himself, but how could he not? As partners, they were supposed to have each other's back, but he'd let her go off on her own knowing someone was after her and that she wasn't one hundred percent focused.

Now he kept his body protectively over Paige's, and scanned the parking lot for any signs that the car was returning. When he was satisfied that it wasn't, Ryan lifted himself a fraction of an inch off her. "Paige? Are you hurt?"

"No," came the somewhat breathless reply. "Let me up."

"We have to get you inside." He stood quickly, yanking Paige up with him and pulling her toward the door.

"Ryan, wait," Paige protested, trying to wiggle out of his grip. "Malachi ran off, we have to go after him."

"Someone just tried to kill you." Fear made his voice harsher than he'd intended. "Right now, keeping you alive is more important."

Dragging her with him, he hustled her quickly back to the hospital, keeping himself between her and any potential threat that still lurked in the dark parking lot. As they walked, he pulled out his phone and called for backup and a crime scene unit.

Jack and Xavier met them at the door. "What happened?" Jack demanded.

"Someone tried to kill her," he replied, shoving Paige inside.

"What?" Jack asked disbelievingly.

"Malachi made a run for it, so we went after him. He took a shot at me, but Paige fired back and he ran off, then someone tried to run her over with a car," Ryan explained, feeling shaky now that it was over. He wasn't the only one who was shaking. As what had nearly happened sank in, Paige had gone pale and was visibly trembling.

"Are you okay?" Xavier asked Paige.

She nodded.

"Can you take her and get her some water and warm her up?" Ryan asked Xavier.

"Sure thing. Come on." Xavier put an arm around Paige's shoulders and led her farther inside the safety of the busy hospital.

"Did you get a look at the car?" Jack asked.

"No, it happened too fast, and it was dark. All I was thinking about was getting her out of the way."

"Her stalker?"

"That would be my guess." He shuddered. "The car was aiming right for her. She'd be dead if I hadn't knocked her down."

"But you did knock her out of the way, and she's okay," Jack reminded him firmly.

"He's left her alone for four years. Why come back now?" They needed the stalker caught. He viewed Paige as a threat to Sofia, but if he succeeded in killing Paige, he could easily pick another target, go after someone else Sofia cared about. Thinking of his wife, he wasn't looking forward to telling her about what had happened. Sofia would blame herself, and he hated to see her beat herself up over something she had no control over.

"I don't know. But the *why* isn't really important. We need to find him before he succeeds in killing her. I'm going to call Mark and ask him to come and examine Paige. She says she's okay, but she's in shock, and she might have an injury she doesn't realize yet." Jack was already pulling out his phone.

"Yeah, good idea," Ryan agreed. He'd feel a lot better if he knew for sure that Paige was all right. "And we're going to have to call everything in. Malachi fired at us, and Paige fired back when he didn't respond to her command to lower his weapon. We can't keep this unofficial any more. I already called for a unit to come and contain the scene, should be here any minute. And we're going to need to go through the hospital's security footage, see if we can get anything on the car that tried to hit Paige."

"Mark's on his way," Jack announced a moment later, shoving

his phone back into his pocket.

"Cops just showed up," Ryan noted as he saw a unit pull up outside.

After quickly showing them where the shooting had taken place, he headed to the office to check on Paige. Xavier had put her coat around her shoulders and a blanket on her lap, and she was sitting with her head in her hands.

He crouched in front of her. "How are you doing?"

Drawing in a deep breath, she responded, "I'm okay, Ryan, really. Thank you, you saved my life."

"And you saved mine," he reminded her.

She nodded distractedly. "But Malachi still got away."

"But now we know he did it. No reason to run and then try and shoot us if he was innocent. How did your talk with Eliza go?" Ryan asked Jack.

"Malachi messed with her head. She's completely terrified, but she's backing him up at the moment," Jack replied.

"And she confirmed the existence of the younger girls," Xavier added.

"We had to stop talking to her because she became hysterical, but Xavier should try again. She seemed to respond better to him than to me," Jack explained.

"We should get Laura to try talking to Maegan." Ryan broached the topic slowly, knowing his brother's instincts would be to say no. "I know you want her to rest, Jack, but we need to find this guy—he's dangerous, and if Eliza has been brainwashed, then Maegan is still our best source of information. She trusts Laura, and she'll be more likely to open up to her than to any of us," he reasoned.

Jack looked conflicted. He was extremely protective of his wife, which was no wonder given everything Laura had been through. And Ryan, too, felt protective of Laura. She was practically his sister. But they needed to end this quickly before anyone else got hurt. The longer Malachi was out there, the greater the chances he'd try this again.

"Okay," Jack relented with a sigh. "She can talk to Maegan. I don't like it, but you're right. Malachi is dangerous, and Maegan is our best chance at stopping him."

"We've identified Maegan and Eliza," Paige told the others. "Once we knew their first names, that they were abducted on the same day, and how they were taken, it didn't take long. Maegan's name is Maegan Masters, and Eliza's is Eliza Donnan. We should contact their families, let them know the girls have been found and are safe."

"Hi, Paigey," Mark announced as he burst through the door.

"Hi, Mark, and don't call me Paigey. What are you doing here?" Paige eyed him suspiciously.

"Checking you out," he replied mildly, pulling up a chair beside her.

"I'm fine; I wasn't hurt," Paige protested.

"And we want to make sure of that. Sometimes adrenalin can mask pain for a while. You know, tending all of you guys and your partners is like a full-time job," Mark observed dryly as he picked up Paige's wrist to check her pulse.

"How is she?" Ryan asked after his brother had taken Paige's blood pressure.

"Considering someone just tried to kill her, she's doing okay," Mark replied. "When Ryan tackled you, did you hit your head?" he asked Paige, running his fingers through her hair in search of any bumps.

"I don't think so," she told him.

"I can't feel anything," Mark confirmed. "What did you land on?"

"My hands," Paige answered.

"Let me see them."

Paige held them out, and it was immediately apparent that one of her hands had been injured—the thumb of her left hand pointed out at an awkward angle.

Brown eyes wide with baffled surprise, Paige said, "I didn't even notice that."

"That's why it was a good idea to check you out," Mark reminded her. Gently, he took hold of her wrist and examined her hand. "It's dislocated. I can probably put it back in for you, or if you want, you can go and get someone in the ER to X-ray it and then relocate it."

Looking dazed and exhausted as she experienced the crash that came following an adrenalin overload, Paige shook her head. "I don't want to go through the ER. You can do it."

"It's going to hurt," Mark warned.

"Here, hold my hand and squeeze as hard as you need to." Ryan held out one of his hands.

Obediently, and without protest, Paige grasped his hand with her good one. That didn't make him feel better. Paige hated to be told what to do.

"Ready?" Mark asked, one hand circling Paige's wrist, the other held the end of her thumb.

Paige nodded, and Mark gave one quick yank. For a second Paige crushed his hand so tightly that Ryan almost yelled out at the pain.

"You okay?" Mark glanced at Paige.

"Yeah," she replied, a little shakily.

Mark raised a skeptical brow. "How does it feel when I move it?"

She winced as Mark rotated her thumb in a circle and bent it at both joints. "It hurts, but it feels like it's moving okay."

"Okay, I'll go get some tape and stabilize that for you. I'll also bring some painkillers. Then I'll go and check on Laura since I'm down here, anyway. I'll be right back." Mark paused at the door. "Let's all please try not to hurt ourselves while I'm gone."

When his brother was gone, Ryan took the seat beside Paige and waited until his partner was looking at him. "You do not go anywhere on your own from now on," he told her firmly.

She rolled her eyes at him. "Even *if* that was the stalker who tried to run me down, he waited four years before trying to kill me again. What if he waits another four years before he makes another attempt? One of you cannot shadow me every second of the day for years."

"We can, and we will," Ryan told her adamantly. Whatever it took to keep Paige safe, he would gladly do so, and he was already trying to figure out how to make it logistically possible.

She rolled her eyes again—more dramatically this time. "You guys have wives, girlfriends, kids; you can't be babysitting me all the time."

"You and Elias can come and stay with us," Ryan ventured, knowing she'd refuse and wondering how to persuade her.

"No." Paige shook her head at him. "And no," she turned to tell Jack before he had a chance to make the same offer.

"Annabelle moved out, so I could come and stay at your place," Xavier offered. "That way you'd be with Ryan when you're at work, and I'd have your back when you're at home."

To Ryan that sounded like the perfect solution. Apparently, it did not to Paige. "No way. Annabelle isn't really going to move out, and you should be working on fixing things with her, not babysitting me."

"Annabelle already moved out, and she's the one who sees problems in our relationship, not me," Xavier countered.

"Paige, do you really think we're going to leave you alone and unprotected while someone wants to kill you? You can agree to let Xavier stay with you or he, Jack, and I will take turns spending the night outside your house," Ryan threatened.

She was wavering, he could tell. Her pride wanted to say that she was a cop, could take care of herself, and didn't need anyone to look after her. But her common sense was obviously reminding her that she'd be safer with them looking out for her.

"I'll think about it," she finally admitted. Which was as good as a yes as far as Ryan was concerned. "I have to call Elias and tell him what happened."

"All right, we'll give you some privacy." Ryan squeezed her shoulder and stood.

"Hey, guys," Paige stopped them at the door. "Thanks for all your offers, you guys are really great friends, and it really means a lot to me. But let's just find this guy so we can all get on with our lives."

* * * * *

12:30 A.M.

"So, you pass Mark's tests?" Jack appeared at the door.

Laura smiled at her husband. Neither she nor Sofia had been able to get any sleep, but they'd both kept the promises they'd made to their husbands and remained in bed. Her brother-in-law had been a welcome distraction when he'd appeared in their room a few minutes ago.

"Mark?" She turned to him, unsure whether or not she had passed.

"Barely," Mark replied. "I'd prefer she remained right where she is, but I get why you want to use her."

"Use me?" Laura turned confused eyes on Jack. "Did something happen? Is Maegan okay?"

"I'll explain everything to you in a minute," Jack assured her, coming to perch on the bed beside her and kiss her lightly on the lips.

Something was wrong, Laura could feel it, but Jack was refusing to meet her gaze, so she couldn't search his eyes for answers.

"Mark, Paige is just calling Elias and then you can go see her," Jack told his brother.

"Paige?" Laura felt a rush of fear flash through her.

"Paige?" Sofia exclaimed almost simultaneously, sitting bolt upright in her bed. "What happened to her? Is she okay? Did the stalker try something with her? I knew something bad was going to happen."

"Sofia, relax," Jack ordered. "Paige is okay. Ryan's going to explain what happened, but I need to grab Laura." He turned to her. "*If* you think you're up to talking to Maegan. I don't want you to push yourself."

"I'm up to it," she replied immediately, already climbing from the bed.

"I'll go check on Paige," Mark announced, ducking out the door.

"Ryan will be right in. You stay in bed until he gets here," Jack told Sofia.

Laura found herself pausing at the door. The last time she'd stepped outside into the busy ER she'd had a panic attack. It had caught her completely by surprise. She hadn't had one in over a year. But as she'd opened that door, she'd felt it coming on and had been powerless to stop it. Her heart had begun to pound, her pulse raced, and she couldn't breathe. She had sunk to the floor, her legs unable to support her—so overwhelmed, she couldn't move. That's where Mark's nurse friend had found her and quickly bundled her back into the quiet room.

"You okay?" Jack's voice rumbled behind her.

Managing a nod, Laura slid her hand into Jack's. His squeezed tightly, and then before she could contemplate the horror that she might have another panic attack when she left the room, she opened the door and stepped through it.

"I'm right here." Jack was so close behind her that his body was pressed right up against hers.

"Why do you need me to talk to Maegan?" Laura asked, needing the distraction.

Knowing that without her needing to tell him, Jack made his voice brisk and businesslike. "Malachi ran. Eliza woke up and we tried talking to her, but Maegan was right, Malachi has messed with her head. She freaked out when I asked her about the baby, so we left her with Dr. Roma and went to find Ryan and Paige. We found them coming in from outside. Malachi had created a distraction and ran. He fired a shot at Ryan, and Paige fired one back at him. Then he got away. We need to find him ASAP. And right now, with Eliza brainwashed, Maegan is our best chance at finding him."

Jack had been walking her toward a small office while he talked, but now Laura stopped and tilted her head back to look up at him. "What happened with Paige? Is she really okay?"

"Paige *is* okay," Jack assured her. "But someone tried to run her down with a car, right after she shot at Malachi. Ryan pushed her out of the way. She dislocated her thumb, but other than that, she's fine—just shaken up."

"The stalker is back. Jack, she can't be alone anymore …"

"Shh," Jack soothed. "We already told her that. Xavier is going to go and stay with her for a while. Try not to worry about Paige; we won't let the stalker get to her again."

Laura knew there was no way they could guarantee that. She and Paige had been friends for a few years now and Laura thought she had a reasonable idea of how Paige's mind worked. And right now, she was worried that Paige was going to want to act as bait to draw the stalker out. When she'd been used as bait to draw out her tormentor, Rose had wound up dead. She didn't want anything like that to happen again.

"Laura." Jack moved so he was in front of her and took her face in his hands. "I know you're worried about Paige—we all are—but right now, I need you one hundred percent focused on Maegan. If we don't find Malachi quickly, he could run, try this again with some other girls. I need you to put everything else aside for now and just work your magic on Maegan. Can you do that for me?"

Setting her concerns about Paige aside, and her concerns about Sofia who was going to blame herself, Laura focused. Maegan needed her, and she wanted to help. She was worried about messing things up, but she was even more worried about doing nothing. "Okay, I'm ready."

Jack held her gaze, searching her eyes to see if he felt she really was ready. Apparently, he decided she was and he nodded. "She's in there. I won't come in. She's not all that pleased with me and Xavier since we wouldn't let her go and see Eliza."

"What do you need me to get from her?" Laura asked.

"Everything you can."

"Okay," Laura hoped she could get Maegan to talk to her. "Can I tell her Malachi ran?"

"Yes, maybe it'll motivate her to talk. And Ryan and Paige IDed Maegan and Eliza; their names are Maegan Masters and Eliza Donnan. Hey," Jack grabbed her wrist when she went to open the door. "I love you, and I don't care if you never get over your agoraphobia. Laura, I love you and our kids more than anything. I don't want you to *ever* doubt that again."

Laura didn't *want* to doubt that ever again. But the problem was, sometimes she didn't have any control over what she felt. "Mark said he thought I should still be seeing my therapist." She watched her husband to gauge his reaction.

"And ...?" Jack prompted.

"And, maybe he's right," she finished, feeling her cheeks flush.

"Good, I think he's right, too. And stop looking embarrassed that you need help. Being a psychiatrist doesn't give you magical powers to fix your problems," he admonished.

She knew that was true, but it had still been an issue for her. She'd been a psychology student when she'd been abducted. She'd finished her degree from her apartment after she'd disappeared and locked herself away. Since then, she'd also gotten degrees in psychiatry and forensic psychiatry.

"I know," she smiled up at him. "I'll try really hard to not feel like a burden," she promised, hoping she could do it.

"You'll do better than try. We'll get you to the point where you believe it."

Laura both loved and hated that Jack always made them a team, facing everything together. She loved it because it made her feel safer and stronger to know he was always right by her side, but she hated that he had to constantly be dealing with her issues.

Jack's unwavering support meant a lot to her, and she wished that she had let him be there for her from the beginning. She knew it had been a mistake not to tell him about her assault and an even bigger mistake to run and hide from her family. She often wondered how her life would have turned out if she had called Jack after she'd been rescued. Still, she knew that what was, was. She had him now, and that's what was important. The best she could do was work on rebuilding the shattered pieces of her life.

"Okay, I better go see Maegan," she said at last, getting herself in the zone where she was completely focused on the task at hand and not distracted by anything else.

"I'll be right out here if you need me."

Inside the small office, Maegan was sitting in a corner, her head on her knees. "Maegan?"

Her head darted up, and Maegan's red-rimmed eyes immediately brightened. "Laura! Jack said you had a panic attack and I couldn't see you." She bounced to her feet and rushed over, throwing her arms around Laura.

Laura didn't really like people to touch her, but she didn't protest and returned the teenager's hug. "Maegan, it's time. You need to tell me everything you can about Malachi."

Pulling back, panic filled her blue eyes. "Did something happen?"

"Malachi disappeared," she told her gently, leading Maegan over to the chairs.

She paled. "Disappeared?" Maegan repeated.

"Yes, he ran. That means that for the moment you are all safe, but we need to act quickly, because Malachi might try to grab some other girls and recreate what he had with his family again.

Or he might decide to try and come back for you and your sisters." Laura didn't want to scare the girl, but she also wanted her to realize just how serious things were.

"You really think he might come back?" Maegan's eyes went wide with fear.

"I think it's a possibility," Laura replied honestly. If she were profiling Malachi, she would certainly put it at the top of his list. He didn't like change. He thought of the girls as his property. Particularly the baby who was the only one who was biologically related to him. "Maegan, I know how horrifying it is to be grabbed by a stranger and locked away someplace where you can't get away. And I know how sick it makes you feel to have to tell someone what happened, especially when the person who hurt you is still out there. But everyone who was responsible for my abduction was found, and we'll find Malachi, too, but only with the information you can give me. My friends found your case. They know your name is Maegan Masters; they know Eliza's name, too. That means your family will be on their way here."

Maegan digested this, her eyes growing teary. "My parents are coming?"

"Yes. Eliza's family, too. And as soon as you tell us the other girls' names, we can call their families, too. Your mom and dad will be so happy to see you. Getting that call will have been the best moment of their lives." Laura knew how much her family had suffered while she had been missing and when she had locked herself away from the world. Now, because of her choice to run and hide, things were still strained between them. She felt so uncomfortable with them. She knew that she'd broken their hearts when she'd disappeared without a word, and she couldn't seem to let go of that guilt. She wished she knew how to fix their relationships. She loved her family so much, and she knew their love for her was unconditional.

"They're really coming?" Maegan couldn't seem to wrap her head around that.

"They're really coming, honey."

"Eliza's family, too?"

"Eliza's family, too," she nodded. Sensing Maegan was almost ready to spill everything, Laura gave her a little push. "You said Arianna is Eliza and Malachi's daughter, that he forced himself on her, did he force himself on you, too?" she asked gently.

Tears began to trickle down Maegan's cheeks. "He started on my thirteenth birthday."

"You were scared he'd start with the others. That's why it was so important for you to make sure this worked out, because you knew if you went back, he'd start on the other girls in a few years."

"Uh-huh," Maegan nodded.

"I understand why you want to protect them. You love them. So, give me their names so we can send them home, too."

Drawing in a deep, shuddering breath, the last of the fight drained from her eyes. "I don't know their last names, but Angela's real name is Bethany, and Abigail's name is Hayley. I assume they were taken on the same day as Eliza and me."

"Okay, I'll give those names to Jack."

"What's going to happen to Arianna?" Maegan asked. "Malachi can't get her, can he? He *is* her father."

"No, honey. Malachi raped Eliza, and even if he wasn't charged with your kidnappings, which he *will* be once we find him, he wouldn't be able to get custody of her. Arianna can go with Eliza."

"Eliza's messed up," Maegan wailed. "Malachi did something to her. He somehow convinced her that she really is his daughter Ariyel."

"Then Arianna can go with Eliza's family while she gets help or she can go into foster care or Eliza can choose to put her up for adoption. But I promise you that she will be safe, just like the rest of you will be safe."

"Okay," Maegan brushed at her wet cheeks.

"Where are the girls hiding? With Malachi on the run, they aren't safe alone. We can't make sure they're protected until we find him, but they need to be with us."

Maegan began to cry again. "I don't know. I told Angela to just take them and hide. I didn't want Malachi to ever get his hands on them, so even if it didn't work and you didn't believe me, and Malachi took me and Eliza home with him, he'd never get the girls. When someone found them, I told Angela to tell them who they were and what happened to them. I thought if I knew where they were, Malachi would be able to force me somehow to tell him. I thought it was safer for them if I didn't know. I'm sorry."

She took the teenager's hand and squeezed it tightly. "Don't be sorry, Maegan. You did what you felt was best, and we'll find the girls."

Looking unconvinced, Maegan gave a half-hearted nod.

"Now, I need you to think." Laura waited until Maegan was looking her directly in the eye. "Can you think of anything that might help us find Malachi?"

"I don't know," Maegan shrugged helplessly.

"Do you think he'd go back to the house? He's on the run; he would go someplace that he feels safe. Do you think that could be the house where he'd kept you?"

She considered this, then nodded. "I think he'd go back there. But I don't know where 'there' is."

There had to be a way to figure it out. Laura went with a few assumptions. One, that the house Malachi had taken the kidnapped girls to was the one in which his family had lived and then died in the fire. Two, that Jack and the others hadn't been able to locate the house by the fire. Otherwise, they would have gone straight there to look for Malachi and not needed her to talk to Meagan. Based on those assumptions, there had to be a way to locate the house. She just needed to figure out what.

Then it occurred to her. "Maegan, Malachi brought you here in a car tonight, right? Not an ambulance?" She was already positive of this because Malachi wouldn't risk someone coming to the house.

She looked confused. "Right."

"What kind of car? A new one or an old one?"

"New. It wasn't the same car as the one he used when he kidnapped us."

"Does it have GPS?"

"Yes, I think so. I rode in the front seat, there was a screen, I assume it was a GPS."

She felt relieved; hopefully that would work. If Malachi used the GPS system, then it would have a record of home, as he would have used it to get to and from there to other places. There was only one last thing to find out. "Maegan, can you find Malachi's car in the parking lot?"

Renewed confidence shone from her blue eyes. "Yes."

* * * * *

12:46 A.M.

"Okay, you can go back to bed now," Jack informed Laura.

She narrowed her eyes at him. "Go back to bed? I'm fine, Jack. Really, I don't even have a headache anymore."

"Angel, just because you helped us out with Maegan doesn't mean you're off the hook. Mark was concerned enough about you to tell you to stay in bed and rest. That means you will be spending the night in bed, sleeping." Jack was still concerned about his wife, but the fact that she was going to go back to her therapist was easing his worries a little. He'd never wanted her to quit in the first place.

"I want to stay with Maegan until her parents get here. They're on their way, right?"

He caught the wistful look in her eyes and wished that he knew how to help her properly reconnect with her own parents. She was so much closer with his than hers these days. Jack knew that Laura had hidden herself away for ten years because she hadn't been able to deal with her own emotions about her abduction, let alone her family's. She had convinced herself that they were angry with her for hiding. Despite the fact that her parents and sister had told her many times that they weren't, Laura continued to believe that they *did* feel angry and were just scared to express it to her because of the trauma she'd suffered.

"Maegan's family are on their way, angel," he assured her, pulling her into an embrace.

"Did you talk to them?" she asked as she snuggled her head against his chest.

"No, Ryan did."

Before he could say more, the door burst open and Paige came in, Mark on her heels. "I found the other girls," she announced.

"Did Mark clear you to work?" Jack asked her. Not only did he not want Paige working tonight, but he'd prefer to lock her away in protective custody until her stalker had been arrested.

She glared irritably at him. "Mark doesn't get to clear me for anything. I'm fine; Mark taped my hand." She held it up for him to see.

Ignoring her, he looked at his brother. "Is she okay to work?"

"I'd prefer she go home and rest. Scratch that, I'd rather she disappeared until you guys find out who the stalker is. But, she's right, I can't stop her from working. If I can't even get Laura to stay in bed, I don't stand a chance against Paigey."

"I hate when you call me that, Mark," she frowned.

"I know." Mark grinned back.

She turned her back on him. "I need to work, Jack. I'll drive myself crazy if I don't."

He relented, because he understood. "Okay, fine. Where are Ryan and Xavier?"

"Right here." Xavier appeared in the doorway. "Ryan is just finishing up with Sofia."

"I'll go back to Maegan. I just wanted you to know everything she told me," Laura announced, putting her hands on his shoulders and tugging him down so she could kiss him. Then she caught Paige in a deadly serious gaze. "Paige, please, promise me you'll be careful."

"I promise. I won't do anything stupid, but I'm not just going to run away and hide," Paige said.

"I have to go back to work. I don't want any more phone calls from you guys. Well, I mean, I want you to call me if you need me," Mark explained. "I just don't want you to need me. I don't want anyone else getting hurt. Paige, be careful, no one wants to bury you. Come on, Laura, I'll walk you back to Maegan, check on Sofia, and head back upstairs."

"He's right, Paige." Jack shot her a serious look of his own once Mark and Laura left. "No one wants you to die, but the stalker seems intent on trying to kill you, so please let us watch your back."

Tears shimmered in Paige's brown eyes. "I don't want to die, Jack. I don't want you guys following me everywhere either, but I'm not going to fight you on it. Let's just hurry up and find him."

He was relieved that they had that taken care of. "You said you found the other girls identities?" he asked Paige.

"Yes, Bethany Christian was abducted from a library the same day Eliza and Maegan were taken. Her mom had taken her to story time for preschoolers. Bethany was playing with the other kids, listening to books, and making crafts. Her mom was talking with the other moms, then when it was time to leave, she went to look for Beth but couldn't find her anywhere."

"What about Hayley?"

"Hayley Newton was six months old when she was taken from her home. Same day as the other girls went missing, Grace Newton says goodbye to her husband, puts the baby down for a nap, then takes a shower. When she comes out, the baby is gone. Obviously, we'll need to confirm with DNA, but the names match. They were taken on the same day and physical descriptions match."

"We contacted the families?" Ryan asked entering the room.

Jack shot his brother an assessing look, trying to determine if things had gone okay when he'd told Sofia about Paige and the stalker. Ryan looked somewhat stressed, so Jack guessed things hadn't gone too well.

Paige's face grew sad. "Yes, Bethany's parents are bringing their three other children and coming straight to the hospital. But unfortunately, Hayley's parents were killed in a car accident a few months after she went missing. The only family I could locate was a grandmother who lives in a nursing home. She was thrilled to hear that we think we found Hayley, but she doesn't think she'll be able to care for the girl. Which means the poor thing will probably go into foster care; not the best option considering she's already going to be traumatized."

"Hopefully, something will work out for her, and foster care isn't always so bad." Ryan consoled his partner. Paige nodded distractedly.

"Now, we just need to find them. Laura said Maegan didn't know where they were, that she just told them to go and hide. Apparently, she never intended for them to go back with Malachi, no matter what happened," Jack informed the others.

"And we have to find the car," Ryan added. "That was total genius on Laura's part thinking of that."

"Maegan gave her a description. Ryan, you and I can go and search for the car, and then if it pans out like Laura thinks, we can go to Malachi's." Jack wanted to get moving, find this man before he had a chance to do anything else.

"I'll try Eliza again," Xavier offered. "I don't know if I can make any progress with her, but it's worth a shot. She's the oldest. Maegan was only ten when she was taken; Eliza was eighteen. She would have picked up things that Maegan missed."

"I'll look for the girls," Paige said. "That means I'll be here—

safe and sound in the hospital—and you guys won't have to worry about me. Plus, Xavier will be here if there are any problems."

Ryan looked like he wanted to argue, presumably in favor of locking Paige away where no one could get to her, but he said nothing. Probably because he couldn't think of a reasonable alternative. They needed to find the children, they needed to find Malachi, and they needed to talk to Eliza again.

"CSU is coming to check out where the shooting happened and where the car tried to run down Paige." Jack tried to glance at her unobtrusively. She paled at his words, but otherwise remained calm. "Okay, let's get going."

* * * * *

12:51 A.M.

Ariyel was scared.

She wanted …

She wanted …

Well, she didn't really know what she wanted.

She didn't know much of anything right now.

Just that she was tired.

Really tired.

So tired that even thinking took up more energy than she had.

She thought it was because the doctor had given her something earlier.

Something to calm her down.

Because those police officers had upset her.

Questions. They had so many questions.

And they kept saying things to her that she didn't understand.

Maegan? She didn't know anyone called Maegan.

Kidnapped? She hadn't been kidnapped.

They had told her she was in the hospital because she'd suffered a drug overdose. They'd asked her if she did it on purpose.

They had said horrible things to her about Arianna.

They had asked her if she needed help.

But she didn't.

Did she?

Her head hurt.

It spun, too.

She couldn't process more than snippets of thought at a time.

Where was her father?

She hadn't seen Malachi since she'd woken up.

But did she want to see him?

Malachi scared her.

She thought he hurt her.

Only Malachi told her that it was what fathers did to their daughters.

Maybe those cops had been right.

Maybe she did need help.

"Eliza?"

The voice at the door startled her.

Scared, she shrunk back into the mattress, pulling the blankets right up to her chin.

It was one of the detectives.

He had light brown hair and unusual eyes, one hazel and one green.

He reminded her of someone. Only she couldn't remember who.

"Hey, Eliza, how are you feeling?" He came and sat on the chair beside her bed.

"Ariyel," she countered desperately. "My name is Ariyel."

"No, it's not," he said firmly, but gently. "Your name is Eliza, Eliza Donnan."

"No," she pressed her hands to her ears. "No, no, no, no, no."

He took hold of her wrists and softly tugged her hands away from her ears. "It's okay, Eliza. Malachi won't hurt you again."

She stared back at him.

Malachi *would* hurt her again.

He always hurt her.

She thought he might be wrong.

She didn't think fathers were supposed to hurt their daughters.

But she had to be wrong.

Malachi was right.

He was *always* right.

"Eliza ..." the detective didn't release her; instead, he slid his hands from her wrists to hold her hands. "Malachi kidnapped you. He took you from your family. He tricked you while you were walking home from college one day. Pretended his car had broken down. You saw the little girls, trusted him. He chloroformed you, threw you in his car, and took you. That was five years ago. Do you remember that?"

He was lying.

He had to be.

She hadn't been kidnapped.

She hadn't.

And yet ...

Fleeting images tumbled through her mind.

A sweet smell.

A phone falling.

A feeling of floating.

"Eliza, do you remember?"

"No," she whispered frantically. "You're wrong. I wasn't kidnapped."

"Honey, I'm not wrong. Try not to be afraid. I won't let Malachi hurt you. I know he messed with your head, convinced you that you are his daughter, but he was lying. Try hard to remember. You are Eliza Donnan. Your parents are Richard and Maggie Donnan. You have an older brother, Michael, and a younger sister, Naomi. You were an early childhood major. You loved to read and go camping and ride horses."

His voice was so gentle, his grip on her hands reassuring, but she was so afraid.

The fear consumed her.

Prevented her from thinking of anything else.

He must have seen it in her eyes because he said again, "Malachi won't hurt you, I promise. I know he did awful things to you, but you're safe now. He can't get to you again. We know who your sisters really are, we've already called their families. They can go home now, they'll be safe from Malachi, too. Maegan said you fought so hard to save them. That's why Malachi had to brainwash you, because you wouldn't stop fighting him."

Cold.

Hungry.

Thirsty.

Dark.

The images flashed into her mind so violently, she cried out. She pressed her hands to her temples as though she could physically stop what she was seeing.

"Eliza? Are you okay?" His voice was full of concern.

"Stop, please," she whimpered. "Make it stop."

"Make what stop, honey?"

"My head, it hurts, stop talking to me. You're lying. You're lying." She began to sob.

She was a bit surprised, but not totally, when he put his arms around her and held her as she cried.

"You're lying," she said again.

Only, the problem was, she didn't think he was.

* * * * *

12:53 A.M.

Paige was so tired, even putting one foot in front of the other was becoming a problem. Yet, as tired as she was, she knew if she were home in bed, she wouldn't be sleeping.

In fact, after tonight, she'd be surprised if she'd ever be able to sleep again.

She was still shaken up by what had happened.

She'd heard the car, but she'd been focused on Malachi and her partner. It hadn't been until a split second before Ryan launched at her, tackling her to the ground and covering her body with his own, that she had realized what the driver intended to do.

She was still struggling to comprehend it.

For the last four years, she had lived with the possibility that the stalker would return, but now that he had, and he'd tried to kill her again, it all felt so surreal. She didn't want to believe that it was really happening.

But it was.

If Ryan hadn't pushed her out of the way, that car would have plowed into her. It had been going fast enough that it probably would have killed her. At the very least, it would have left her fighting for her life. Again.

Paige didn't really remember the attack that had almost ended her life. Her head injuries had been too serious and had wiped out most of her memories. All she did remembered was pain and fear. She liked it like that. She didn't want to remember details. It was terrifying enough without having every awful second seared into her mind.

She wanted to end this before the stalker made another attempt on her life. She didn't want Ryan, Jack, and Xavier hovering over her every second. It could be years before they caught him. Or, what if they never did? She couldn't spend the rest of her life with bodyguards shadowing her every move.

So, she was going to do something about it.

In the morning she intended to talk to their lieutenant about using herself as bait to try to trap the stalker. She couldn't live like this any longer. The fear of knowing he could come after her again at any moment was too much. Using herself as bait was risky, but she was willing to take the risk to bring this to an end. She wasn't, however, going to tell Ryan, Jack, and Xavier what she was planning because they would veto the idea immediately. They were *way* too overprotective of her.

Right now, though, her focus was finding these little girls.

Tonight was not the best night to be working a case with kids. Having anything to do with children always made her heart ache. She wanted to be a mother so badly. But she meant what she'd told Ryan earlier. She was done. She couldn't go through another failed adoption.

When she had seen Elias' name pop up on her phone while she'd been in the bathroom earlier, she had known immediately that it was bad news. Apparently, the young woman whose baby they had been going to adopt had changed her mind. Amy had been scared to take on the responsibility of raising a child on her own. She was only nineteen. Her parents had refused to help and she hadn't known who the father was. Then, an aunt had offered to let her move in and even to look after the baby once it was born so she could continue her studies and work. So, the young woman had decided to keep her baby. Wanting them to know immediately, Amy had called Elias, and Elias had called her.

Of course, she totally respected Amy's decision and sincerely wished her and her baby all the best, but she just couldn't deal with getting her hopes up again only to have them dashed to pieces.

So, she was done.

She wasn't doing it again.

She was just going to have to accept that however much she wanted to have children, it just wasn't going to happen for her.

Paige was glad that the boys had agreed to let her search for the little girls on her own. They hadn't had much of a choice. If Malachi had fled to his house, then two of them needed to go, since he was clearly dangerous. And Eliza seemed to respond to Xavier, so he was the logical choice to talk to her. Laura was still with Maegan. Which only left her to look for the girls.

And she had needed the time to process her feelings about what had happened. She couldn't do that while the guys were watching her closely to make sure she didn't fall apart. She knew they meant well, and that her near death experience had created this overprotectiveness, but their hovering and constant worrying was stifling.

Still, she'd do as she'd promised and remain here in the hospital where she should be relatively safe. She wasn't stupid and she didn't take stupid risks, and even though she didn't like it, she would agree to let them babysit her because it would make her safer, and she really didn't want to die.

A shiver suddenly rocked through her.

Someone was watching her.

She was sure of it.

Was it the stalker?

Was he still here in the hospital?

He could have parked his car somewhere after his failed attempt at running her down and then doubled back here to take another shot at her.

The halls were quiet. It was nearly one in the morning, and the hospital was virtually empty. The patients were all in bed, and the few nurses on duty were mostly sitting and chatting at the nurses' stations.

Discreetly, she checked over her shoulders, searching the dark corridors for any movement.

She saw nothing.

Was she just being paranoid?

She was wired and stressed and on edge tonight; maybe her fears were just making her imagination fly into overdrive.

Paige continued walking, but she hadn't gone more than a few yards when the feeling of being watched swamped her again.

Someone was definitely there.

Should she go back down to the ER? It would be busy and

Xavier would be there. She could tell him that she thought someone was following her.

No, she didn't need to tell Xavier. She could handle this herself.

She took a few more steps and the feeling that someone was following her was so overwhelming that she caved and yanked out her phone, noting with irritation that her hands were trembling. She didn't want to need Xavier, but she wasn't so stubborn that she was going to risk her life to keep her pride.

Typing in his number, his concerned voice answered almost immediately. "Paige? What's wrong?"

"I think someone is following me," she whispered.

Xavier muttered something she didn't catch, probably a curse. "Where are you?"

"Third floor, I was heading for the play therapy room. Jack and I checked the day care room earlier because we thought the girls might hide there. But then I was thinking if I was little and scared I'd want to hide someplace smaller, safer feeling, and then I remembered interviewing a kid in the play therapy room a couple of months ago."

"Okay, I'm on my way. I'll get to you as quickly as I can. Just be careful."

She debated her options once she hung up. The play therapy room was just at the end of the hallway. If she was right and the girls were there, they needed to be found. If, on the other hand, she was right, and someone was following her, then she could be putting the girls in danger.

Scanning the hallways, they appeared empty, and she made her decision. She had to see if the girls were there; she could protect all of them if the need arose. And Xavier would be here in minutes. Besides, she didn't really think the stalker was a threat to anyone other than herself.

She hurried the rest of the way down the hall and opened the door to the play therapy room.

Two scared little faces peered up at her.

The oldest girl tugged the baby and the smaller girl into her arms.

Paige took a slow step into the room. "You're Bethany, right?" she addressed the oldest girl, squatting down so she was eye level with the child.

Slowly, Bethany nodded.

"And this must be Hayley." She tugged gently on one of the little girl's tangled pigtails. "And Arianna." She rested a hand on the baby's silky soft head. "My name is Paige, and I'm a police officer. Your sister, Maegan, told us that you need help."

She wasn't sure what to expect from the terrified children, but it certainly wasn't for Hayley to launch off her sister's lap and throw herself into her arms.

She held the child close as the little girl cried into her neck. "It's okay ... shh ... it's okay. You're safe now. You're safe."

Footsteps sounded outside the door, and Paige reached for her gun with one hand while maneuvering Hayley so that her body protected the little girl from any potential threats.

"Paige? You in there?"

Hearing Xavier's voice, she relaxed. "It's okay," she assured the children, "it's just Xavier. He's my friend and a police officer, too. Yeah, I'm in here!" she called out.

The door opened, and Xavier stood there, scanning the room to confirm that everything was okay. His gaze fell on the children. "You found the girls." He smiled.

Picking up baby Arianna, Paige stood, holding the baby in one arm and Hayley in the other. "And now you guys get to go home," she told the kids.

"Home? Really?" Bethany scrambled to her feet, her scared expression had changed to one of excitement.

"Okay, everyone, let's go back down to the ER to wait." Xavier began to herd them toward the door. "And you," he whispered in her ear, "do not leave my sight."

Some of her elation at finding the missing girls faded. Xavier was right. She wasn't safe. This time the stalker wasn't giving up. This time he seemed intent on killing her. And with a shiver of fear, she realized that this time she might not be lucky enough to survive his attempt.

TWENTY-NINE YEARS AGO

6:29 P.M.

Malachi was excited.

Although he was trying to contain it, as bouncing around was hardly appropriate behavior for a thirteen-year-old.

Today was his thirteenth birthday, and he had been milking every second of it from the moment he'd awoke this morning.

In fact, he intended to milk his birthday at least until the weekend when he had his party. His entire seventh grade class had been invited. His mom had gone all out, hiring a conference room at a fancy hotel and several suites so he and his friends could stay the night. There'd be food and music and dancing, and they could even go swimming in the hotel's pool.

Turning thirteen was a big deal in his family. It signified becoming a man.

And he *was* becoming a man.

Samantha Ingham was coming to his party. They'd known each other since kindergarten. They'd been friends and then enemies and then friends again, and now … now what Malachi felt for her was more than friendship. She was so pretty. She had long dark hair and blue eyes, and she was smart and funny and good at sports.

Every time he saw her, he wanted to kiss her, but he was embarrassed. He'd never kissed a girl before. None of his friends had. His friends teased him about his crush on Samantha, but he didn't care. He knew they had crushes on girls, too. They were just scared to admit it.

He was going to kiss her at his party.

He'd been working up the courage to do it for weeks now.

He was going to ask her to dance, then wait for a slow song, and then after that, he was going to kiss her. He was as excited as he was nervous about it. What was it like to kiss a girl? He had no idea, but his parents seemed to like kissing each other, and so did people in movies, so it had to be pretty awesome.

"You can wait in the car, Malachi, while I run a quick errand." His father's voice pierced his thoughts.

Blinking, he peered out the window. They weren't at the ice-cream parlor. After finishing his family birthday dinner, he had insisted on ice cream. And not just any ice cream, but a selection of his favorite flavors from his favorite store.

His dad had wanted to go alone, but Malachi had insisted on coming along, stating that he wouldn't know which particular flavors he'd feel like until he saw them. And it was his birthday, after all.

"Where are we?" he demanded.

"I just have to run a quick errand before we go get the ice cream," his father replied. "Wait here." He slipped from the car and hurried off.

Malachi looked around; they were in a small alley. Garbage cans and rubbish piled up on both sides. Graffiti covered the brick walls of the buildings that backed onto the alley.

What were they doing here?

What errand could his father possibly have to run in a place like this?

Wanting to find out what his father was up to, he wondered in the back of his mind whether it was some special surprise for his birthday. Malachi climbed out of the car and went in search of his father.

He found him at the end of the alley, standing in front of a locked wire gate, talking in hushed whispers with a woman.

The woman looked vaguely familiar.

Quietly he crept closer, sensing that whatever was going on

was something big.

"I told you 'no,'" his father was saying to the woman.

"I don't accept that. I *won't* accept that," the woman replied.

"You don't have a choice," his father shot back.

"No, it's *you* who doesn't have a choice. I won't let it end. I don't want it to be over."

Over? End? What were they talking about? And why would his father be meeting with a woman in an alley to discuss it?

"I'm leaving." His father turned his back on the woman.

She grabbed his arm. "No, please. Please, don't leave. I'm begging you ... I can't live without you." The woman began to cry.

Couldn't live without him? Were his dad and this woman ...?

No, it couldn't be. They couldn't be having an affair. His dad loved his mom.

"I love my wife. It's over. I don't want to see you again," his father told the woman.

"I won't let you go. I'll tell her. I'll tell her everything. I'll tell her how we met; I'll tell her how long we've been together. I'll tell her what you like in bed." The woman shrieked at top pitch and Malachi jumped.

His father noticed the movement and turned toward him. "Malachi. I'm sorry." His blue eyes were sadder than Malachi had ever seen them, and watery with unshed tears. He had *never* seen his dad cry before.

Still clawing at denial, he shook his head vehemently. He couldn't accept that his father and this woman were having an affair.

"Let's go." His father walked toward him, taking his arm and propelling him back towards the car.

The woman sprang at them, triumphant. "Now you'll have to tell your wife—your son knows—he won't be able to keep it a secret. She'll leave you, and you'll come crawling back to me."

"I'll never come back to you, and I'm going to tell her myself."

His father opened one of the car's back doors and shoved him inside, then climbed in the driver's seat.

Throwing open the passenger door, the woman clambered inside, too. "She won't forgive you."

Ignoring her, his father started the engine and reversed the car out of the alley.

Malachi was in shock.

He couldn't believe this was happening.

And today of all days.

This day was supposed to be special. His thirteenth birthday. The day he became a man. And in a way, he had. His childhood naïveté was shattered. His childish illusions destroyed.

"Martha, I'll drop you off at home on the way," his father was telling the woman.

Martha? Wasn't that the name of his father's secretary? Is that where he'd seen the woman before?

"No," Martha wailed, tears streaming down her cheeks.

Malachi studied the woman. She was pretty, he had to admit that. She was tall, had long, wavy blonde hair and large green eyes. But as pretty as she was, Martha had nothing on his mother. His mother was good and kind and sweet and hardworking. She'd do anything for him or his father. And this was how his father repaid her? By cheating on her with his secretary?

"Please, please," Martha continued to sob. "I won't tell. I promise. I won't tell your wife. She never has to know, and we can just keep doing what we've been doing." She reached out a hand and traced it down his father's cheek. "I love you."

For a long moment his father said nothing. Just drove. Then he reached up a hand, covered Martha's, and gently pulled it away from his face, he brought it to his lips and kissed it. Then he set it on her lap. "I'm sorry, Martha. I never wanted to hurt you, but I don't love you. I love my wife."

Martha sat there, staring at him and crying.

Malachi wondered whether he hated his father or his father's mistress more.

His father continued to drive the car.

Then Martha howled—a sound Malachi would never forget. She lunged at the steering wheel, yanking it sideways. "If I can't have you, then no one can!" she screamed.

The brick wall was upon them before his father could stop the car.

With an almighty, earth-shattering, bone-crushing bang, the car hit the wall and the world exploded into nothingness.

NOVEMBER 4TH
1:00 A.M.

1:04 A.M.

"That was Xavier." Jack hung up his phone and looked over at his brother. They were in Ryan's car driving to the address that showed up as home on Malachi's GPS. Thankfully, Malachi had never entertained the possibility of being caught and he had often used his GPS to look up how to get from his home to various locations.

"What did he want?" Ryan cast him a quick glance then returned his gaze to the road.

"He said they found the girls, safe and sound," he replied.

Sensing there was more, Ryan tensed. "That's great. But there's more, isn't there?"

He sighed. He may as well just tell him. "He also said that someone was following Paige while she was searching for the kids."

Ryan didn't comment. Then he thumped a fist into the steering wheel and growled. "Is she okay?"

"Xavier said she's fine, just shaken up. He said he won't let her out of his sight," Jack assured him.

"Jack."

That was all Ryan said, but he didn't need to say more. Jack already knew how worried his brother was about Paige. With good reason. For the stalker to come back after the failed attempt at running her down showed just how serious he was about killing her.

"I know, try not to worry about her. Xavier won't let anyone get to her. We'll keep her safe, Ryan."

His brother said nothing. There was nothing to say. There was no way they could guarantee Paige's safety, short of locking her up some place.

"We're here," Ryan announced a few minutes later.

They pulled to a stop in front of a large, fully-fenced property. Wire topped the brick fence and a large gate blocked the driveway. Behind the high fences, a large house could just be seen. It was a three-story brown brick structure with metal bars on all the windows.

The house positively oozed gloom and doom.

They were definitely at the right place.

Climbing out of the car, they headed for the gate, and Jack was surprised to find it unlocked. Malachi must have been in too much of a hurry to lock it. It had only been an hour since Ryan and Paige had encountered him in the parking lot of the hospital, most likely not enough time to gather some belongings and flee, especially since he'd left his car behind. Hopefully, he had made it back here and hadn't left yet, then they would be able to arrest him.

Ryan put a hand on the gate, pushed it farther open and stepped into the driveway. Jack stopped him. "Ryan, what's our probable cause?"

"I thought I heard someone call for help," Ryan replied calmly.

He raised a brow. "Neither Maegan nor Eliza mentioned Malachi having any other children here."

He shrugged. "Maybe he grabbed another girl on the way back here." Ryan started walking up the drive.

They both knew there was no one else here, except perhaps Malachi, but Jack went along with it and followed his brother toward the house. Both of them pulled out their guns as they reached the front door. Malachi had proved how dangerous he was when he'd shot at Ryan earlier tonight.

Just like the gate, the front door stood open and they

cautiously made their way inside. They stood in a foyer surrounded by steel bars. There would have been no way for the girls to get through it and to the front door. There were several locks on both the foyer door and front door, including a deadlock and a padlock, as well as a combination lock. Malachi had made sure that those girls were trapped inside this house.

Quietly, they made their way from room to room. The more of the house they saw, the sorrier Jack felt for the girls Malachi had abducted. This place wasn't a home. There were no photos on the walls, no kid's artwork on the refrigerator, there were no toys lying about, no piles of laundry waiting to be folded, no stack of dishes waiting to be loaded into the dishwasher. Laura was a bit of a neat freak and kept their house well organized, but with both of them working long hours, a toddler, a baby on the way, friends and family, there were times when household chores got left behind.

With no signs of Malachi on the first floor, they headed for the stairs.

The second floor had four bedrooms. One was clearly Malachi's, although once again, there were no personal touches. The other rooms looked to belong to the three youngest children, but they weren't like the typical little girl's bedroom. The few toys were packed away on shelves and the beds were made with military precision. There were no clothes on the floor or hair accessories on the dresser or anything else that usually came with children. The only things that softened the rooms and made them a little childlike were the motifs on the walls. Fairies in the nursery, safari animals in Hayley's room, and a circus theme in Bethany's.

Malachi's room looked undisturbed. No clothes appeared to be missing from the closet or the dresser. A laptop remained on the small desk by a window, and the alphabetically arranged bookcase didn't have any gaps.

They moved onto the third floor. There were two bedrooms—

Maegan and Eliza's. Both were simple and unadorned, and neither expressed the personality of its occupant. Once again, there were no signs of Malachi.

Starting to wonder whether Malachi had already come and gone, Jack was getting frustrated. Someone like Malachi would never stop. They had taken his girls from him; he would want to replace them. If he couldn't do it here in this home, he would simply find another house and more girls and continue to attempt to recreate the family he had lost.

They needed to stop him.

Jack glanced at Ryan. "Basement?" he asked.

Ryan nodded. "I saw a door in the kitchen that looked like it would lead to a basement."

Still moving carefully, it was plausible Malachi had squirreled himself away in some secret place they hadn't been able to find, they headed for the basement.

The large space was mostly empty. There were a few tools on one wall and a couple of boxes in one corner and a door in the far corner. Together they crossed to the door. Ryan covered him as he put a hand on the knob and turned. Jack pushed the door open to reveal a small room, the walls of which had been painted black.

"He put Eliza in here," Jack said to Ryan, his eyes roving the room. He was positive he was right and pictured a terrified Eliza trapped in here, probably for days or even weeks on end.

"It's how he brainwashed her," Ryan agreed.

"We should call Xavier and tell him. He might be able to use that with Eliza to get her to open up." He pulled out his phone, ready to call his partner.

"I saw an office upstairs; we can go through that. Maybe we'll get lucky and find something that will lead us to where Malachi went—he's obviously not here." Ryan was already heading for the stairs.

Jack followed, dialing Xavier's number, and hoping that they located Malachi quickly because he had a bad feeling that if

Malachi wasn't stopped soon, a lot more lives were going to be destroyed. As he waited for Xavier to answer, he said a little silent prayer of thanks that all his family and friends were safe and sound.

* * * * *

1:11 A.M.

"You came back," Eliza's pale face relaxed when she saw him.

"Of course, I did. I said I would," Xavier admonished gently as he came and resumed his seat beside her bed.

Eliza had been crying in his arms when Paige had called him to say she was being followed. He had immediately eased the sobbing girl back against the pillows, told her he had to attend to an emergency and assured her he'd be back shortly, then hurried after Paige. He hadn't wanted to leave Eliza alone in that condition, but he also couldn't leave Paige alone and unprotected if the stalker was back.

He had run through the hospital's halls, ignoring the odd looks from nurses, wanting to get to Paige as quickly as possible before the stalker had a chance to make another attempt on her life. Thankfully, he'd found her safe and sound with the little girls Malachi had kidnapped.

Wanting to get all four of them back down to the relative safety of the busy emergency room, he had hustled them quickly through the corridors, constantly scanning all around them for any potential threats. Once they'd arrived in the ER, he had put them in the small office they'd been using. While he wanted to keep Paige in his sight, he had to get back to Eliza, so he had called in one of the officers who was outside at the shooting scene and asked him to stand guard at the office door, not allowing entrance to anyone.

With Paige at least temporarily safe, he focused on Eliza. They would find Malachi, and then they'd pull out all the stops and find the stalker so Paige would stay safe.

"I was scared," Eliza whispered. Her blue eyes seemed too big for her thin face.

"You don't need to be afraid anymore, Eliza," he promised.

"Stop calling me that; it's not my name," she said, but the conviction had gone from her voice.

He was making progress with her. When he'd been talking to her earlier, reminding her of her abduction and about how Malachi had brainwashed her, she'd been having flashbacks, he was sure of it. She just needed a little bit more of a push.

"Eliza, you're starting to remember, you know that everything I've said is true. Malachi is not your father, he kidnapped you and three other girls. Maegan, Bethany, and Hayley. We contacted their families, they can go home, your family is coming to get you, too. You're going home."

"Home?" she repeated, looking conflicted.

"Not Malachi's house, you never have to go back there, you get to go back to your real home. Your family loves you so much, they missed you."

"Family?" her brow scrunched in concentration. Then she studied him. "You remind me of someone, but I can't remember who."

Before he could push her to try and remember who, his phone buzzed. For a moment, he thought it was going to be Paige telling him the stalker was back, but his partner's name was flashing on the screen. "Jack, what's up?"

"Ryan and I are at the house. There's a room in the basement painted all in black, and I think that's where Malachi put Eliza to break her down so he could brainwash her. We also found bottles and bottles of sleeping pills in the bathroom cabinet. He's probably been feeding them to her daily to keep her under control."

"Okay, thanks." Xavier hoped he could use the additional

information to get Eliza to open up. "Any sign of Malachi?"

"Looks like he's been here at some point, but he's not here now. Any more issues with Paige?"

"No. I've got an officer on her, and I'll check in with her again soon," he replied.

"Okay, good luck with Eliza."

"I'm going to need it. Talk to you later."

Once he hung up, he turned back to Eliza, who had been watching him closely during his phone call. "Who was that?" she asked.

"That was my partner, he's at Malachi's house. Eliza, he found the room in the basement." He paused to gauge her reaction. If he hadn't been looking for it, he wouldn't have seen her near imperceptible shudder. "Did he lock you in there, Eliza?" he asked gently.

She shook her head, but her eyes filled with tears.

"Was it dark in there? Did he feed you?" Going with a hunch, he asked, "Did he take your clothes?"

Eliza clutched at the blankets and pulled them tighter around herself.

"How long did he keep you in there, Eliza?"

"A long time." Her voice was barely a whisper, and he noted that she was no longer contesting the fact that her name was Eliza.

"It was dark in there." He made it a statement not a question.

Eliza nodded.

"And you were cold because you didn't have your clothes," he continued.

Another nod.

"Did he make you beg him for water and light and food?"

"I wouldn't the first time," she murmured, squeezing her eyes closed.

Malachi had needed to break Eliza, so he had taken everything away: sight, sound, food, water, clothing. He had deprived her of everything then made himself her only way to get those things thus making her utterly dependent on him. Her environment would have made her weak, disoriented, vulnerable, and completely susceptible to Malachi's manipulations.

Bit by bit he was getting through to her. She had all but admitted the abduction and that she was really Eliza Donnan and not Malachi's daughter, Ariyel. Xavier was fighting his instincts to push her hard because he didn't think she was emotionally stable enough to handle it. But time was not on their side. In order to keep Eliza and the other girls safe, they needed Malachi caught.

"Eliza." Xavier waited until she opened her haunted eyes to look at him. "You were so strong. Malachi had to fight so hard to try and squash you, but he didn't. You're here; you're alive; you're safe. But Malachi is still out there. And he could do this again. You were the oldest; you might have seen or heard things Maegan missed. I need your help to find Malachi, so he can never hurt anyone else."

Her face had grown progressively paler as he spoke, now a completely unnatural shade of grey, and Xavier was relieved she was lying down; otherwise, he feared she would have collapsed. "He's still out there?"

"Yes, but we'll find him," he assured her.

She shook her head violently. "He'll come back!" she wailed.

"No, Eliza, he will never hurt you again. I promise."

"No. Ariyel. I'm Ariyel. Malachi is my father," she said desperately.

As quickly as he'd been making progress with her, it all fell away, and now he was right back where he'd started with her complete denials of everything. Xavier wondered whether Laura, with her degrees in psychology and experience with trauma victims, might have better luck with Eliza.

Reaching out and grasping her hands, he expected her to wrench them free, but instead her thin fingers latched onto his, clinging as if her life depended on it. "Eliza, I know you're scared.

I know what you've been through is horrendous, and I know how overwhelming this must all be for you, but I am promising you right here and now that I will keep you safe. Okay?"

Again, he expected her to recoil, to express the facts that she had no reason to believe that he could keep her safe, but instead she nodded slowly. "You remind me of George," she whispered.

"Who's George?" he asked.

Tugging free one hand, she traced her fingertips down his cheek. "I think ... I think ... I think he was my boyfriend."

"Xavier?"

* * * * *

1:22 A.M.

"Xavier?"

He turned to face her, but the young woman in the bed didn't seem to notice her presence. She was staring in wide-eyed adoration at Xavier.

"Annabelle." Xavier seemed surprised to see her. "What are you doing here?"

"I wanted to talk to you," she replied, although what she wanted to do now was find out who the woman in the bed was. Annabelle recognized the look on the woman's face when she looked at Xavier, because it was the same way she had looked at Xavier when she was lying in a hospital bed scared, traumatized, and alone.

Xavier arched an eyebrow. "I'm a little busy right now."

His rejection hurt, but Annabelle reminded herself that he was entitled to be frustrated with her. After all, she *had* moved out of their house. "Please. It won't take long."

He stared at her so long that she thought he was going to refuse, but then he nodded. "Fine." Turning to the woman in the bed, Xavier said, "I'll be right back. I'm just going to be outside the door. Are you going to be okay?"

The woman gave a shaky nod.

Squeezing her hand, Xavier gave the woman a final smile, then stood and stalked out of the room. Annabelle followed, feeling a stab of jealousy toward the woman.

Apparently in no hurry to talk to her, Xavier went straight through the ER, stopping to talk to an officer standing outside one of the offices. "Any signs of him?" he asked.

"No, sir."

"Okay, let me know if anything happens."

Xavier looked concerned as he slowly made his way to a relatively quiet corner of the waiting room. "What's wrong?" Annabelle asked as she trailed after him.

"The stalker tried to kill Paige tonight, then he was following her. I've got her tucked away in there with an officer watching her, but I'm still worried about her. The stress of having him still out there is getting to her."

Annabelle knew exactly how Paige felt. Ricky Preston had been on the run for close to a year before he finally made his move. "Is she okay?"

"Minor injuries from when Ryan tackled her out of the way of the car. Other than that, she's just shaken up." His eyes were cold and distant as he looked at her. "What do you want, Annabelle?"

"You're calling me Annabelle again," she noted. He only ever did that when he was annoyed with her.

Xavier simply shrugged. "What's up?"

Shoving away her own frustrations, again she had to remind herself that Xavier had a right to be annoyed with her. "Just because I'm moving out doesn't mean I want us to break up," she said.

"You came all the way down here to tell me that while I'm working?"

"Earlier at the house, I tried to explain why I'm moving out, but you don't understand. I just wanted to try and explain again. I just need some time—"

"I've given you time, Annabelle," Xavier interrupted. "I've been patient; I've been supportive; I've been there for you every step of the way. I've given you time, but I don't know that I can wait for you forever."

She staggered back as though he'd slapped her.

She thought Xavier loved her. That he would never leave her. That he would wait for her forever.

Which, logically, she had to admit was unfair.

"Don't look at me like that, Annabelle. You're the one who keeps pushing me away, not the other way around."

That was true, and yet it still felt so unfair.

Unfair mainly because it made her feel bad.

She had pushed Xavier away, but she didn't know why she kept doing it. Even now, looking at the man she loved, Annabelle knew that all she needed to say was that she was sorry and that she wasn't moving out. Then he would take her in his arms, hold her, kiss her, and tell her he loved her, and they could go home—together.

"I love you, Annabelle," he continued. "I just don't know if I can be in a relationship with someone who isn't all that committed to it."

She frowned. "That's not fair. I love you, too, and I *am* committed to our relationship."

He raised a disbelieving brow. "We've been together for five years now. I've proposed to you twice; both times you turned me down. I've given you time. I've done everything I can think of to help you, but I want a family. I want a wife and kids. And if you don't, then maybe we shouldn't be together."

"You're giving up on me." She could hardly believe it was true. "You promised me you never would, but you have."

He shook his head. "I've never given up on you. It's you. You've given up on yourself."

Was that true?

Had she given up on herself?

Was that why she kept pushing Xavier away?

He had done so much for her. Even little things. Like he knew how self-conscious she was about her unusually pale eyes, so he had stopped wearing the hazel contact lens over his green eye, so that everyone who looked at him could tell he had heterochromia.

She had never believed that she deserved to be loved. Her parents had stopped loving her after something had happened to her when she was four. She didn't clearly remember what it was. Just flashes of images and sounds. But whatever it was had to be bad if her own parents had stopped loving her afterward.

Xavier had broken through that barrier. He had somehow managed to convince her that he loved her. That as long as he was around, she wasn't alone.

And yet, one part of her brain remained stubborn. Refusing to accept it. Needing him to prove over and over again that he wasn't going anywhere.

"Take your time moving out the last of your things; I won't be staying at my house for a while." Xavier announced. "With the stalker upping the ante with Paige, we don't want her alone and unprotected, so I'm going to be moving in with her and Elias for a while, until we catch him."

She felt a sudden stab of jealousy toward Paige. Her friends would and were doing whatever necessary to protect her. And not just physically. Xavier, Jack, Ryan, Laura, and Sofia would all be doing their best to lift her spirits and make sure she didn't become depressed or paranoid. Annabelle knew that if she let them they would do the same for her, but she never let them.

"The ball is in your court, Annabelle." Xavier watched her closely, tensely, to see what her reaction would be.

And of course, ever the coward, she said nothing. She didn't know how to express to Xavier everything that was going on inside her right now.

He sighed. "I have to go back to Eliza." He turned, took a few steps, and then paused. "You have to decide what you want—constantly jerking me around isn't fair to me. You know what I want."

"Do I?" Her emotions were bubbling too close to the surface to hold them back. Before they burst out, she fled. Not stopping until she was outside, she took huge gulps of the cold night air as she struggled for control.

Annabelle half expected Xavier to come walking out behind her, gather her up in his arms and promise her that they could work things out. That he was still right there beside her, ready and willing to help her however he could.

But he didn't come.

She wanted him to, she realized.

Needed him to, even.

Needed him to follow her just one more time to prove to her that he really loved her and would never leave her.

* * * * *

1:25 A.M.

"I don't think we're going to find anything helpful," Ryan announced, sitting back in the chair at the desk in Malachi's office and stretching.

They'd been going through Malachi's paperwork, trying to find anything that might hint to where he'd flee. They hadn't found anything. Well, basically nothing. There were a few old bills from several years ago and a couple of bank statements—again, several years old.

At least they now knew that Malachi's full name was Malachi Rivers. With that information, they would be able to do a complete background search on him, including finding out about the fire that killed his daughters.

However, that wasn't going to help them find him quickly.

Those things would take time to find out and then investigate. By then, Malachi could have disappeared, be gone forever. He was clearly clever enough to interact with others without arousing suspicions.

With the bank statements, they could monitor his accounts, then they'd know if he withdrew anything and possibly locate him that way. Although if he was smart, Malachi would have other accounts that he had access to, perhaps even cash hidden in his house in case he needed to make a quick getaway.

So, while their search of his files had produced evidence that might eventually lead them to Malachi, there was nothing that would get them there quickly. And they needed something quickly. Of course, the house would be searched more thoroughly, and more evidence may turn up that would help, but for now, they may as well head back to the hospital. Their most useful resources were still Maegan and Eliza.

"I agree," his brother nodded then yawned. "We may as well head back to the hospital, check on Laura and Sofia, then we can work Maegan and Eliza and see if they can tell us something that would indicate where he'd go."

Ryan stood. "That way we can keep an eye on Paige, too." He was so concerned about his partner, it was hard not to let his fears dominate his thoughts. Not only was he scared that the stalker would get to her and kill her, but he was also worried about what would happen to Sofia if her stalker killed Paige. He didn't want to lose his partner and best friend and he didn't want to see his wife consumed with unwarranted guilt. The stalker needed to be stopped.

"I'm going to run upstairs and grab the laptop. We can go through it at the hospital with Paige. That way we can watch over her without making her feel like we're babysitting her," Jack announced.

"Okay, I'll stack up what we have here and meet you at the car."

Ryan had gathered all the paperwork from the office and was halfway to the front door when the house suddenly exploded.

The ground shook.

Bits of the ceiling came crashing down.

Fires started up in several locations.

Knocked to his knees by the force of the explosion, he clambered to his feet. "Jack!" he yelled, heading for the stairs.

His brother didn't answer.

Fighting a stab of fear, Ryan took the stairs two at a time, heading for Malachi's bedroom.

There he found his brother lying on his stomach on the floor by the window.

He wasn't moving.

In the explosion, a tree had come crashing through the window, seemingly hitting Jack and knocking him out.

His brother better not be dead. No way did Ryan want to face Laura and tell her that her husband had died.

Hurrying to his brother's side, Ryan knelt, pressing his fingers to Jack's neck. He detected a pulse, but his brother still wasn't stirring. Carefully rolling him over, he noticed a bloody head wound, but other than that, he couldn't see anything of immediate concern.

Around them, Ryan could hear the crackling of the fire as it quickly spread throughout the house.

They had to get out now.

Only, getting his brother out wasn't going to be easy.

Jack was only eighteen months older than him and they had been pretty much the same size since they were teenagers.

And right now, Jack was unconscious—a dead weight.

If it had been his partner here with him, he simply would have picked Paige up and carried her out of here, but that wasn't going to work with Jack.

He needed his brother to wake up.

Like right now would be good.

He slapped at Jack's cheek. "Jack. Wake up."

No response.

The floor beneath them felt like it was starting to weaken. There wasn't time to wait any longer. The fire was eating away at the house. Ryan was sure that help would already be on the way, but he didn't have time to wait.

Hooking an arm around Jack's shoulders, he managed to haul him up to his feet. Hoisting his brother over his shoulders in a fireman's carry, he hurried to the door and out into the hall.

Flames were dancing in both bedrooms on the other side of the hallway and Ryan noticed a huge hole in the floor.

Had that hole been there when he'd come up looking for Jack or had the house disintegrated that quickly?

He wasn't sure. When he'd come up, his sole focus had been finding his brother.

Carrying Jack, he maneuvered around the hole in the floor and somehow managed to get both of them down the stairs.

The first floor was full of smoke. Thick smoke. Making visibility extremely low.

The fire was raging down here, making Ryan think that Malachi had used some sort of accelerant.

He must have doused the house when he was here earlier collecting his things. He must have figured that now that they had the girls, they'd find the house and wanted to make sure any evidence he'd left behind was destroyed.

Ryan was figuring that Malachi had to have set a bomb on a timer. Given himself enough time to flee then wiping away any traces the house held of the girls he'd kidnapped.

He was also wondering whether Malachi had hoped to take out a few police officers along the way.

Needing to pause to catch his breath, Ryan lowered his brother to the floor, then fell to his knees beside him. Dropping onto all fours, he attempted to drag what oxygen the fire hadn't devoured into his burning lungs. The smoke along with the strain of dragging his brother through the house was wearing him out.

Heat from the fire was debilitating. Sweat poured down his back and dripped down his forehead into his eyes, making them sting.

Jack still wasn't moving, and Ryan was weakening, but leaving his brother behind was not an option. Not only would it devastate him and his entire family to lose Jack, but there was no way Ryan could ever face Laura again if he didn't get her husband out alive.

"Come on, Jack," he begged.

Again, there was no response.

Fear was niggling relentlessly at him. How serious were Jack's head injuries? Did he have other injuries? It would have been preferable to leave Jack for the paramedics to move, but that was not an option. Getting out of the burning building was their number one priority.

Eyes stinging, Ryan straightened, grabbed Jack under the arms and began to drag him toward the door.

It wasn't too far.

And there was no more time to rest.

They had to get out before the whole building collapsed.

Already as they moved, Ryan could feel the house around them weakening.

The flames were everywhere.

Eating at the building relentlessly.

Destroying everything in their path.

Dodging several patches of burning floor, Ryan got both himself and his brother to the front door.

Out in the cold night, Ryan choked as his aching lungs attempted to suck in as much fresh air as they could hold.

He paused only for a moment. It wasn't safe to remain close to the house. It was a raging inferno by this point. He had to get his brother as far away as possible.

Taking hold of Jack's shoulders once more, he pulled him down the driveway and out onto the street where he was met with the sound of sirens.

Help was coming. Although it would have been too late to save them if they'd waited inside.

Behind them, with an almighty crash, Malachi's house imploded.

Sinking down to rest against the side of his car, Ryan focused on calming his ragged breathing.

Beside him, Jack moaned.

Ryan kneeled over his brother. "Jack?"

"Ryan?" Jack sounded groggy and disoriented.

"I'm here," he assured him, his voice a hoarse croak, throat raw from all the smoke he'd inhaled.

"What happened?" Jack's eyes struggled open, and he tried to sit up.

He held his brother down. "Don't move," he instructed. "The house exploded, and you were knocked out."

"I smell smoke."

"House is on fire."

Jack nodded and sank back down against the asphalt.

Ryan relaxed a little. Despite the lump on his brother's head and the gash that would no doubt need stitches, Jack appeared lucid and coherent. He'd most likely avoided a concussion.

The house along with any secrets it held were gone.

Malachi probably thought he had won. Outsmarted them.

But he was wrong.

He and Jack hadn't been killed in the fire, and they still had their most valuable tool of all. Eliza Donnan. Ryan was positive that her drug overdose had been intentional. And not administered by either Malachi or Maegan.

Eliza was the key to finding Malachi.

Now, they just had to convince her that she was safe so she would tell them what she knew.

* * * * *

1:33 A.M.

"Paige?"

"Yeah, honey?" Paige looked down at the little girl in her lap. Hayley had refused to leave her since she'd found the children in the play therapy room.

She had carried Hayley and Arianna as they'd made their way back to the ER. Tired, overwhelmed, and as she reluctantly admitted to herself, scared, Paige had trusted Xavier to watch out for the stalker. In the emergency room, he had put them all in the office, forbidden her to leave the room unless he was with her, and put an officer on the door.

Someone had brought them a baby carrier and some formula, and Paige had fed, changed, and put Arianna to sleep all while balancing Hayley on one knee.

"Can I go and see Eliza?" Hayley asked.

"Not right now, sweetie." Xavier was still in with Eliza. Hopefully, he was making progress with her.

"Are you sure it's okay to use our real names?" Hayley continued, her big blue eyes more serious than a little girl of five should ever be.

"I'm positive."

"But it will make Malachi mad," the child protested.

Paige squeezed Hayley tightly. "You don't have to worry about Malachi ever again," she promised.

Before Hayley could respond, the door opened, and Paige instantly tensed, part of her thinking it was going to be the stalker. But it wasn't. Laura and Maegan entered the room.

"Maegan," Bethany smiled and bounded to her feet, throwing herself at the older girl.

"Laura told me you guys were here. Are you okay?" Maegan hugged Bethany.

"We're fine," Bethany assured her.

In her lap, Hayley was looking conflicted, not quite wanting to leave Paige's arms just yet but also wanting to go to Maegan. Paige made the decision for her. "Go say hi." Paige set the little girl down and watched as Maegan picked her up and Hayley wrapped her thin little arms around her neck. Tears pricked at her eyes. She was getting attached to Hayley already and that was a mistake.

"You okay?" Laura asked quietly as she sat down.

She nodded because her throat was too tight to squeeze out any words.

"No, you're not," Laura contradicted. "I'm so sorry, Paige. Jack told me how the adoption fell through."

She was way too transparent these days. She hadn't told anyone other than Ryan, yet everyone seemed to know. "Did he also tell you I'm not going through that again?"

"Yeah, he did, but you're not thinking straight right now. Give it some time; something will work out."

"No, it won't. I have to accept that, or I'll never be able to move on." Paige couldn't take her eyes off the girls. Hayley had no family who could care for her, and Paige felt a connection to the child. She wanted to entertain the notion of becoming a foster parent so Hayley could live with them. She and Elias had talked about fostering before. But she just didn't think she could cope with any more disappointment. It was better not to get her hopes up. Besides, someone wanted to kill her, that was hardly the environment for anyone to place a child into.

Laura followed her gaze. "Jack told me about Hayley," Laura said. "Her parents are dead, and she only has a grandmother who can't care for her. You and Elias could take her. She seems to really like you, and Maegan said that she's usually very clingy to Eliza."

"She wouldn't be safe with me," Paige murmured. The stalker was ruining her life. Again. She couldn't take any more of it.

"Paige, look at me." Laura's voice had lost its soothing gentleness and gone deadly serious.

Complying, she found Laura's violet eyes full of fearful concern.

"Are you thinking of making yourself bait?" Laura asked.

Surprised that Laura had figured that out, although she shouldn't be, Laura was extremely intuitive. She shrugged. "I can't live like this anymore."

"Paige, I get it, I really do. I know how I felt when someone was hurting and killing people to get to me. The fear of knowing he would come after me at some point was like a weight crushing down on me. But it's too dangerous. Something could go wrong. He could get to you. When you guys tried to use me as bait, Rose was killed."

She winced at the reminder of her friend. She was already struggling to keep control of her emotions, and thinking of Rose again was making it harder.

"I'm sorry, Paige. I know how much you miss her. Jack does, too. But it's too risky, no one wants to lose you. You just have to keep faith. We'll find him, don't do anything rash. Promise me, Paige."

She wanted to. She didn't want Laura or anyone else worrying about her, but she just couldn't go on this way. "I'm sorry, Laura. I can't promise that."

"The boys aren't going to let you do it," Laura contested desperately.

"I'm not going to tell them. And even if I did they can't stop me."

"Paige, they'll keep you safe until they find him."

Paige shook her head. "I can't live with them hovering at my side like bodyguards until we get him."

"Paige," Laura protested.

"Please don't tell Jack. He and Ryan and Xavier are likely to try to forcibly lock me away somewhere if they know that I want to try and trap him."

Before Laura could agree or disagree to keep her secret, there was a knock at the door. Again, Paige tensed, wondering whether she would ever relax again.

An officer appeared as the door opened. "I have Bethany Christian's parents out here," he announced.

Bethany froze, her face a mixture of excitement and apprehension. "They're here?" she repeated.

"It's okay, Bethie," Maegan assured her. "I'm a little scared about seeing my family again, too."

Hayley came back over and climbed into Paige's lap, resting her little head on her shoulder. "Everything okay, honey?" Paige asked her. The little girl nodded, but she sensed that wasn't true.

"I'll go with Bethany," Laura volunteered, standing and gesturing to the two older girls.

"What's wrong, Hayley?" Paige asked when they were alone.

"Bethany's going home with her mommy and daddy?"

"Yes, she is."

"And Maegan and Eliza, too?"

"That's right." Paige wondered where this was heading.

"Am I going home, too?"

"I'm sorry, baby ... but your mommy and daddy died," she told the child gently.

"What's going to happen to me?" Hayley asked solemnly.

"Well, you have a grandmother."

"Am I going to live with her?"

"I don't think so, honey. Your grandmother is old and sick, but we'll find a wonderful home for you."

The little girl tilted her head up to look at her. "Can't I live with you?"

Fighting back tears, Paige so desperately wanted to say yes to that. "I don't think so, sweetheart."

"But what if the home I go to is scary, like my last home?"

"It won't be, I promise. We will find you a fabulous home with the best mommy and daddy." Paige hoped that was true. This little girl was unlike any other child she had ever dealt with. She deserved the best. "Why don't you close your eyes and try to get some sleep; it's very late."

Obediently, the little girl rested her head on Paige's shoulder again and closed her eyes. Hayley must have been exhausted. Within a couple of minutes, her little body relaxed in sleep. Stroking the child's hair, Paige studied her. For the first time since she'd found the girls, Hayley's face had lost its worry lines. The little girl was so serious. Paige wanted to pick her up and take her home and make her feel safe and loved and teach her how to be a happy, carefree, normal five-year-old, to give her the kind of childhood Paige and her brothers and sister had had.

"Everything okay in here?" Laura asked as she and Maegan returned.

Too overwhelmed to talk, Paige just looked at her friend. Why was life so cruel sometimes? It felt like the universe was deliberately torturing her.

Apparently, Laura read that in her face. "Maegan, can you go get some blankets for Hayley?"

Sensing something was up, Maegan nodded. "Sure."

"Make sure an officer stays with you at all times," Laura added.

"I will," Maegan assured her with only a small eye roll, despite everything she had been through the girl was still a teenager.

"Aren't you supposed to be in bed?" Paige asked wearily as Laura sat beside her.

"Shh, don't tell Jack." Laura gave her a small smile.

"That depends," Paige began warily, "on whether you're going to tell him what I want to do."

She sighed. "Honestly, I don't know, Paige. I'm your friend, and I don't want you to feel like you can't talk to me with the expectation of privacy. And I don't want you to not talk to me in the future because you don't trust me. But, on the other hand, I am extremely concerned about you. And not just your physical safety. And I don't want to say nothing and then something happens to you."

"It's my choice," Paige protested.

"Did you tell Elias what you're thinking of doing?"

No, she hadn't. And she didn't intend to. Her husband would be totally in sync with the guys in attempting to forbid her to do it. "I'm a big girl; I can make my own decisions."

Laura arched a worried brow. "Normally I'd agree with you, but you're so stressed out right now, I think your judgment is skewed."

"I just need this to be over."

"Have you thought about how Sofia is going to feel if you throw yourself at the stalker and no one can get to you before he hurts you? Or kills you?"

She flinched. "That's not fair." Paige would never intentionally do anything to hurt her friend.

"I know," Laura agreed unapologetically. "But I'm not playing fair. I'm playing hardball. I'm trying to save your life."

"I promised you I wouldn't do anything stupid," Paige reminded her.

"I know you did, and I believe you. The problem is, I think we have a completely different opinion on what stupid is right now."

Paige looked down at the little girl asleep in her arms. "I was pregnant," she said quietly.

"What?" Laura sounded confused.

"Four years ago, when he tried to kill me, I was pregnant. I didn't know at the time, but I found out later. I was only five weeks along." Elias had broken the news to her while she'd still been in the hospital. It had come as a major shock. She and Elias had not been planning on getting pregnant. They hadn't even been married two years and had decided to wait at least another year before they began trying.

"Oh, Paige, I'm so sorry." Laura wrapped an arm around her shoulders. "Does anyone else know?"

She shook her head. "Only Elias, and now you. He took so much from me, Laura. I lost my baby, and I lost the ability to ever have kids of my own. I can't lose anything else. What if he did something to Elias? Then I'd have nothing. I have to stop him. Surely, you can understand that."

Laura was wavering. Paige could see it in her eyes. She needed to convince her to keep quiet. If she couldn't and Laura told Jack, then there was a very real chance that she would find herself put into protective custody against her will.

On the desk beside them, her phone began to buzz. Unable to reach it with Hayley asleep in her arms, Paige asked, "Can you pass me that?"

"Sure. It's Ryan," Laura informed her as she picked up the phone and handed it over.

"Hey, Ryan," she answered. In the background she could hear sirens and shouting. Instantly, she was concerned. "What happened?"

"Malachi rigged the house to explode," her partner answered. His voice was hoarse, and he sounded a little breathless.

"With you inside?" Her tone must have conveyed something was wrong because Laura tensed beside her.

"Yep."

"Are you okay?"

"What happened?" Laura demanded. "Is Jack okay? Is Ryan okay?"

Paige waved her quiet as she awaited Ryan's response.

"I'm fine, extremely mild smoke inhalation, but Jack was injured."

"Is he all right?"

"Paramedics are checking him out. He was knocked out, but he seems okay. Firefighters are putting out the fire, but the house is gone. We won't be getting anything from it. As soon as the medics are done with him, we're heading back to the hospital."

"Ryan, Laura's with me. She knows something's up. I'm going to have to tell her."

"Tell me what?" Laura was sounding completely panicked

207

now.

"Jack's going to be mad that she's not in bed. Just make sure she knows that he's okay. Really, Paige, he's fine and I'm fine. I have to go, but we'll be there soon. Xavier told us about the stalker following you earlier, so please be careful. Don't go anywhere on your own."

As Paige hung up her phone and prepared to tell Laura what had happened, Hayley sighed in her sleep and shifted closer, and Paige wondered whether making herself bait for the stalker was a good idea after all.

* * * * *

1:44 A.M.

"Laura, try to calm down." Xavier took her arm and tried to push her into a chair.

"Calm down?" she all but screeched at him. "I can't calm down."

She had been in a complete panic since Paige had told her about the explosion at Malachi's house.

Jack had been injured.

Just like in her dream earlier.

Only in her dream, he'd been dead.

What if he was more seriously injured than Paige had told her?

Paige had said that Ryan had told her that Jack was okay, but was he really?

Had Ryan been lying?

Wanting to protect her?

Apparently, Jack had been knocked unconscious, so how okay could he really be?

"Laura, now, sit!" Xavier barked, his tone stern.

She allowed him to guide her into a chair.

Maybe she did need to sit.

She wasn't feeling so great.

Fear over Jack was even overriding her agoraphobia.

Every single part of her felt wobbly.

Including her mind.

She couldn't lose Jack.

She couldn't survive it. It was as simple as that.

Fear was clogging her body.

Almost literally.

White dots began to dance in front of her eyes, and she realized that she was gasping for breath.

"Laura?" Xavier's voice had jumped from stern to concerned. "You need to calm down. Now. You're hyperventilating."

She struggled to calm herself but thought it was probably a losing battle.

"Laura, listen to me." Xavier was kneeling beside her chair. "I spoke to Jack on the phone. He really *is* okay. He doesn't even have a concussion. Just a bump on the head and three stitches. That's it. He's fine. Now if you don't calm down, I'm going to get someone to sedate you."

She fought to get control of herself. She didn't want to be sedated. She needed to see Jack for herself before she could believe that he was okay.

"Okay, that's better," Xavier nodded approvingly as she managed to marginally calm her ragged breathing. Then his gaze shifted to something behind her and he bounded to his feet. "What are you doing out here? It's not safe for you."

"I wanted to see Ryan and Jack when they get here," Paige replied.

Going to her and shielding her body from the majority of the room, Xavier escorted Paige to the seats where Laura was. "Like they couldn't have come and seen you in the office," he scoffed, pushing Paige into a chair and then positioning himself so he both blocked her from any potential threats and could monitor everything happening around them.

"I didn't want to scare the girls," Paige explained. "Plus, I promised I wouldn't go anywhere alone, and I'm not. I'm sitting here right beside you, bodyguard."

Xavier glowered at her. "You're going to make guarding you a nightmare, aren't you?"

Shrugging fitfully, Paige didn't respond, and Laura made up her mind immediately to tell Jack what Paige was planning. She understood where Paige was coming from, she had suffered an enormous loss and almost died, but she was going to get herself hurt or killed if she tried to make herself bait. Laura didn't want to jeopardize their friendship or Paige's trust in her, but keeping her alive was more important. If need be, she could work on rebuilding trust later.

"There they are," Xavier announced, gesturing to the door.

Both she and Paige stood and hurried toward them. Xavier muttered something and caught up to Paige, remaining at her side as she threw her arms around Ryan.

Laura froze a few feet from Jack. Her eyes traveled his body, trying to convince herself that he was alive. That he was here and in one piece. Other than smelling of smoke and a darkening bruise around a white square bandage on his forehead, he looked fine.

And yet, she still couldn't believe it.

"Laura, I'm okay." Jack closed the distance between them and pulled her into his arms, crushing her against his chest.

She breathed in deeply, trying to inhale his scent as though that might convince her stressed out mind that her husband was really all right. She shuddered violently in Jack's arms, wrapping her own arms around his waist and clinging to him desperately.

"Shh, angel, I'm right here." Jack's hand cradled her head, his warm fingers threading through her hair and gently kneading the back of her head. "Are you okay?"

For a long time, she just rested against him, letting him hold her up, and letting her fears slowly trickle out of her head. Jack was okay—warm and strong and solid. Aside from a scratchy voice, he sounded normal, like his usual strong, confident self. "I'm okay," she whispered at last.

At her acknowledgement, she felt Jack relax. Kissing the top of her head, he told her, "You're supposed to be in bed."

"And you," Ryan was saying to Paige, "are supposed to be in the office with a cop on the door so the stalker can't get to you."

"I'm not a prisoner, Ryan, and I stayed right here with Xavier, just like I promised," she retorted. Then she shivered and hugged Ryan again. "I'm really glad you're okay."

"Right back at ya," Ryan hugged her back. "I freaked out when Xavier said the stalker had been following you."

"I'm really glad you're okay, too." Laura tugged herself out of Jack's arms to hug her brother-in-law. She didn't want to lose anyone she loved and tonight had been a bad night for all of them.

Paige turned to Jack and hugged him, too. "I'm glad you weren't hurt worse. Are you sure you're okay?"

"I'm fine, Paige, really. No concussion. All I have is a mild headache," he assured her.

"Did you at least find anything helpful at the house before it blew up?" Paige asked.

"Before we discuss that, can we please go somewhere that isn't a security nightmare?" Xavier was still looking at Paige in frustration and constantly surveying their surroundings. "Out here, there are too many people, too many doors, too many windows."

"He's not going to come back tonight," Paige protested.

"Do you want to be safe or do you want to be sorry?" Ryan asked her.

She groaned but didn't protest as Ryan and Xavier flanked her as they walked back to the office. Laura took Jack's hand and hoped that he wasn't going to try to order her to go back to bed. Not that she had to accept his orders, of course, and usually she didn't, but she didn't want to stress him out when he'd been injured. And he would stress if he was worried about her. But she didn't want to sleep. She was probably too wired to anyway, but if exhaustion did take hold and she slept, she would almost definitely have nightmares. Which would almost certainly feature her husband's near death experience.

Jack must have been preoccupied because he squeezed her hand but didn't say anything as they followed the others to the office. Inside, Xavier remained at the door while the rest of them sat.

"The house was a bust," Ryan informed them. "We got Malachi's name, and thankfully we sent off some bank account information before we lost it all in the fire."

Laura shuddered again at the mention of the fire.

She had come so close to losing Jack.

And to lose Jack would have been to lose her life.

Jack had been knocked unconscious in the explosion. If Ryan had been, too, then both of them would have perished.

Somehow, Jack sensed her increasing anxiety levels and reached for her hand, pulling her onto her feet and then down into his lap. She pressed against him, hoping his strength could seep into her. He was the one who'd been injured, she should be comforting him instead, once again, Jack was the one to comfort her.

"I don't think the house was ever going to give us the answers we need. Eliza is. I don't think Malachi or Maegan was the one to drug her. And I don't think it was a suicide attempt or an accident. I think she deliberately overdosed herself so that Malachi would bring them all here," Ryan was saying.

"I started making progress with her, but then when I told her Malachi had run, she shut down again," Xavier explained.

"She knows Malachi brainwashed her. He had to have told her things about the real Ariyel to make her believe that she *was* Ariyel. If we can get her to open up, we'll know where Malachi went," Ryan said.

"You stay with Paige, and I'll try talking to her again," Xavier said.

"Actually, I think we should send in Maegan and Laura." Ryan cast her a careful glance, attempting to gauge whether she was up to it.

"No," Jack said immediately.

"You really think it'll help?" Laura asked.

"Yes," Ryan nodded emphatically. "You need to push her hard though, and since you're a psychiatrist, and she's extremely emotionally vulnerable right now, I think you'll do better than the rest of us. Maegan should help to ground her, make her feel safe, and act as additional motivation to talk, and you'll know what's best to say and how and when to say it."

"I'll do it." Laura wanted to end this for Maegan and Eliza and the other girls. She didn't want them living with the threat of Malachi still being free. Then she wanted to go home with her husband and her son, curl up in bed, and sleep for about a week.

"No, you won't," Jack protested. She could feel the tension rippling through him. "You can take yourself right back to Sofia's room and hop back into bed. And you can take Paige with you, so she stays out of trouble." Her husband shot a glare Paige's way. "Xavier can continue to work on Eliza; he's already built trust with her."

"I agree. Eliza trusts Xavier, so we want him as a backup in case Laura pushes her hard enough that she cracks. He can then come in and see what else he can get out of her. I don't want to sound harsh. I feel sorry for her, and we'll make sure that she gets the very best counseling, but right now we need to get Malachi off the streets, and she's our best chance of achieving that," Ryan reminded them.

* * * * *

1:55 A.M.

"Is Eliza okay?" Maegan asked Laura as they stood outside Eliza's hospital room.

"She's very fragile right now," Laura replied.

"Then why are we doing this?" Maegan didn't want to put Eliza through anything more than she had already endured.

"Because Malachi needs to be stopped," Laura answered.

"But that's your job. Well not *you* specifically," she corrected herself, "but your husband and his friends. They should be the ones out looking for Malachi."

"They were, and Malachi blew up the house with my husband and my brother-in-law inside. He could have killed them." Laura drew in a shaky breath and looked like she was struggling to calm herself.

"I'm sorry."

"It's not your fault."

Maegan disagreed. She had messed up; she knew she had. "I should have told you everything from the beginning. Then Jack could have arrested Malachi and he'd be in jail. Your husband wouldn't have nearly been killed, no one else would be in danger from him, and Eliza wouldn't have to go through this."

"What's done is done, honey." Laura took her hand and squeezed supportively. "Malachi messed with your head, too. He abducted you and kept you locked away from the rest of the world. You were scared, but you still came forward; don't beat yourself up."

Well, Maegan was beating herself up, and she didn't know how to stop. "Let's just get this over with," she muttered, putting her hand on the door handle.

Laura stopped her. "Maegan, she's already stressed out. She needs you to be calm."

She held her breath and counted to ten, then Maegan slowly let it out again. "Okay, I'm ready."

"He's been feeding you sleeping pills since he brainwashed you, to keep you under control. But he stopped while you were pregnant. You started to remember things. When the baby was born, he wanted you to start taking them again, but you didn't. You kept them. You wanted to get yourself and the others out of that house, so you took the pills. You knew Malachi would bring you here, because you're his daughter's mother. He couldn't risk anything happening to you."

"He's obsessed with having children," Eliza whispered. "He was so pleased when Arianna was a girl, but I wanted her to be a boy. So he couldn't do anything to her."

"How long after he took you did he starting abusing you?" Laura asked gently.

"Immediately," Eliza sniffed. "But he didn't start with Maegan until her thirteenth birthday. I knew he'd do the same to Bethie, Hayley, and Arianna. I couldn't protect Maegan, so I had to protect the others."

Finally, Maegan crossed to the bed. "It wasn't your fault, Eliza. What Malachi did to me, there wasn't anything you could have done to stop it."

"I failed you," Eliza cried.

"No. No," she repeated. "You did everything you could to save us. To protect us from Malachi. I know he did terrible things to you every time you tried to get us help." Maegan was crying now, too, and threw herself into Eliza's arms.

Laura gave them a moment before she continued. "Eliza, we need you. You know Malachi better than anyone else. Do you know where he would go?"

"The house," Eliza replied immediately.

"We found the house. Malachi blew it up," Laura told her.

That surprised her. "He loved that house, he was obsessed with it. He must be desperate."

"Can you think of any other place he may go?" Laura pushed.

She closed her eyes in concentration. Tears continued to trickle out. After a couple of minutes of silence, Eliza opened her eyes, looking at them apologetically. "I'm sorry, my head is all fuzzy. I can't think properly. I remember Malachi talking to me, but I can't make out the words."

Perfectly hiding the disappointment Maegan knew she must be feeling, Laura smiled reassuringly. "That's okay, Eliza. It will come to you. You just have to keep trying. I know those memories can be scary, but you can't run from them. We need you. Maegan needs you. Bethany, Hayley, and Arianna need you."

Maegan wanted to tell Laura off for pressuring Eliza, even though she'd known that was the whole point of talking to her. But before she could, there was a knock at the door.

A moment later, it swung open and Jack stuck his head in. "Maegan, your family is here."

TWENTY-NINE YEARS AGO

9:22 A.M.

Was he awake?

Malachi wasn't altogether sure.

The last thing he remembered was his birthday.

He and his father had gone for ice cream. Only his father had stopped at an alley on the way to run an errand. The errand turned out to be a secret meeting with his mistress. His father had wanted to end things with her, but she hadn't wanted to. She'd jumped in the car with them. Continued to beg his father not to break up with her.

Then she had grabbed the steering wheel, causing the car to crash into a brick wall.

Had he been killed?

Had he just woken up in heaven?

Or hell?

He really didn't know.

Perhaps it was because his head was aching so badly it felt like it was on fire.

Maybe he really was in hell.

It couldn't be heaven, because there was no pain in heaven, right?

Counting heaven out, he was either dead and in hell or alive and badly hurt.

Was he still in the car?

Had the accident just happened?

No, it couldn't have because he was someplace quiet. Not on a busy street.

And he was someplace soft and comfortable. Not still in a car.

Someone was holding his hand.

Malachi tried to open his eyes but found he could only crack them open a slit.

He wasn't dead.

He wasn't in hell.

He was in a hospital room.

Now that his eyes were opened, he realized his head wasn't the only thing that hurt.

His entire body ached with an agony he had never experienced before.

Beside his bed sat his mother.

She was clutching his hand.

She didn't notice he was awake.

As he looked at her, he realized something was different.

Not her, him.

Something was different with him.

He had changed somehow.

He could feel it in his bones.

* * * * *

7:58 P.M.

The next time he awoke, Malachi found he wasn't in pain.

Only he wasn't sure if that was a good thing or a bad thing.

This time he didn't hesitate to open his eyes.

He was still in a hospital.

And his mother still sat at his side.

Almost immediately, she noticed he was awake.

A smile lit her pretty face as she jumped to her feet and began to smother him in kisses.

"Malachi, you're alive, you're awake. They said you wouldn't survive. They said you'd never wake up."

"How long?" he tried to ask, but all that came out was a croaky squawk.

"Here, baby." His mother held a straw to his lips, and he drank greedily, albeit clumsily.

"How long?" he asked again. His voice was weak, faint, insubstantial.

"Seven months." Tears were streaming down his mother's beautiful face. How could his father even think of cheating on such a woman? "You've been in a coma for seven months."

Seven months?

How could so much time have passed while he'd been just lying here sleeping?

"I thought you'd never wake up," his mother sobbed. "They said you wouldn't. I kept praying you'd come back to me, but the days and weeks and months kept ticking by. I love you so much, my sweet little boy. I couldn't handle losing you, too."

Losing him, too?

That must mean his father ...

"Your daddy didn't survive, baby." His mother held his face in her hands. "The car was going too fast; he was killed instantly."

Something was wrong with him.

He didn't feel anything.

No anger, no hurt, no disappointment, no grief over his father's death. No thankfulness at being alive, no joy, no excitement, no trepidation or apprehension at the long recovery process to come. No fear at whether or not he would be the same as he'd been before.

He already knew he wouldn't.

He was different.

Changed.

He had lost the ability to feel emotion.

It was gone.

Simply gone.

"Oh, baby, are you okay? Are you really okay?" Not waiting for an answer, she began to kiss him all over his face again. "I love you, baby. I love you so much. I love you. I love you. I love you."

He loved her, too.

His mother.

His responsibility now.

He was thirteen.

A man.

The man of the house now that his father was dead.

It was Malachi's job to take his father's place.

And he would do a better job of running the family than his father had.

His father was a cheater. He had jeopardized the family by his affair. He was weak and pathetic. A useless excuse for a man.

A man should be strong. A leader. A man should demand respect from those around him. He should be confident and self-assured. A man should always be in control.

A man should take care of his family. Provide for them. Protect them.

A man should be everything that his father wasn't.

Malachi would learn from his father's mistakes. He wouldn't repeat them.

He had learned a lot about women, too.

A woman should be subservient.

She should obey.

She should respect a man as having authority over her.

Not like that woman. Threatening his father. Trying to tell him what to do. Trying to break up his family.

That woman had tried to kill him.

He would never let anyone be in a position to do that to him again.

He would lead his family. Guide them. Rule them.

He would not let his sisters turn out like that willful woman.

Ariyel was sixteen, Alice was ten, Angela was four, and Abigail just a baby.

FIVE

They were his responsibility, too.

And he took his responsibilities very seriously.

NOVEMBER 4TH
2:00 A.M.

2:08 A.M.

Home.

Maegan couldn't believe that she was really about to see her family again after five long years.

Her stomach was an absolute swirling mess of nerves.

Her parents were waiting for her in an unoccupied hospital room. All she had to do was open the door and walk inside. Yet something was stopping her.

"You okay?" Laura asked quietly.

She nodded. She was okay. Wasn't she? Why didn't she just go into the room and throw herself into her parents' arms? What was stopping her?

"It's okay to be nervous. Five years is a long time," Laura said gently.

"Things won't be the same." Maegan knew she could never, no matter how much she wanted and no matter how much her parents wanted, go back to the way they'd been before.

"No, they won't," Laura agreed.

"Was it hard with your family after your abduction?" she asked. She knew that Laura didn't like to talk about it, but she needed answers from someone who'd been through something similar to what she had.

"Yes, it was," Laura answered honestly. "I was struggling to make sense of what had happened to me, to process it, to deal with my own feelings and emotions. I couldn't deal with theirs, as well. I ran. I hid from them—from everyone—for ten years. If

Jack hadn't stumbled upon me, I'd still be hiding. Now I wish I hadn't hid. I wish I hadn't lost ten years of my life—I can't ever get them back."

"Are things okay with your family now?"

"Not really. They're better, and I see them, but I feel guilty for shutting them out when they were suffering, too. I feel like I was selfish. I should have let them help me. They needed to be there for me for their own healing, and I denied them that. My guilt makes me not like to be around them. I'm much closer with Jack's family than my own. I have a lot of regrets, Maegan. I don't want you to have them, too. I wish I could give you a magic answer that will make your transition back into the normal world smooth, but I can't. There isn't one. You just have to do what feels right for you at the time."

It both reassured her and stressed her more to know how difficult things had been for Laura. What they'd been through was different. Laura's abduction had been only a few days but extremely intense and left her fighting for her life. Hers had been much longer but not as intense. But both had been terrifying and life changing.

"Laura, do you think it would be okay if—"

"Of course," Laura cut her off, "you can talk to me any time you want."

"Thanks." It made her feel a little better to have a safe place to go when she needed someone to talk to.

There was no putting it off any longer. That wasn't going to make things easier. With a steadying breath, she pushed open the door and stepped inside.

Her mom and dad were holding hands. They both turned toward the door when they heard it open. For a long moment the three of them just stared at each other. Her parents looked so much older than she remembered. But, at the same time, they still looked the same.

Maegan had been unsure right up until she saw them about

how she'd feel. Now that they were standing right in front of her, watching her closely, presumably unsure about how she would react to them, she felt a wave of relief wash over her.

Everything was going to be okay.

Rushing at her parents, she threw herself into her mother's arms.

Five years' worth of tears came out in a flood. Clinging to her mother like she used to when she was a very little girl, Maegan wept for what felt like forever.

Her mother cried, too, holding her tightly, stroking her hair, and murmuring soothingly in her ear.

Her father held them both. He was crying, as well.

She had missed them so much.

She loved them so much.

Loved them so much her heart was aching with it.

"Mommy," she whimpered, her face in her mother's neck.

"I'm here, baby," her mother whispered back. "I'm here and no one is going to take you from me ever again."

Maegan wished her mother could really guarantee her that. But she knew no one could. Not only was Malachi still on the loose, and as such a threat to her and her sisters, but there were more monsters out there than people realized. And any one of them could hurt her.

"Are you okay, princess?" her father asked, picking her up as though she were a child. His eyes scanned her frantically as though he was worried she might be injured.

Malachi had never hurt her in a way that had left physical scars, so she didn't know how to answer her father's question. She wasn't comfortable talking about being raped with anyone, let alone her parents. And even though she didn't have any noticeable wounds, she wasn't okay. She would never be the same person she'd been before. She would never grow into the same woman she would have had she not been kidnapped. She felt so many things that she didn't think she could untangle them all and explain them to anyone.

Knowing her father needed an answer, she mustered up a smile for him. "I'm all right, Daddy."

And she would be.

Jack and Xavier would find Malachi. They would arrest him, and he would go to jail where he couldn't hurt her or anyone else ever again. She would go home where her parents and the rest of her family would help her to heal.

Maybe one day, she would get better.

Maybe one day, she would move past what had happened and have a normal life.

Right now, though, she had to take it one day at a time, and when that was too hard, one minute at a time.

* * * * *

2:12 A.M.

"Hey, I thought you were sleeping." Xavier smiled at Eliza as she opened her eyes.

She shook her head. "I'm tired, but I can't sleep. Not knowing he's out there somewhere."

Xavier wished there was something he could say to take away Eliza's fears, but he knew there wasn't.

He wished there was something he could say to work things out with Annabelle, too.

He should have gone after her when she was here earlier. He knew she wanted him to, but how many times could he go running after her before she finally realized that he was always going to be there for her?

Xavier didn't want her to keep testing him. It made him feel inadequate, and he had done everything within his power to help Annabelle.

It was just never enough.

Would it ever be enough?

He was beginning to think it wouldn't be.

He had meant every word he'd said to Annabelle. He loved her very much, but he wasn't the one pushing her away. And if she wasn't one hundred percent into their relationship, then he would reluctantly move on.

Xavier wanted it all: wife, kids, a family. And if Annabelle didn't want those things, then he would find someone who did. It had been a complete surprise when she'd turned down his first proposal. A horrible surprise. He had gone all out. They'd been on vacation at the beach; they'd ridden horses through the shallow waves, then had a romantic picnic on the soft white sand, then he'd gotten down on one knee and asked her to marry him. It had never occurred to him that she's say no. She had assured him that she loved him and that she did want to marry him, but that she needed more time.

Like an idiot, he had given it to her.

When he had proposed again, he'd been positive that this time Annabelle was going to say yes.

He'd been wrong again.

This time, not only had she said no and that she wasn't ready, but she'd also broken the news that she was going to be moving out for a while.

There wasn't going to be a third time. He wasn't so stupid that he couldn't take a hint. Annabelle didn't want to marry him. And since she had moved out, he was taking it as a sign that it was over between them.

Xavier didn't want to move on. He wanted things to work out with Annabelle. He wanted them to have their happily ever after. Badly. But he also knew that, sometimes in life, you don't always get what you want.

He focused his attention back on the terrified woman in the bed. Annabelle may not want him anymore, but Eliza needed him. And sometimes it was nice to be needed.

"We are going to find him, Eliza," he promised.

She looked back at him doubtfully.

"You know, the more you can tell us about Malachi, the quicker we can find him," he reminded her.

"I don't remember anything else," she whimpered forlornly. "I keep trying to, but I can't."

"It's okay." He took her hands and held them. "Your memories will come back, but you have to be patient."

"I don't want to be patient. I want him caught. I can't live like this. Knowing he's out there." Fresh tears were brewing in her haunted eyes.

"The more you force the memories to try and come, the more you're stressing yourself and making it harder for you to remember."

"But I came here to get help," Eliza protested.

Laura had told him that Ryan had been correct and that Eliza had deliberately overdosed herself to force Malachi's hand and get him to bring them here so she had a chance to get them help.

"If I did this on purpose, then why can't I remember?" Eliza continued, becoming increasingly distressed. "I don't understand. I did it on purpose. I must have remembered what Malachi did. But then when I woke up here, I couldn't remember anything. When you were telling me that my name was Eliza and that I had been kidnapped, I didn't believe you."

"But now you do, honey." He tried to make his voice soothing. They needed information from Eliza, but the more she worked herself up, the harder it would be to get that information.

"But I want to remember everything." Her eyes pleaded with him as though he could make those memories return.

Maybe if he got her talking about Malachi and what he'd done to her, it would help to spark her memory. Gently, he released her hand and grasped her wrist. His other hand traced a scar on her left forearm. "How did you get the burn? Did Malachi do it to you?"

Beneath his hands, she trembled violently. "Yes."

"Why?"

"Because I set fire to the house to try and escape. He had the house rigged with sprinklers. They put the fire out as soon as it started. He took a candle and held my arm over it until it burned me."

His hatred of Malachi grew. Fighting down his rage, he kept his voice soft. "Is this the only place he burned you?"

"No." The word was barely a whisper.

Forcing himself to keep going, Xavier wanted to stop pushing her, let her overburdened mind recover first. If it wasn't so imperative they find Malachi ASAP, then he would stop. "Where else did he hurt you?"

"One of my breasts. He cut it all over, dozens of slices. He said now even if I managed to escape, no man would ever want me." Tears were streaming down her cheeks.

"Is that the only time he hurt you?" Xavier knew it wasn't, but he wanted to keep her talking. It seemed she remembered things when he prompted her with direct questions. Only he didn't know what questions to prompt her with to find out more about Malachi. Perhaps once Paige and Ryan had run a background check on him, it would provide him with information like details about Malachi's childhood, family, wife, kids, job, which would in turn help trigger Eliza's memory.

"No. When I tried to dig a hole under the fence, he dug his own hole in the backyard, put me in it, and then buried me alive." Her eyes went vacant and her voice dull. "Dirt was in my eyes and up my nose and in my mouth before he dug me back out. I was so scared. I didn't want to die, but I couldn't stop trying to get away even though I knew he was going to punish me."

He resisted the urge to coddle her. "What else did he do to you, Eliza?"

"When I cut the electricity, he took a knife and cut my arm open. He let it bleed a lot before he stitched it up."

Xavier released her left arm and picked up her right. "This scar?"

"Yes. One time I jumped out a third-story window. I was badly hurt, but he wouldn't take me to the hospital. He didn't punish me that time. He said my injuries were punishment enough. I kept trying to get away, but it didn't work. Nothing ever worked."

Xavier wondered how she had known that this time he would bring her to the hospital.

"After I flooded the house, he put me in that room in the basement," she continued.

By now, Eliza was looking so devoid of emotion that Xavier was beginning to seriously worry about her. It was time to stop pushing her. He didn't want to cause her permanent damage. He needed Laura here. She would know how hard to safely push.

"Okay, Eliza, you should try to get some rest." He pressed on her shoulders to lay her back against the mattress, then he reached for the bed's controls and pressed the buttons to lower it so it was flat.

"I can't rest," she murmured even as her eyes fluttered closed.

"Yes, you can. I'm going to go and get Dr. Roma and see if she can give you something to help you sleep."

She caught his hand as he stood. "No. No more drugs. Malachi's been drugging me for two years."

"I know he has, honey, but right now you need rest, and I don't think you're going to get any on your own."

"Will you stay with me while I sleep?"

"Of course, I will," he assured her.

"Will you hold my hand?"

Annabelle had held his hand while she slept that first night she'd spent in his house. And she had looked at him the same way Eliza was looking at him now. Like he was the only thing that could keep her safe and sane. It felt odd to be here with Eliza like this, being the strength she needed, comforting her, supporting her. It felt almost like he was betraying Annabelle.

But she was the one who had walked out on him. And while he knew nothing romantic would ever happen between him and Eliza, he had to start getting used to the idea of Annabelle not being a part of his life anymore.

"Of course, I will."

* * * * *

2:19 A.M.

A spear of jealousy shot through her as she stood at the door listening in on the conversation going on inside the room.

For the first time, Annabelle realized that she really might have lost Xavier.

How stupid could she be?

Why on earth would she want to push him away?

He was perfect.

In every way.

And she loved him so much.

That he hadn't followed her earlier still hurt. That he'd told her he wouldn't wait for her forever hurt, too. As did the fact that he thought she wasn't committed to their relationship.

All of those things were her fault.

Why would he think that she was invested in their relationship when she'd said no both times he proposed to her? She hadn't wanted to. The desire to say yes had been overwhelming. But, she had said no. Twice.

Why was she so self-destructive?

Why couldn't she accept her good luck in finding a wonderful, caring, thoughtful, sweet guy who loved her so much?

Why did she want to deprive herself of happiness?

There was something wrong with her. There had to be. Annabelle could think of no other reason why she would keep doing things she didn't want to do, and that didn't make her happy except that there was something wrong with her.

Now she had to decide what to do about it.

She could give in and make it a self-fulfilling prophecy that she remain alone, unhappy, and unloved for the rest of her life. But that seemed stupid. She had truly believed for most of her life that she was destined to never be loved by anyone. And then Xavier had come along and changed all of that.

He had given her everything she had ever dreamed of.

And she was throwing it back in his face like it wasn't good enough for her. Like *he* wasn't good enough for her.

Well, he was good enough for her.

Maybe her problem was that she didn't believe she was good enough for him.

She wasn't. She knew that. Xavier deserved so much better than a messed-up woman like her.

He had never walked away from her, though.

When her fears overwhelmed her, he was always right there by her side. Holding her, soothing her, calming her, making her feel like she *did* have enough strength to keep going.

Without him, she probably would have just withered away and ended up taking her own life.

She had thought about suicide so many times in the last five years. Even gone so far as to actually begin planning things out. But she'd never followed through. Because of Xavier.

Annabelle didn't want to lose him.

Strike that. She *wasn't* going to lose him.

She was going to do whatever it took to get him back, to convince him that she wanted to be with him, so they could spend the rest of their lives together.

First thing's first. She had to get herself some help. Until she learned why she kept sabotaging herself and then started to work on stopping it, she was never going to be able to give Xavier what he needed.

They had done therapy together, and it seemed to have helped

Xavier, but Annabelle had felt like she was just going through the motions, turning up to each session to please Xavier.

Now, though, she wanted to get better.

She wanted to find out what was wrong with her and do something about it.

She wanted to find her own strength.

She wanted to learn to stand on her own two feet.

She wanted to learn not to fear happiness.

She wanted everything she had ever dreamed about.

She wanted exactly what Xavier wanted.

She wanted to marry the man she loved, have children with him, and grow old together.

Annabelle didn't want to go back to the therapist she and Xavier had gone to. She didn't really like the woman. She could always talk to Laura, but if she wanted to work on better connecting with her and Xavier's friends, maybe it would be better to keep the relationship strictly friendship rather than mixing in therapy. Maybe she could ask Laura for the name of her counselor. Laura was a good judge of character, so whatever therapist she had been seeing was sure to be one of the best.

"Oh, Annabelle." The door to the hospital room suddenly opened and Xavier stood there. Obviously, he was surprised to see her. "I thought you went home."

She shook her head. "No, I wanted to wait, talk to you again."

"I'm going to be a while."

"I don't mind waiting," she told him, and she really didn't. Now that she had decided to get help and get better, she felt so much lighter, like the weight that had been crushing her for years was suddenly lifted.

He narrowed his eyes at her, seemingly unsure about her calm tone. "Once I'm done here, I'll be taking Paige home."

"I don't need to talk to you for long," she assured him.

His gaze shifted from her to the door behind him. "I have a quick minute now. What's up?"

"I just wanted to apologize," Annabelle told him. "I'm sorry that I've been pushing you away."

"Yeah, I'm sorry about that, too, because I have never given you a reason to do it." Xavier's face didn't soften at her apology as she had hoped it would.

She forged on, despite the fact that her insides were quivering. She so hated for anyone to be angry with her, and she so hated to have any sort of confrontation. But this wasn't a confrontation. The first step in her getting better was for her to learn to stop obsessing over what other people said and did and thought about her. She couldn't control that. All she could control was herself.

"I love you, Xavier. And I'm sorry that I've given you reason to doubt that. I'm sorry I turned down your proposals. I'm sorry that I've kept myself closed off from you. I'm sorry that I messed things up between us. And I'm sorry that I moved out of our home. But I'm going to change all of that. I'm going to go back to therapy and I'm going to get better and I'm going to work hard to fix things between us."

Xavier said nothing. Just stood there and looked at her.

"You don't believe me." She felt crushed as she looked at his stony face.

He shrugged unapologetically. "I've had my blinders on with you because I love you, but you keep doing things that surprise me. I've asked you time and time again to talk to me; I've asked you time and time again not to move out; I've asked you time and time again to let me help you. You keep turning me down. I guess actions speak louder than words. You're not the only one who doesn't want to get hurt again. I lost a lot with Julia, and I've lost a lot with you. I guess I'm hesitant to trust you again."

"I want to change," she protested, hurt that Xavier wasn't being more supportive. But she had to accept that. She'd hurt him. She'd been selfish, thinking only about how she felt, about what she needed. But now she knew what she had to do. She knew that she needed to learn to help herself and not just keep letting other people do it for her. That wasn't a long term solution. It was just like slapping a Band-Aid on, the cut was still there, it didn't make it disappear, it just hid the problem. She had finally realized that she was the only who could heal herself.

"I hope that's true. But are you only wanting to change for me? What if it's already too late for us? What if things between us are over, are too broken to fix? Do you still want to change for you? Because that's the only way that it's going to work. You have to want it for you, Annabelle, not for me."

"Is it too late for us, Xavier?" she asked in a whisper.

"I honestly don't know," he replied.

At least his eyes had finally gone from deliberately empty to sad. Annabelle took that as a good sign. "I know you've given up on me. I know you only gave up on me because of me and my behavior. But I'll prove to you that I'm going to change. I haven't given up on us. Or on myself."

He remained unconvinced. "I have to go back to Eliza."

As she turned and walked away, Annabelle couldn't help but hope once more that Xavier would come after her. Declaring his love and his faith in her.

He didn't.

She managed to hold her tears in until she climbed into her car. Then she let them flow. Fighting, once again, a surge of jealousy toward Eliza. The young woman was lucky to have Xavier's care and support. She remembered what that was like. He had given it to her and she had thrown it back in his face.

Maybe he was right.

Maybe things between them really were too broken to fix.

Maybe it really was too late.

* * * * *

2:27 A.M.

Malachi hoped it wasn't a mistake to come back here.

It was risky.

Extremely risky.

The cops were swarming all over the place. It had been difficult enough just getting in the building, let alone getting back out again.

It probably hadn't been the best of ideas to shoot at that cop earlier, but he hadn't had a choice. He had needed to get away from the hospital before they tried to arrest him. But now it was coming back to bite him.

It was only by the skin of his teeth he'd managed to get away the first time. He hadn't realized there were two cops chasing him. He'd thought he could shoot the cop and then run in the ensuing commotion. But then, that lady cop had pulled a gun on him. If it hadn't been for that car that tried to run her down, he wouldn't have made it away.

But made it away he had, and that was what was important.

Although, he'd had to sacrifice his house.

As soon as he'd left the hospital, he'd fled back there, managing to grab a few of the most important papers and photos and then he'd had to rig it to explode. He couldn't risk them finding anything there to use against him.

As he'd been driving off, he'd seen the cops pull up outside the house. He didn't know how they'd found him, but he guessed it must have been through the car that he had left behind at the hospital. Maybe they had used the GPS to track down the house.

Malachi wondered absently whether the cops had been killed in the explosion.

He didn't really care one way or the other.

He didn't enjoy killing, although he'd certainly done it before.

He didn't not enjoy it either.

He hadn't enjoyed or not enjoyed anything in twenty-nine years.

The accident that had killed his father and left him in a seven-month-long coma had taken his ability to feel anything either good or bad.

The serious head injuries he had suffered could have made him lose the ability to talk or walk or remember things. Instead, they had made him lose the ability to feel.

Since the day of his thirteenth birthday, he hadn't felt sad or happy or scared or apprehensive or guilty or anything at all. He was like a robot. In all those years, he hadn't judged his actions as right or wrong. He simply did what he wanted. Killing when necessary, hurting when necessary, taking what he wanted when he wanted it.

And what he wanted now was his girls.

The police had no right to take them from him.

They were his, and he intended to get them back.

The problem was, he didn't know if the police already had all the girls. If they didn't, he could search the hospital, find the little ones, and disappear with them again. If, on the other hand, the police had them, then getting to them would be nearly impossible.

He was going to have to decide how hard he wanted to work for this.

Even if the girls had been found and returned to their families, it didn't mean he couldn't grab them again. He was smart. The head injuries hadn't robbed him of his intelligence; he could figure out a plan to go after them.

But did he want to?

It would be risky, especially if he went for them soon. The police might have them guarded, believing he would come back for them. If he waited a while, the risk would go down. The police would become complacent, suspect he had fled the state, or perhaps even the country. They would no longer view him as a threat, thus leaving the girls vulnerable and providing him the perfect time to strike.

But did he want to wait that long?

After all, it wasn't like he couldn't find more girls who fit his profile. Perhaps, that was the better solution after all. He loved a full house, and he needed to have women around to attend to his needs, both physical and sexual. It wouldn't be hard to find some more black-haired, blue-eyed girls to take with him.

And getting a new house wouldn't be all that hard, either. He had access to enough money. He always kept several accounts, as well as huge stashes of cash for an emergency. Losing his home was a tragedy but one he could overcome quite easily. Sure, the house had memories, but the good thing about memories was that you could always create more.

So, decision made. He wouldn't bother with the girls. He'd just find more. They were important to him, but not important enough to risk his freedom. So, he would let them go—all except Arianna and Eliza.

Arianna was his child. His own flesh and blood. He could not abandon her. He *would* not abandon her. And Eliza was her mother. He must have them both.

Malachi remembered his own mother fondly.

He wished things had turned out differently with her.

But she had turned the way all women go in the end. Disrespectful and disobedient. With Eliza, it had been different. He'd made sure that she truly understood that he was her master. He would make sure Arianna learned the same lessons as her mother.

Heavily disguised with a blond wig, brown contact lenses, and a fake nose, he strode through the emergency room. He was unsure how he was going to get Eliza out. The police were on her. They knew she knew things and know things she did. She knew it all. Everything about him. Because he had told her. It had been part of her reprogramming.

He was confident he could come up with some plausible reason to gain access to her, right up until the moment he approached her room. There was an officer standing outside, plus the pretty detective he'd been watching earlier was chatting with

Detective Xander and two other guys he assumed were also cops right outside the door to Eliza's room.

Muttering under his breath, he kept walking so as not to draw suspicion, making his stride purposeful. No one gave him a second glance, and he continued down the corridor and away from all the people.

He needed a new plan.

Grabbing Eliza right now was obviously not an option. He would have to come back for her and the baby.

Malachi didn't want to leave empty-handed.

He could try and lure the pretty detective away and take her with him. But she wouldn't satisfy him long-term. She didn't fit his physical requirements. She may do until he got someone else or until he was able to come back for Eliza.

Wondering how he could get her on her own, he rounded a corner and saw the answer to his prayers standing right in front of him.

Pacing up and down just a few yards away from him was a beautiful, raven-haired woman.

He quickly glanced around to see if anyone was about. Once again, he was in luck. This corridor was deserted. No one in sight.

He fingered the gun in his pocket.

He didn't want to shoot her, but he could use the gun to gain her compliance.

She didn't register his presence as he walked toward her.

It wasn't until he wrapped an arm around her neck and pressed the gun into her side that she realized he was there.

"Make a sound and I shoot you," he whispered in her ear. "Understand?"

Against his chest her body trembled, and she didn't answer at first. Presumably, she was weighing up her options. It was possible she could survive the gunshot, if it missed her vital organs. And the sound of the shot would bring people immediately. Fleeing would be difficult.

At last, the woman nodded, one hand pressed to her swollen stomach. If she hadn't been pregnant, Malachi thought she would have risked it and screamed for help.

"Okay, I don't want to hurt you, but I will if I have to. We're going to walk out of here nice and calmly. If you do anything to draw attention to us, I won't hesitate to shoot the closest person. Understand?" he asked again. The safest way out for him was to make sure she didn't do anything stupid.

Again, she gave a harsh nod.

He walked her toward the nearest door, avoiding the main doors where there were too many people and cops. He had stolen a car earlier, so all he had to do was get the woman into it. That should be easy enough. So far, she was complying. The threat of being shot or getting someone else shot was enough to ensure she did as he said.

That all changed when they stepped through the door and out into the night.

The woman began to pant, her breath coming in short, sharp, gasps. She began to shake violently, and she stopped walking, her body all but going limp in his arms.

Malachi didn't know if she'd gone into shock or she was trying to get him to leave her behind, but whatever the reason, he didn't have time to figure it out. He needed to get her out of here immediately, before someone stumbled upon them. And even if he wanted to, which he didn't, he couldn't leave her behind now. She would go running straight to the cops, and despite the disguise, they could easily figure out it was him behind the attempted abduction.

Picking the woman up, he ran to his car and threw her inside.

* * * * *

2:34 A.M.

Cold metal pressed against her side.

This couldn't be happening.

Laura was so scared, she couldn't move.

It was an effort just to nod her head in response to the man's instructions.

She had weighed up her options and she didn't like her chances if she tried to call for help or make a run for it. If she hadn't been pregnant, she might have risked it. It was one thing to risk her own life, but she couldn't risk her child's.

So she had let the man walk her through the hospital with his gun digging in her flesh.

Deciding her best chance at surviving was to be as compliant as possible, she made no attempts at escaping. It was hard, though. She knew that Jack and the others were just a few corridors away. And she knew that her chances of getting out of this alive decreased dramatically if he got her into a car.

But what choice did she have?

He had threatened to shoot her or any innocent person he came across if she did anything.

How could she have been so stupid?

She didn't even hear him until he was upon her. She knew better. She knew not to be so distracted that she wasn't paying attention to her surroundings.

Only she had been thinking about her family. Seeing Maegan reunite with hers had gotten her thinking. She wanted to let go of the guilt that prevented her from becoming close with them again. She missed them. As a child, she had been very close with her big sister and her parents. She wanted that back. She just didn't know how to get it back.

That was the least of her concerns at the moment, though. If she didn't get herself out of this alive, then she would never see them again, so the condition of their relationship would be irrelevant.

She tried to calm herself. Tried to focus all her energy on

keeping control of her emotions.

But then, he took her outside.

Already totally stressed out, her agoraphobia kicked into high gear as soon as the fresh air hit her.

And she was unable to do a thing about it.

She struggled to draw enough air into her lungs. Her body shook uncontrollably. Her heart was pounding. And she couldn't walk even if she wanted to.

She couldn't move. Couldn't breathe. She was completely helpless. Completely at this man's mercy.

The only part of her mind still functioning knew her panic attack could anger her abductor. If he was angry enough, he could shoot her right here and now.

He didn't, though.

Instead, he picked her up and ran with her toward the parking lot. Stopping at a black SUV, he opened a door, threw her inside, then jumped into the driver's seat, roaring out of the hospital's parking lot.

All Laura could do was close her eyes and attempt to talk herself through the panic attack.

After several minutes, she had it under control enough to start to think clearly again.

Precious minutes lost, she tried to play catch up, gather as much information as she could so she could try to talk her way out of this.

The man in the driver's seat was lean but obviously strong as he hadn't struggled at all as he'd carried her to the car. Laura knew she wasn't going to be able to out muscle him, especially since she was eight months pregnant.

That left her with taking advantage of any opportunity that presented itself to run.

Or making a connection with him.

But that depended on who he was and why he had taken her. For all she knew, the man who had her could be Sofia and Paige's stalker who had decided that she had somehow hurt Sofia and deserved to be punished.

Thinking about that made the panic inside her swell so much that it was almost physically choking her.

Deliberately, she stamped it down.

Jack would notice she was missing soon. He didn't like to have her out of his sight for too long, especially if he knew she was on her own, so he'd go looking for her. When he didn't find her, he would know something was wrong. All she had to do was keep herself alive long enough for him to find her. And he *would* find her. She just had to keep believing that.

She studied the man closely. He didn't look familiar. He had curly black hair and brown eyes. Or did he? The light in the car was dim, but she thought one of his eyes might be blue.

Then it clicked.

Curly black hair and blue eyes. This was Malachi. He must have come back to the hospital to see if he could get his hands on the girls. Only he must have realized that it would be impossible. So, he'd grabbed her. She fit his profile—almost—her eyes were more violet than blue.

The knowledge that Malachi had her in a car and no one knew where she was, was so terrifying that she had to fight off another panic attack.

She had to get herself under control.

Her life depended on it.

And not just her life, but her baby's, too.

She had to get them both out of this alive.

She forced herself to at least project an air of calm. "You're Malachi," she said, her voice coming out wobbly despite her best efforts.

He was surprised that she knew that. Obviously, he hadn't bargained on abducting someone who knew who he was. "How do you know that?" he demanded.

"My husband is Detective Jack Xander. He spoke with you at

the hospital. I'm Laura. I'm the one that Maegan first talked to," she explained, pleased that she had managed to eradicate the wobble from her voice.

He burst into peals of laughter. "Well, of all the coincidences. Of all the women in the hospital, I pick the one person who started this mess."

A stab of fear shot through her. If Malachi blamed her for him losing the girls, he could take that anger out on her.

"Relax," Malachi correctly interpreted her fear. "I don't want to hurt you."

"You want to keep me," she whispered. How would she cope with that? Four days of hell at the hands of Frank and Francis Garrett had been bad enough. How would she endure years? Or forever? She couldn't discount that possibility. If Eliza hadn't gotten Malachi to take her to the hospital, then those girls would likely have lived out their entire lives in his house.

"You make that sound like a bad thing." His voice was conversational. "It's not. Or at least it doesn't have to be. I took good care of those girls. So long as you follow the rules and respect me as the head of the house, you'll be fine. You and your baby," he indicated her pregnant stomach.

Laura believed that. Malachi didn't enjoy hurting people. He simply used it as a means to an end. He wanted to be in control, and he would do whatever it took to make sure those around him bowed down to him. If she could make herself obedient, then she could survive.

Realizing with a start that she still had her cell phone, hope surged through her. She'd dropped her bag somewhere along the way, but her phone had been in her pocket. Malachi hadn't thought to check for one. That was a gift from God. And one she would have to use carefully. She needed to wait until Malachi was distracted before trying to make a call. If she messed it up, she'd lose the phone for good.

"We're here." Malachi suddenly stopped the car.

She scanned their surroundings. It looked like they were in a cemetery. What was Malachi doing here? Had he come to visit the graves of his dead daughters? If he had, that could turn out to be good news. Once they had the details of Malachi's background, Jack and the others might think to come and look for her here.

Or even better, if Malachi got distracted at the gravesites, that could be her opportunity to run. There would be plenty of places to hide, and if she could call Jack, then he'd come and get her.

Hopefully, Malachi would leave her in the car when he went to visit the graves. Not only would it increase her chances of slipping away unnoticed, but Laura wasn't sure she could handle going outside again. She needed a moment to prepare herself so she could make a run for it. If Malachi left the keys in the car, maybe she could avoid going outside altogether and climb into the driver's seat and drive off.

Unfortunately, Malachi seemingly had no intention of leaving her alone in the car.

He climbed out and then came to retrieve her, dragging her out and into the night. Laura fought her rising fears. Repeating over and over to herself that she needed to stay calm to escape. She couldn't condemn her baby to a life of imprisonment in Malachi's house.

Once he had her out of the car, he didn't drag her off toward some graves as she had anticipated. Instead, he pushed her up against the hood of the car, bending her over it as his hands slid under her sweater.

She knew what his intentions were.

He was going to rape her.

Already, she could feel his erection pressing against her back.

"I've never done it with a pregnant woman before." His mouth was so close to her neck, she could feel his breath warm against her icy cold skin.

He hadn't done it with a pregnant woman before and she wasn't about to let it happen now. She was *not* letting this man rape her in a cemetery. She had been raped before, and she had no intention of going through that hell again.

Biding her time as Malachi caressed her stomach with one hand, the baby in her womb kicking its tiny legs as though it too wanted to fight off this horrible injustice. His other hand was fumbling with the zipper of her jeans.

In order to undo her pants, he had to move her a little away from the car. Taking advantage of this, Laura spun around and rammed her knee into his groin in one fluid movement. Hours of self-defense drills with Paige had her hitting her target perfectly.

As Malachi's howl of pain echoed through the silent cemetery, Laura ran.

* * * * *

2:42 A.M.

Something was wrong.

Jack could feel it.

Laura should be back by now.

She had said she needed some time. She had been thinking about her family. Jack knew she had. Watching Maegan reunite with hers had gotten Laura thinking.

Stressed out enough after the night they'd had, he hadn't wanted to let her go off on her own, he had wanted to keep his wife where he could see her. But he was trying hard not to be too overprotective. He knew Laura didn't like that. He had to try to accept that he couldn't keep her in his line of sight permanently. It was hard. He loved her so much and the thought of losing her terrified him almost to the point of paralyzing him. But Laura was strong, and tough, and smart, he had to learn to trust that she could take care of herself.

Right now, though, he knew this was different.

This wasn't paranoia talking.

Nor was it his head injury.

He didn't remember the explosion or the tree coming through the window and striking his head. He didn't remember the fire or Ryan dragging him through the crumbling house. He didn't remember anything until he woke up on the sidewalk. But he didn't have a concussion, only a couple of stitches and a headache, which was currently pounding at his temples as his fear amped up several notches.

Apparently noticing this, Paige narrowed her eyes at him. "What's wrong?"

"I have a bad feeling about Laura," he replied.

"Want me to go and find her?" Paige offered.

"No." Not only did he not want Paige going off on her own, but when he found Laura, he wanted a moment alone with her. He needed to reassure himself that his wife was okay. Maybe that head injury had messed with his head more than he'd thought. "You stay here with Ryan; I'll go look for her."

Jack didn't wait for any response, just jogged off in the direction Laura had gone earlier. He expected to find her pacing in a nearby hallway. Instead, he found nothing.

Nothing.

Not a single thing.

The corridors were empty.

Laura was nowhere to be found.

Terror swirled inside him. Burning hot. Smothering him.

What he saw next made him nearly pass out in horror.

Laura's bag lay on the floor.

He fell to his knees beside the bag. He was sure it was Laura's, but maybe he was wrong. With shaking hands, he reached inside, finding the purse, and pulling it out. Opening it confirmed his worst fears. Laura's driver's license was inside, as were pictures of the two of them and Zach.

This *was* Laura's bag.

And she wouldn't leave it, with her license, credit cards and cash still inside, lying on the floor in a hospital corridor.

At least, she wouldn't leave it on purpose.

Something had happened to her.

Something bad.

His feelings of foreboding had been spot on.

"Xavier," he yelled. He was aware of the fact that there were patients asleep in the rooms that lined the hallway, but right now he didn't care in the least.

"What's wrong?" Xavier appeared beside him moments later.

"Laura's gone. I found this." Jack thrust the bag at his partner.

"Gone?" he repeated, confused.

"Disappeared, missing, lost, taken, abducted," he raved. His terror was rising. Choking him. Laura had been through enough, and now she was suffering again.

"Are you sure?"

He thrust the bag at Xavier. "This is hers. Do you think she'd just leave it here?"

Xavier rifled through the bag and checked the wallet just as Jack himself had done, his face growing progressively more concerned. "Okay, let's check outside. She might not have been gone long."

Jack pulled out his gun and rushed for the nearest door. If someone had abducted Laura, they wouldn't have used the ER's main entrance.

He scanned the dark parking lot.

But saw nothing.

No signs of Laura.

No signs of anyone at all.

His headache morphed into a raging tornado.

"Jack, look," Xavier pointed at something on the ground a few feet away.

Kneeling beside it, Jack picked it up. It was a wig. A blond wig. A blond man had walked past them not long ago while they'd been standing talking outside Eliza's room.

It was Malachi.

Jack knew it.

Malachi had wanted to come back and make an attempt at reclaiming the girls he thought of as his own. Only he'd known they were looking for him, so he had to come in disguise.

Seeing them blocking his access to Eliza, he must have decided to grab someone else.

Laura fit his profile.

He had taken her.

Malachi had Laura.

A glance at his partner confirmed that Xavier had come to the same conclusions.

"Looks like they're already gone," Xavier said softly.

"We might never find her." Jack was in shock. He could barely think straight. Malachi kept his victims indefinitely. His wife and unborn baby could be gone forever.

"But he probably won't hurt her, Jack. He wants her alive. He didn't hurt the other girls, only Eliza as punishment," Xavier reminded him.

"He raped them, though," Jack said tightly. He didn't think Laura could survive going through that again. He didn't think he could survive knowing Laura had been put through that again.

"I know." Xavier looked pained. "Right now, let's just focus on the knowledge that it's highly unlikely that he'll hurt or kill her. That gives us time to find her."

He had to force thoughts of Malachi raping his wife from his mind. If he let himself be consumed by what might be happening to Laura, then he wouldn't be able to function. And if he couldn't function, then he couldn't work on getting his wife back. And Jack had no intention of allowing Malachi to keep his wife and unborn child.

"We need to talk to Eliza," Jack stated.

"Laura said that she thought Eliza was blocking her memories because she's still scared. What Malachi did to her isn't going to be overturned instantaneously. But I made some progress with her earlier. If I ask her direct questions she seems to know the answer," Xavier explained. "We can use some of the information that Ryan and Paige found to try and prompt her memories, but there are no guarantees, Jack. We can't pin all our hopes of finding Laura on Eliza. If she hadn't already been off the sleeping pills during her pregnancy and then the two months since Arianna was born, then we wouldn't be getting anywhere with her. We have to be grateful to get whatever information she can give us. You can't be getting frustrated with her if she doesn't remember, that's not going to help."

Not wanting to waste another second, Jack nodded vigorously and started for Eliza's room.

"Jack, Laura is smart and intuitive and good at reading people. She will know what to do and say to keep herself alive. She'll do her part and survive until we find her. You just have to keep believing that."

Clinging to that thought as though he were drowning and it was his life preserver, Jack prayed that it was true.

* * * * *

2:51 A.M.

"Eliza?"

The voice startled her out of sleep.

She hadn't thought she'd be able to sleep and yet she must be so exhausted she had dozed off. She'd even been dreaming about her sisters and their families. Maegan's family had come for her, and Bethany had gone home, too.

Apparently, her family was on their way here.

But did Eliza want to see them?

She wasn't sure.

She wanted to go home. Well, more accurately, she didn't want to go back to Malachi's. The alternative to Malachi's was her parents' house, but right now Eliza couldn't imagine going back there.

She had changed so much in the last five years.

Mentally and even physically.

She had scars from where Malachi had hurt her during his punishments following all her failed escape attempts.

And she had a daughter.

How could she raise Arianna?

Did she even love the baby?

Could you love a baby that was a product of your rape?

Eliza didn't know.

But she did know that she wanted the baby to be safe, to be happy, and to have a normal life.

How could she go back to a normal life after what she'd lived through the last five years?

How could she be a part of her family again?

What would she do?

Would she go back to college and complete her degree? Would she work? Would she fall in love, get married, and have a family?

She couldn't imagine doing any of those things.

So where did that leave her?

"Eliza?"

She blinked, realizing she had zoned out and concentrated on Xavier's concerned face. She was finding it difficult to focus. She recognized the effects of the drugs the doctor had given her. They always left her feeling woozy and disconnected.

"Honey, we need to talk to you. Do you think you're up to it?"

Why did he keep calling her honey? He didn't know her. He had no reason to be nice to her. And yet he had been. He had made her feel safe. Or at least as safe as she could feel under the circumstances.

But she wanted more.

She wanted to feel safe. Really safe.

She wanted to feel loved.

She wanted to feel not alone.

She wanted her family, but she also wanted more than that.

She wanted George.

Her memories were coming back. She had been dating George for nearly a year when she'd been kidnapped. She had known that he was the love of her life. They had even talked about marriage. Did they want to get married while they were both still in college or should they wait until they graduated? They had never come to a decision.

By now, George must have moved on. He could be married to someone else by now. Had kids. Five years was a long time. She didn't expect him to have waited for her. But did he still love her? Or even care about her? Or even think of her from time to time?

Eliza hoped he did, but she couldn't blame him if he had simply forgotten about her and gone on with his life.

"Eliza?" Xavier repeated her name. "Are you with me?"

No, she wanted to reply. She was so tired. Too tired to try and concentrate. Instead, she gave a small nod.

"We need to talk to you about Malachi," Xavier informed her.

An involuntary shudder rippled through her, and she clutched at the blankets as though they were really a magical force field capable of keeping all the evil in the world away rather than a simple piece of material.

"Eliza, you've been through so much, and that it's not over has to make it so much harder. But I am promising you that we will find him. Okay? I don't want you to worry about that," Xavier soothed.

How could she not worry?

She knew Malachi.

He wouldn't give up on her and the others so easily.

Especially her and Arianna.

He knew that they weren't really his daughters. But Arianna was, and he wouldn't give up his daughter without a fight. Her either. She was the mother of his child. In his mind, that made her his property.

"You're worrying." Xavier tilted her face in his direction. "I can tell. We need you focused; can you do that for me?"

Unsure whether she could, Eliza nodded anyway. Something was wrong. She could read that in Xavier's face and in his voice.

"You remember Laura?"

Eliza did. Laura had been in here earlier with Maegan, asking her questions. Laura had been abducted, too. She understood. She had understood a lot of things. Things Eliza hadn't even told anyone. Laura had figured out that she had deliberately overdosed herself to get Malachi to bring her to the hospital. Last time she'd tried that it hadn't worked, but she had known this time it would. Now that she was the mother of Malachi's daughter, he wouldn't let anything happen to her.

"Malachi took Laura. He came back to the hospital, probably for you and the others. When he realized he couldn't get to you, he took Laura instead," Xavier gently informed her.

For a moment, the world stopped.

At least, that was what it felt like to Eliza.

Her eyes stopped working, her ears stopped working, her heart stopped working, her lungs stopped working.

"Eliza."

The sharp voice pricked through the haze she was trapped in. She blinked and the world seemed to start up again.

"Are you okay?" Xavier was peering down at her, his eyes dark with concern.

"He came back here?" her voice a breathy whisper.

"Yes, and he might come back again. He won't get to you; there's an officer on your door. But we need to find him, Eliza. Before he hurts Laura and before he hurts anyone else."

"Eliza, we have Malachi's house and some of his bank account details, would he have access to money we don't know about?"

She shifted her gaze from Xavier to the other man in the

room. It was Xavier's partner, Jack. She remembered him asking her questions earlier tonight. Laura had said that Jack was her husband. He must be in a blind panic knowing Malachi had his wife, and yet he appeared calm and in control.

Slowly, she nodded. "Yes, he has lots of cash in his house from the settlement."

"What settlement?"

"From the car accident."

"What car accident?"

"When Malachi was thirteen, he was in a car accident. His father was killed, and he was left with serious head injuries. He was in a coma for seven months. The doctors never expected him to wake up."

"But he did," Jack stated the obvious.

"And he was never the same afterward. The accident changed him." Eliza wondered whether if Malachi had never been in that accident then none of this would have happened.

"What can you tell us about Malachi's family?" Xavier asked.

Her heart started to pound again. Memories flooded into her mind so quickly she couldn't cope. They were overwhelming her. There were too many. Things she didn't want to remember.

Eliza whimpered, pressing her eyes closed and her fingertips to her temples.

Desperately, she tried to will the memories away.

But the flashbacks were so vivid.

So real.

Like she was back in Malachi's house.

In the basement.

In the dark room.

Her naked body was so cold. She was huddled in a corner, her knees tucked up to her chest. She was so used to being hungry by now that her stomach didn't really notice. But the lack of water was awful. Her body craved it so much it was often all she could think of. She didn't sleep much, or maybe she did, she couldn't really tell the difference between asleep and awake. The dark was so complete, so impenetrable, that it seemed alive.

"Eliza."

Someone took her shoulders and shook her. The movement seemed to transport her out of the basement and back into her hospital room.

"Eliza? Are you with me?" Xavier was perched beside her on the bed, his hands still clutched her shoulders.

"I don't want to talk anymore. I'm tired," she whispered.

"You remember." Jack was looming over her.

She shrunk away from him. "Please, leave me alone."

"You're going to tell me what you remember, Eliza," Jack commanded fiercely. His anger seemed to reverberate off the walls of the small room, growing exponentially larger.

"Jack, ease up," Xavier warned. "Pushing her that hard isn't going to help."

He softened his tone, his blue eyes bright with fear. "Eliza. Please. Help me find Laura before it's too late. She's eight months pregnant. If we don't find her before Malachi disappears, then she and our baby will be stuck with him forever."

She wanted to help. She really did. But she was so afraid.

"Eliza, did Malachi talk to you about his family while he had you in that room?" Xavier asked gently.

She focused on Xavier. Jack's terror was too much to bear. It made it difficult to concentrate, and it made her own horror grow. But Xavier calmed her somehow. "It was so dark in there," she said softly.

"I know, honey. He did that to break you down. But you're safe now. You're here in the hospital. Your family is coming, and we're not going to let Malachi hurt you again," Xavier soothed.

"The darkness got inside me," she continued. "I don't know how to get it out."

"I'll help you; your family will help you," Xavier assured her.

Nodding absently, Eliza wasn't sure it was possible to remove the darkness that filled her soul. "Malachi doesn't have any daughters. Well, except Arianna," she amended.

"But the fire." Jack looked confused. "Maegan said he told you all that you were replacements for his daughters who died in a fire."

"It wasn't his daughters who died in a fire. It was his sisters. Ariyel, Alice, Angela, and Abigail were Malachi's sisters," she explained.

"Then why did he tell you that they were his daughters?" Xavier looked just as confused as his partner.

"Because after his father's death, Malachi thought of himself as the man of the house. It was his thirteenth birthday. They were meant to go for ice cream, but his father stopped to see someone on the way. Malachi's father was having an affair. He tried to end it, but the woman wouldn't. She climbed in the car with them. When she realized that she couldn't have what she wanted, she crashed the car." The more Eliza spoke, the more details came back to her. "After the accident Malachi wasn't the same."

"How was he different, Eliza?" Xavier prompted her when she didn't continue.

She shivered as she pictured the lifeless light in Malachi's eyes. "He was evil. He thought his father had failed his family. He vowed to be different. He was thirteen—a man. He believed it was his job to care for his family, to protect them."

"What did he do to them?" Jack asked, his voice quietly menacing.

"He didn't let them leave the house. He had ... he had a ... a sexual relationship with them." Eliza struggled to force the words out of her throat. "His mother and Ariyel, who was sixteen, right away. His younger sisters from their thirteenth birthday."

"Because in his mind, they became adults once they hit thirteen," Xavier murmured.

"Malachi was only thirteen. Why did his mother let him do that?" Jack asked.

"Malachi was evil. He punished them when they disobeyed. His mother was grieving the loss of her husband, and she had nearly lost Malachi, but she was scared of him. Of what he would do. To her and his sisters. He kept them locked up in that house for twenty-three years."

"Until the fire?"

"Yes."

"They died in the fire?"

"Yes. His mother, too. And I think some other woman, but I'm hazy on the details." Eliza was tired now. Exhausted, really. Completely mentally and emotionally drained.

Seemingly sensing this, Jack asked, "Do you know where he would go?"

"He would want to feel close to his family." Eliza closed her eyes as she thought. "Since the house is destroyed, he can't go there." Suddenly, it occurred to her. "Their graves. Malachi will be at the cemetery where his mother and sisters were buried."

SIX YEARS AGO

4:18 A.M.

Something woke him up.

Malachi wasn't sure what it was.

A bad feeling, maybe.

Glancing at his watch, he saw it was after four in the morning. He was supposed to work until six, but that bad feeling was growing.

He decided to risk it. Nothing ever happened here, anyway. Malachi worked as a security guard, driving around patrolling the schools and businesses who hired the firm he worked for. Most nights he just drove around a bit then parked his car somewhere and napped. Sure, there had been the odd night where someone had actually attempted a break in, but usually it was just some stupid kids.

What were the chances that tonight would be one of those rarer than rare nights where he actually had to deal with something?

Slim.

Turning the ignition on, Malachi started toward his house. It wasn't more than a ten-minute drive away. Less if he broke the speed limit and ignored any red lights. There weren't usually many cops about at this time, so he decided to risk it and do both.

In seven minutes, he was pulling into the street where the house he had lived in his entire life was situated.

Nothing appeared out of sorts.

For a moment, he'd panicked that someone had stumbled upon his home. It had been twenty-three years since his accident.

Twenty-three years since he had been changed forever. Twenty-three years since he had taken over running his family.

They all bowed to his every whim now.

They no longer asked to leave the house. They no longer talked about leaving and getting married and having families of their own. They no longer talked about getting jobs and contributing to the running of the household.

They had learned that he was the man of the house and that he alone ruled.

As he pulled into his driveway, nothing appeared out of the ordinary.

And then he saw it.

Smoke.

His house was on fire.

Malachi was in such a hurry to get to the house that he put the wrong code in at the gate four times before his trembling fingers could do it correctly.

Then he bolted for the front door.

Again, it took him several tries to get through the locks and padlocks and codes that protected his family from anyone who wished them harm.

As soon as the door was open, it was like the smoke exploded out. Flames were consuming the house, devouring it from the inside out.

Out of his mind with fear, Malachi's first concern was the woman he loved, Samantha Ingham.

He had brought Samantha to live with them six months ago. She was supposed to be his. If he'd never been in the accident, then she *would* have been his. At the time, Samantha had been married with three kids, but Malachi had known that she wasn't really happy. How could she be without him?

So, he'd rescued her. Brought her back here to his safe haven. She had resisted at first. She'd been scared. But he knew that she loved him. They were destined to be together since they were kids. He knew she felt the connection between them.

Not only was Samantha the love of his life, but she was also the mother of his child. She was six months pregnant, and he could hardly stand to wait another three months for the baby to arrive.

He headed straight for Samantha's room in the basement. She had been a little off lately, defiant and reckless and endangering their baby. Malachi was sure it was just pregnancy hormones throwing her off, but he had to protect his child. So, he'd built a special room for her in the basement.

He barely noticed the smoke as he ran. It was there, filling his lungs with each breath he took and filling the house just as thoroughly.

In the basement, he found his mother.

She was lying on the floor by the door to Samantha's room, an axe in her hand.

What was she doing here?

The basement was forbidden.

And why did she have an axe?

It became apparent, when he got closer.

She'd been trying to chop through the door to Samantha's room. This was, of course, impossible. Even for someone strong like himself. Let alone a feeble older woman.

Was his mother still alive?

He couldn't go past her without checking, so he dropped to his knees beside her and pressed his fingertips to her throat.

At his touch, his mother's eyes struggled open. "Malachi." She said just the one word. But it communicated enough. She wasn't happy to see him.

"Mother, how did the fire start?" Suspicion was already creeping inside him. Had she betrayed him? Gone against him? Tried to get the fire department and the police department here?

"I'm sorry," she croaked. "I love you, but you're wrong. The world isn't a dangerous place. It's in here that's dangerous."

Then his mother closed her eyes, and he knew she was gone.

Unsure how he felt about her betrayal, he jumped to his feet. He had no time to worry about that now. He pulled a key from his pocket as he strode for the door, fearing he was already too late.

When he yanked open the door, he found Samantha lying in a huddle on the floor.

As soon as he saw her, he knew.

Yet it didn't stop him from flinging himself down at her side and desperately searching her neck for a pulse.

He found nothing.

Samantha was dead.

His baby was dead.

"No!" he howled, gathering her limp body into his arms as though his life could seep out of him and into her.

Tears streamed down his cheeks. His eyes stung from the mixture of smoke and tears. Gathering the woman he loved into his arms, he carried her from the house.

Sirens sounded in the distance.

Police and firefighters were coming.

They would want to take Samantha and the baby from him.

He couldn't allow that. He couldn't bear to part with her just yet, so he put her in the trunk of his car where she would be safe. So he could say his goodbyes later when he could be alone with her.

As the sirens got closer, some of his common sense kicked in. The house was now a raging inferno, but the police would be suspicious if he hadn't gone in and made an attempt at rescuing his family.

The neighbors already thought he was odd. He and his whole family. Because only he ever left the house. They thought it was because his family had strange religious beliefs that prohibited them from interacting with the outside world.

He didn't want to raise the policemen's suspicions. So,

ignoring his burning lungs and stinging eyes, he went inside to look for his sisters.

NOVEMBER 4TH
3:00 A.M.

3:02 A.M.

Laura ran.

Her well-placed kick to Malachi's groin had given her a small head start. Enough for her to be off and running through the cemetery before Malachi recovered enough to take off after her. It was barely a minute, but she tried to make the most of it.

She was running as fast as she could.

But everything was working against her. It was November and cold and she wasn't dressed properly to be out in the night air. The cemetery was wooded, and what little moonlight filtered through the heavy cloud cover was cut out by the trees. Not only was it dark and cold, but she was fighting off the panic that being outdoors in this wide-open space invariably brought on.

What Malachi had nearly done to her was swirling around in her mind, too.

Threatening to clog up her already terrified head.

She couldn't think about that right now.

Malachi hadn't raped her; that was the important thing. That and keeping away from him long enough for someone to find her. Because she had no doubts at all that if Malachi found her and took her away, raping her would be pretty high on his to do list.

So instead, she pushed all her fears away and ran.

Footsteps sounded around her—the unmistakable crunch of shoes on dry leaves. The huffing and puffing of someone who was breathless from so much running.

Malachi was close by.

"Laura," he called. "Come out, come out, wherever you are. I'm going to find you, you know. You can't hide from me forever."

Ignoring the burning in her chest and her aching legs, Laura continued to run. She couldn't really see where she was going, but still, she ran.

She was always running.

This was the second time she had been chased by a violent psychopath. Forced to run for her life. Last time, she had spent four days running through the woods, desperately seeking an escape she knew didn't exist. That time she had been abused every time Frank and Francis Garrett caught her, her body growing progressively weaker with each assault.

This time, she wasn't going to let anything like that happen.

This time, she was going to get away before she got hurt.

She still had the phone. She just had to find someplace to hide, so she could call Jack.

Laura weighed up her options on finding a hiding place.

She could go into a mausoleum, but if Malachi started searching them, she would be trapped. Maybe it was better to stay outside, hide amongst the trees, and hope he didn't stumble upon her. But at least if he did, she wouldn't be trapped and she'd be able to run again.

The chances of her outrunning him if it came down to it probably weren't all that good, though.

Not that she would give up without a fight.

"Laura," Malachi's voice boomed through the still night. "It's the middle of the night. No one else is here. No one is going to find you. It's cold, and you're not wearing a coat. Let me take you back to the car. You must be tired; you're pregnant, you should be resting."

Laura knew she didn't have any time left. Malachi was close. Too close. He could find her at any second. And she didn't think that she could run much longer. Slowing down, Laura crept into a small grove of trees and ducked down. Catching her breath, she leaned against a tree trunk and pulled out her phone. It was now or never. There wasn't going to be a perfect time to do this.

She dialed Jack's number with trembling fingers.

"Laura?" Her husband's panicked voice answered almost immediately.

"Found you."

Startled, Laura dropped the phone as her gaze darted up.

Malachi stood over her.

A smirk on his face was just visible in the dark.

He stamped a foot on the phone and Laura's hopes shattered right along with her cell. She hadn't even been able to tell Jack where she was. He was never going to find her. She was going to be trapped with Malachi forever.

Battling her fears once again, Laura shrieked and darted to her feet as Malachi reached for her.

Catching him off guard, he stumbled, and Laura ran.

Malachi recovered quickly and was soon after her again.

Exhausted and terrified, Laura was slowing. She wouldn't be able to run much longer.

He was gaining on her.

He was going to catch her.

Any second now.

Then all of a sudden, the earth disappeared beneath her feet.

She was falling.

In the dark, she had stepped off the edge of an incline. Tumbling down a grassy bank, Laura rolled over and over again down the fifteen-foot drop, until at last, with a bone shuddering thud, she finally came to a stop at the bottom.

Mercifully, she had somehow managed to avoid crashing into any of the trees or rocks that dotted the bank on her crazy descent and it didn't seem like she had sustained any serious injuries. Still, every inch of her body ached, and she knew she would be covered in bruises tomorrow.

Dizzy, dazed, and disoriented, Laura could do nothing but lie there and attempt to still her spinning head.

"Don't try that again." Malachi's voice sounded close by.

Ignoring her aching limbs and wooziness, Laura attempted to roll over onto all fours. She didn't think she could walk but she might be able to crawl.

"You could have been seriously hurt," Malachi reprimanded as he snatched her up, walking with her in the direction of the car.

He carried her easily, highlighting his strength, and Laura knew she ought to do something. Fight him off as best as she could no matter how fruitless it was. But the fight had seemed to drain out of her. She was sore and cold and scared, and she just wanted to go home.

Only she couldn't.

She would never get to go home again.

Jack didn't know where to look for her, and Malachi would never let her go.

She would never get to see her husband or her little boy again. She would never get to tell them one more time that she loved them.

In Malachi's arms, Laura began to cry.

* * * * *

3:06 A.M.

What was wrong with these women?

Didn't they know he only wanted to help them? To protect them?

Malachi didn't want anything to happen to Laura and her baby. They would make a wonderful addition to his family. And the baby would only be a little younger than Arianna. Once he got his daughter and her mother back, the two little ones would grow up together. Raised as siblings.

Eliza really did remind him of his deceased sister Ariyel. Three years older than himself, Ariyel hadn't responded well to his taking over the running of their household.

Him becoming the man of the house had been a gradual transition. When he had been released from the hospital eight months after the accident, his mother had been so glad to have him alive and back home that she had given him whatever he wanted.

Then bit by bit, he had taken over.

He had convinced his mother that it wasn't safe for him and his sisters to continue to attend school. She hadn't understood, but he had insisted, thrown a fit, broken things, screamed, and she had given in. Each time he had demanded something, she had given in with less fuss and less resistance. Eventually, she had bowed to his every whim, forcing his sisters to do the same.

But Ariyel had resisted.

Strongly.

He had been forced to punish her.

Several times, in fact.

But in the end, she had learned.

Just like Eliza had.

Just like Laura would.

In the end, they all learned that he was the one in charge.

Laura had grown quiet in his arms. Her tears spent, she rested heavily against him. After a quick visit to the graves, he would take her to his cabin. He had bought it years ago, kept it in a different name so it wasn't traceable to him. The police would never find him there. It would be the perfect place to hide out until he bought another house.

Once he had Laura tucked safely away, he would go back for Eliza and Arianna.

He wasn't giving them up.

They belonged to him. It was as simple as that. And *no one* took away anything that belonged to him.

Before he went anywhere, though, he needed to say goodbye to his family. Explain to them why he may not be able to visit for a while.

Reaching the gravesites, he let Laura's feet slide down to the ground, then held her against his chest. He didn't want to risk her running again. Next time, she might not be so lucky and may cause herself injuries, so he pulled a knife from his pocket and held it to her neck.

Laura flinched and tried to shrink away from the cold metal blade, but the only way to move was backward, and she apparently didn't want to be too close to him. There was nowhere for her to go, though. She was trapped between him and the knife. And Malachi wasn't worried that she would try anything else.

He could have used the gun. It was still in his other pocket, but he could subdue her easier with the knife than the gun should she make another attempt at running. The gun was more likely to cause serious injuries, whereas the knife could inflict a painful, yet minor wound very easily.

With Laura under control, he focused his gaze on the headstones.

There were six of them. All in a row.

Martin Rivers. On his headstone, it claimed he was a beloved husband and father, but Malachi disagreed with that statement.

Next was his mother, Anne Rivers. He had chosen not to put anything on her headstone. He hadn't felt it was necessary. He was going to be the only person visiting her at the cemetery and he already knew what kind of woman his mother had been.

Ariyel had been thirty-nine when she died.

Angela had been thirty-three.

Alice twenty-seven.

And Abby twenty-three.

The two youngest girls didn't remember their father. They only knew Malachi as the head of the household. They had never been to school. Malachi had educated them himself within the safety of their home. They'd had no friends, never held a job, and they didn't know what life was like outside the house. But Malachi hadn't cared about any of that. All that mattered to him was that they had been safe.

They had not had to suffer any of the atrocities that came with existing in the outside world.

Because of him.

He had protected them, and he would protect his new family.

"Malachi."

* * * * *

3:14 A.M.

Malachi's head snapped in his direction when he heard his name called.

Malachi wasn't the only one whose head snapped up at the sound of his voice. Laura looked toward him, too. Even from several yards away and in the semi-dark, Jack could see her relax at his presence.

His wife was trembling, tear tracks marked her cheeks. She was dirty and there was grass in her hair, but she looked okay. She was alive, and it was his job to keep her that way.

As soon as Eliza had told them where she believed Malachi would go, Jack had jumped in his car and started driving here. He hadn't been too far away when his phone had started ringing. When Laura's name had shown up, he hadn't known whether to shout for joy or scream in fear. He had hoped that Laura was calling to tell him she was safe, but he hadn't even known if it would be Laura on the other end of the phone. It could have been Malachi calling to taunt him.

When he'd answered only to find no one there, fear had nearly overpowered him. Then the line had gone dead. In a panic, he had called Xavier and asked him to bring Eliza to the cemetery. If they could convince Malachi that he could take Eliza and the baby home with him, then they might be able to get him to give up Laura.

Right now, though, he had to remain calm.

His wife and unborn child's lives depended on it.

Ryan and Paige were here with him, but they'd decided it would be best if Malachi didn't know that. More cops were on the way, too. At the moment, no one would have a good shot at Malachi. He had Laura as a human shield and the headstones behind him were a good five or six feet tall. Shooting around them in the dark probably wasn't an option.

For now, everything rested on him.

He had to hold it together. To that end, he deliberately blocked out Laura's petrified eyes and focused on Malachi.

Malachi held a knife at Laura's throat and pushed it deeper into her flesh, causing Laura to cry out in pain, and a thin line of blood to dribble down. "Go away, Detective Xander."

"I can't do that, Malachi," Jack said calmly. It took every bit of his self-control not to lose it at Laura's cry of pain.

Malachi moved the knife from Laura's neck to hold it poised above her pregnant belly. "If you don't leave, I can either kill your wife or your child. Or, if you get unlucky, both of them."

Laura whimpered and tried to angle herself so the knife wasn't over her stomach. "It's okay, Laura," Jack soothed. He didn't think Laura would panic and do anything to startle Malachi unless it came down to protecting the baby. "You're not going to hurt her, Malachi. You want to protect her, not hurt her."

Malachi tilted his head to the side and studied him quizzically. "You really love your wife?"

"More than anything in the world. She and our son are my life."

"You have another child?"

"A little boy. His name is Zach; he's eighteen months old."

"You would do anything to protect her?"

"Anything," Jack echoed, wondering whether a trade might be possible. Laura would freak if he traded himself for her, but at least she'd be safe, and he could deal with her anger later. Laura's furiously terrified eyes tried to seek his, no doubt to try to forbid him from attempting any sort of swap, but Jack refused to meet her gaze.

"That's how I felt about my family." Malachi looked thoughtful. "I kept them safe. I taught them. I learned medicine so I could help them when they were sick. I looked after them financially."

"You loved them." Jack felt like he was making progress with Malachi. Maybe he could talk him down without needing to use Eliza. He didn't want to put her in the middle of a potentially dangerous situation if he didn't have to.

"I loved them before, but after the accident I couldn't feel things anymore."

"That's not true, Malachi," Jack contradicted. Paige and Ryan had managed to track down a lot of background information on Malachi, and he intended to use as much of it as possible to attempt to talk him down.

Frowning, Malachi moved the knife back to Laura's throat. "I don't have emotions anymore."

Given that Malachi was an imminent threat to the safety of others, they'd been able to get his psychiatric history. The psychiatrist who had seen him shortly after the accident had determined that Malachi had lost the ability to empathize with others, but he could indeed feel emotions. Anger, joy, excitement, fear, frustration—Malachi could feel it all. In fact, the brain damage he suffered made his emotions stronger, but his ability to deal with them appropriately was severely diminished. Combine that with his impaired capacity to empathize, and he had become a virtual ticking time bomb.

"After your father's death, you were angry," Jack reminded

him. "Very angry. At everyone. You were getting into fights at school. Beating up the other kids. You got expelled."

"They kept saying they were sorry about my father's death," Malachi growled. "I didn't want them to be sorry. My father was having an affair. He didn't take care of his family. He deserved to die."

"You blamed him."

"It was my birthday. We should have been celebrating with our family; instead, he went to his mistress," Malachi spat the word out like it was poison. He tightened his grip on Laura, digging his arm into her neck and cutting off her air supply. Laura's eyes grew even wider with panic, and she clawed at Malachi's arm, standing on her tiptoes so she could breathe.

"She tried to kill you." Jack stomped on the rage that spouted inside him as he watched Laura's terror. "No one would blame you for hating her."

"She thought she could order my father around. He told her it was over. She didn't listen. That woman was disobedient and disrespectful. I didn't want my sisters to turn out like her. I made sure they didn't."

"You abused them, Malachi," Jack said softly. He didn't think Malachi would hurt Laura. He'd truly believed he was protecting his sisters, and now Laura. His best bet was to keep Malachi talking and distracted. Xavier and Eliza should be here now. The prospect of getting Eliza back would hopefully be enough to cause him to let his guard down, and once he released Laura, then Ryan, Paige, or one of the many cops he was sure were surrounding them, but that he couldn't see, could take a shot at him.

"I protected them. I made sure they were safe."

"You kept them locked in that house for twenty-three years."

"I kept them safe," Malachi repeated.

"You had sex with them." Jack worked to keep the disgust from his voice.

He shrugged indifferently. "Women have urges that they can't control. I simply took care of them so they wouldn't go and ruin other families."

The accident and the events leading up to it, plus the brain injury, had really messed Malachi up. He had referred to his sisters as women, but at the time of the accident, they had ranged in age from sixteen to infancy. Clearly Malachi identified turning thirteen with becoming an adult, and in his mind, he became the head of the family at the age of thirteen. Maegan had told them the sexual abuse began on her thirteenth birthday.

"How did the fire start?" Jack asked. There was no point in discussing what Malachi had done to his sisters and mother—to him, it all made perfect sense.

"She tried to let them out of the house."

"Who tried to help who out of the house?"

"My mother tried to get Samantha out."

Samantha Ingham had gone to Malachi's school. She had disappeared almost a year before the fire that had killed Malachi's family. At the time, she had been happily married with three kids and worked as a prominent defense lawyer. It had been deemed that her abduction was a result of one of the cases she had worked on, but the police had never been able to prove which criminal she had represented had repaid her by kidnapping her. Apparently, the police had been wrong.

"You had liked Samantha since you were kids. You wanted her to have a good life."

"I had been going to kiss her at my party. We would have gotten together, and we would have been married once we graduated school. We would have been a family. My father ruined all of that. She was supposed to be mine. She *was* mine. I only reclaimed her because that was the way it was supposed to be. I rectified my father's mistakes. Samantha was happy with me. We were expecting a baby."

"How did the fire get started?"

"I wasn't there that night. My mother thought she could start a fire, get the fire department to come, and get Samantha out. Only the fire spread too quickly. They couldn't get out."

Eliza had tried the same thing, only a sprinkler system had thwarted her attempt. Malachi must have learned his lesson from his mother's actions. "The police never found Samantha's body."

"I got there before the fire department. I tried to rescue them. I got Samantha out first, but she wasn't breathing, I put her in the trunk of my car."

"Where is she buried?" Jack asked, positive that Malachi would have wanted the woman he loved properly laid to rest.

He gestured his head at the graves behind him. "She's with my mother. The two women I loved most in the world. I thought it was fitting that they should spend eternity together."

"But your mother betrayed you," Jack reminded him. Anne Rivers must have finally realized what a mistake she had made letting her son rule their household with an iron fist—forbidding anyone to leave and sexually abusing them all.

"She made a mistake. Everyone makes mistakes sometimes," Malachi retorted.

"Like your father made a mistake in having an affair. A mistake he tried to rectify. Your mother made the same mistake."

Malachi went deadly still. "What do you mean?"

"Your mother had an affair, too. Abby wasn't your father's daughter."

For a long moment, Malachi didn't say anything, just stood there and processed this new information. Then he chuckled. "Nice try, Detective, but I don't buy it. My mother would never have cheated on my father. She would never have risked her family's happiness. And now, as lovely and as therapeutic even, as this little chat has been, we have to leave now. Come along, Laura." Malachi tried to pull her backward, but Laura resisted. "Don't worry, Detective. I'll take good care of your wife and your baby. I'll treat them like my own, because they are now."

Jack readied himself to attempt a shot. He knew Ryan and Paige would be, too, as would every cop out there. There was no way Malachi was walking out of this cemetery with Laura.

Then Jack heard footsteps approaching. Xavier and Eliza had arrived. Now they just had to hope their plan worked.

* * * * *

3:22 A.M.

"I don't think I can do this." Eliza paused to whisper in Xavier's ear. She hadn't wanted to leave the hospital to come to the cemetery to try and talk Malachi down. She was petrified at the prospect of seeing him again. And what if something went wrong? Xavier had assured her that he wouldn't let Malachi hurt her, but that was no guarantee.

Still, she couldn't do nothing.

That wasn't the kind of person she was.

If there was anything she could do to stop Malachi from hurting Laura, then she had to do it.

Plus, she didn't want to live with the knowledge that Malachi was free to come back for her at any time he chose.

So, she had agreed to come.

Only now that they were actually here at the cemetery, she was having second thoughts. Serious second thoughts.

"You can do it, Eliza," Xavier whispered back.

His words strengthened her. She wasn't sure why. In just a couple of hours, this man had become very important to her. He gave her strength when she didn't have any of her own right now. Eliza didn't understand it. Maybe it was because he reminded her of George. But maybe it was okay that it didn't make sense. Maybe he was just her guardian angel, sent by God to help her during this horrible time.

"Whoa, easy, I got you," Xavier grabbed her elbow as she

stumbled, steadying her. "Take it slow. It's dark out here and you're still weak."

And weak she was. When she had climbed out of her hospital bed to come here, her knees had buckled, and she would have hit the floor if Xavier hadn't caught her first. Now walking through the wooded cemetery in the dark, she barely had enough energy to walk in a straight line. She kept tripping over sticks and rocks and tree roots. The drugs she'd taken were still in her system, leaving her feeling woozy and not quite all there.

"We're almost there." Xavier stopped, and Eliza stopped with him. "You remember what you need to do, right?"

Eliza could feel his worried gaze on her. She knew the plan. She just wasn't sure it was a good one. Or that she wanted to be a part of it. Still, she had agreed, and she wasn't going to back out now. "I know what to do," she assured him.

"All right. Jack and I will be right there, and Ryan and Paige and lots of other cops are surrounding the area. Malachi won't be leaving here, and he won't hurt you, okay?"

"Okay," Eliza echoed with a lot less conviction.

They walked a few more yards, and then on the other side of a small group of trees stood Laura's husband, Jack Xander. A few yards in front of him were the gravesites of Malachi's family. Malachi stood in front of the headstones. Laura was pressed against his body, a knife at her throat.

"If you try anything stupid, Detective, I'll make sure you regret it," Malachi was saying. Moving the knife from Laura's neck, he traced the tip down her cheek, leaving a trail of blood behind it. Laura whimpered and tried to shrink away from the knife, but there was nowhere for her to go. She was trapped. Eliza knew the feeling.

"I don't think you want to leave just yet, Malachi. There's someone here who wants to see you." Jack waggled a finger at her, urging her forward.

Reluctantly, Eliza complied. She didn't want to see Malachi.

She didn't want to talk to him. She didn't want to pretend that she would go home with him. She didn't want to claim that they would raise their daughter together.

"Eliza?" Malachi sounded surprised to see her. "What are you doing here?"

Taking a deep breath, she took a step closer. "Who's Eliza?" On the drive over, Xavier had coached her on a few things to say and do and advised her to pretend she still believed she was Malachi's daughter Ariyel.

Even in the dark, she could see he was suspicious. "Do you really expect me to believe that these cops didn't tell you that your name is Eliza and that I kidnapped you and Maegan and Bethany and Hayley and held you all against your will for five years?" Malachi scoffed.

She made herself sound timid, which wasn't a stretch. "They told me that, but I told them they were lying."

He was confused now. "You really believe you're Ariyel?"

"I am Ariyel."

"Why are you here?"

"I asked them to bring me to you."

He directed his attention to Jack. "Someone else is here?"

"Only my partner." Jack gestured to Xavier.

Scanning the area and seeing no one else, Malachi nodded. "Come closer," he ordered her.

Complying, she left the relative safety of Xavier and Jack and crept across the grass toward Malachi. When she got closer, she met Laura's violet eyes. Beneath the terror, Laura was clearly commanding her not to risk herself. Ignoring her, Eliza focused on Malachi. "I want to go home," she whispered.

"Home? What home?"

"Our home."

"The other girls can't come back with us. Maegan convinced the cops that I hurt her, and they took the girls away." Malachi was focused solely on her now, his grip on Laura loosening. She just needed to keep him talking a little longer, and then as soon as he let Laura go, the cops would take him out.

"We just need Arianna."

He looked around. "Where is the baby?"

"She's in the car. It's too cold out here for her, she's so little." Of course, that wasn't true. Arianna was safely back at the hospital. Eliza may or may not love the baby, but she certainly intended to protect her.

Thankfully, Malachi seemed to buy her bluff. He nodded and smiled at her. "Come here," he said almost tenderly.

Fighting her instincts, which were screaming at her to run as fast and as far away as she could, Eliza walked closer. Close enough now that he could reach out and touch her. She wanted this over. Being this near to Malachi was making her whole body tremble and her stomach turn vicious circles.

"You can have Eliza and Arianna. You can take your daughter and her mother and disappear again. Just let Laura go," Jack's voice spoke softly.

"You mean you're letting me go even though you know what I've done?" Malachi sounded incredulous.

"I just want my wife back. I told you I would do anything to protect her." Jack's voice was completely calm.

Malachi was wavering, Eliza could see it in his eyes. Why didn't he just release Laura and be done with it? She couldn't last much longer. The desire to run back to Xavier was near overwhelming, and she feared she would give in to it soon. But if she did, there would be nothing stopping Malachi from hurting or even killing Laura. It was that knowledge alone that kept Eliza's feet rooted to the spot.

"Please, let her go," Eliza murmured.

"Why would you care if I let her go or not?" Malachi demanded.

"I ... I don't ... I don't care," Eliza stammered. "I just want to go home." She was unable to stop her eyes from darting around.

Xavier had said there were cops surrounding them, remaining out of sight so as not to spook Malachi, but Eliza couldn't see anyone.

Her panic was quickly rising.

What if there weren't any other cops here?

What if Xavier and Jack truly intended to trade her for Laura?

What if Malachi was going to take her with him and keep her locked away—forever, this time.

Following her darting gaze, a slow and resigned smile lit Malachi's face. "Well played, Detective. It almost worked perfectly. You kept me talking, Eliza almost had me distracted enough to release your wife. Once I let her go, I'm guessing one of the dozens of cops surrounding us were going to take me out."

"You're not walking out of here alive, Malachi," Jack told him.

"If I'm not walking out of here alive, then neither are they."

What happened next happened so quickly, Eliza didn't have time to react.

Malachi lunged forward, Laura still in his arms.

The knife swung in a huge arc down toward her, glinting in the moonlight as it moved.

There was an explosion of pain in her shoulder.

Something warm and wet spilled down her chest.

She dropped to the ground, her legs no longer strong enough to support her.

There was screaming.

A loud bang.

Then footsteps.

Content in the knowledge that the bang was a gunshot and that the bullet had most likely killed its target, Eliza let her body and her mind go completely limp, closed her eyes, and rested.

* * * * *

3:34 A.M.

Everything happened so quickly.

In Laura's mind, it was nothing more than a jumble of sounds and sights.

Malachi lunged at Eliza, plunging the knife deep into her shoulder.

Then he brought the blade back to her neck and sliced into it.

As he released her, she dropped to the ground. It wasn't a planned move in anticipation of the cops she knew were all around them firing a shot at Malachi. It was simply because she didn't have enough strength left to remain on her feet.

A gunshot sliced through the night.

Someone dropped to the ground beside her.

Laura wasn't unconscious, but she also wasn't really aware of anything happening around her.

Voices yelled.

Footsteps pounded the earth.

Someone knelt at her side.

Something pressed to her neck, and she heard a voice yell, "I need medics here."

"Me too," someone else yelled.

"On their way," a third voice spoke.

Her body was shaking. She couldn't stop it. The constant trembling was hurting her already bruised and sore muscles.

"Laura?" Fingertips brushed hair off her cheek. "Can you hear me?"

She was struggling to open her eyes. Dazed and disoriented at first, she wasn't quite sure where she was or what was happening.

Then she panicked. Where was Jack? He'd been here. He had tried to talk Malachi into letting her go. At one point she had been sure he would be willing to trade himself for her. She had been so furious. How could he even think of doing that? Didn't he know that if anything happened to him her life would be over? She had tried to catch his eye, order him not to even consider it, but he had refused to look at her. Had he done it? Had he traded himself for her?

Then as her eyes settled on the face hovering above her she relaxed. "Jack."

Relief flooded his blue eyes. "I'm right here, angel, and I'm not going anywhere. Try not to talk. It'll make the bleeding worse."

She barely registered his words. "Where's Malachi?" She wiggled beneath him, trying to twist sideways to find him. She had to know where he was. She had to know if he was still a threat.

"Lie still," Jack instructed, placing a hand on her shoulder and forcibly holding her down

"Is he dead?" she asked, refusing to follow his orders.

"Yes, Laura, he's dead," he reassured her. "Now, please stop moving."

"He cut me." Her eyes widened with surprise, registering what Jack's hands on her neck were doing. He was trying to stem the flow of blood from the gash on her throat. As if remembering Malachi cutting her made the injury real, it began to throb with a horrible burning pain.

"Yeah, he did, angel, but paramedics will be here any second. Are you hurt anyplace else?" He kept one hand on her neck while his other quickly skimmed her body in search of other injuries.

"All over," she replied. "I fell when I was running from Malachi. Jack, he … he …" Tears brimmed in her eyes and began to roll down her cheeks, making the cut on her cheek sting. "He tried to rape me."

"I'm so sorry, honey," Jack murmured, leaning down to kiss her forehead.

"I fought him off," Laura continued as though he hadn't spoken. "And then I ran. I was so scared. I thought he was going to take me away. I thought I was never going to see you or Zach ever again." Her fear was still so real, so vivid, it hadn't diminished yet. In fact, it seemed to be growing exponentially inside her. Her sobs grew, becoming more earnest.

"Laura, baby, you have to calm down." Jack was sounding

panicked now, too. "The more upset you get, the more you bleed."

Laura knew he was right. A neck wound was serious, even if it hadn't gotten an artery. She was becoming hysterical, but powerless to do anything about it. Her rising stress levels were not good for the cut on her neck or her or her baby.

"Here." Ryan suddenly knelt beside them and draped a thermal blanket over her violently shaking body. It didn't help. She knew she was going into shock. Nothing was going to warm her right now.

Jack spared his brother only the most fleeting of glances. "Thanks."

"Let me hold that; you try to calm her down." Ryan took over putting pressure on her bleeding neck.

Her husband took her face in his hands and angled it in his direction. "Laura, honey, look at me. Come on, sweetheart, I really need you to calm down right now. Can you do that for me?"

"Eliza?" Fresh anxiety sliced through her. "Malachi stabbed her, is she okay?"

He glanced over his shoulder. "She's alive. Xavier's with her," Jack answered vaguely.

"Jack, I'm sorry," she began to sob again.

"Why are you sorry, angel?" he asked, confused.

Fear that she had somehow done something to bring this on herself was plaguing her. "I shouldn't have been walking off on my own, then Malachi wouldn't have grabbed me. You always tell me to ..." She knew it wasn't possible to spend every second with someone by her side, nor did she want to, but she wasn't thinking logically right now.

"Shh, shh." Jack stroked her tangled hair. "Sweetheart, please, please try to calm down, you're scaring me."

She was scaring herself. Her breathing was growing erratic, and her heart was hammering in her chest.

Two paramedics dropped down beside them. "Let's see what we've got here." A middle-aged woman unsnapped her case then pulled away the scarf from Laura's neck to examine the wound.

As the paramedics began to treat her, Laura let herself fade again. Everything happening around her dissolved into the background. She was vaguely aware of an oxygen mask being slipped on and her breathing eased a little. Hands were skimming her body in search of other injuries and bandages were being applied to her bloody neck. Medications were administered.

Jack just knelt beside her, stroking her dirty hair, untangling the knots with his fingers. Laura worried about putting her husband through another round of traumatized hysteria. It was bound to happen. Tonight's events wouldn't leave her any time soon. The feel of the cold metal blade of the knife against her neck was seared into her memory. Knowing that not only could Malachi kill her if he wanted but any accidental slip or movement could also end her life. She was going to have nightmares again and panic attacks. Her agoraphobia would probably also get worse.

Then all of a sudden, something pushed all her fears to the background. "Jack," she reached blindly for his hand.

"What's wrong?"

"The baby, I think I just had a contraction." Her eyes sought his, begging him to do something. It was too soon for the baby to be born.

He turned his own panicked eyes on the paramedics. "Is she going into labor? Can you stop it? She's only thirty-five weeks."

"Let's just focus on getting her to the hospital; they can give her drugs that should hopefully stop the labor, or at least delay it. If she's even in labor. This may just be Braxton Hicks contractions. Let's not panic yet. Right now, I'm more concerned about the wound on her neck, and the fact that she's going into shock," the paramedic said.

That didn't help to relieve her anxiety.

It was too soon for their baby to be born.

And it wasn't just that it was early that was stressing her. It was the birth itself. She couldn't have people seeing her scarred body. Not even doctors. With Zach, she had had to be sedated and have a cesarean because the thought of a natural delivery had caused several hysterical outbursts.

As Laura was bundled onto a stretcher and hurried toward an ambulance, she kept a hold on Jack's hand and prayed.

Less than an hour ago, she had prayed that she might survive Malachi, and she had. Now she prayed that if she were going into labor the doctors would be able to stop it, and if they couldn't, that her baby would be born healthy.

* * * * *

3:49 A.M.

"I can't believe I missed so much." Sofia was staring at her husband in shock.

Ryan had turned up in her hospital room a couple of minutes ago, rousing her from a sleep she hadn't even known she was in. Apparently, she had finally fallen sleep after Ryan had told her about the stalker trying to run down Paige with a car. She would have thought she was wound way too tightly for sleep, but seemingly not.

Rest had helped, and she was feeling much better. She wanted to get up and out of this bed, but she was still hooked up to an IV. After what Ryan had just told her, she wanted to go and see all the people she loved to make sure they really were okay and her husband wasn't just sugarcoating things so she didn't stress too much.

"Malachi kidnapped Laura?" Sofia couldn't believe that had happened. How was Laura going to deal with that? She already struggled to cope with everything else she'd been through.

"Yes, he came back for Eliza and the baby but couldn't get to them, so he took Laura instead," Ryan confirmed.

"But she's okay, right?" She tried to read in her husband's eyes if he were telling her the truth.

"She has some injuries. Malachi cut her neck. It was bleeding pretty badly, but she's going to be okay," Ryan assured her.

"Cut her neck? She could have died!" she exclaimed.

"She was lucky the knife didn't get an artery," Ryan agreed.

"There's something else." Sofia could tell by the way her husband wouldn't directly meet her gaze.

"Laura thought she may have been having contractions," Ryan reluctantly admitted.

"She's going into labor? It's too early. I have to go see her." She tried to pull out the IV, but Ryan preempted her by sitting on the bed beside her and clasping her hands.

"Honey, I know you love Laura, and I know you want to be there for her, but Jack's with her right now, and I think they need some time alone. Plus, he already called her family, and they're on their way here."

"Laura won't want her family here, they stress her, and she'll already be over the top stressed after being held hostage and nearly killed," Sofia protested.

"Jack thinks it's important for her to know that her family is here for her, that they aren't angry with her. You know she struggles with that," Ryan reminded her.

Grudgingly, Sofia had to admit that Jack was probably right. "How's Eliza?"

"The knife nicked an artery. She lost a lot of blood, and it's still touch-and-go with her. They're rushing her into surgery. Xavier is with her, and her family should be here within a few hours," Ryan explained.

She frowned at her husband. "I can't believe you let her do that. After everything Malachi did to her, you shouldn't have put her through that and used her as a pawn."

"She agreed," he protested. "And it was the only way we could think of to get Laura out alive. Besides, Eliza didn't want the threat of Malachi being free weighing down on her."

"You still used her. She's not a hostage negotiator or a cop. She has no experience or training, and you walked her into a hostage situation where she could have been killed. She could still die from her injuries." Sofia studied her husband. She wasn't really mad about Eliza, she understood why they had used her even if she didn't agree with it. And she had allowed herself to be used as bait in an attempt to catch the person murdering her family. What was really making her angry was that Ryan himself, and Jack, had nearly been killed in an explosion. Okay, so she was going with angry because it was easier to deal with than horribly scared.

Seemingly reading her mind, he said, "I'm okay, Sofia." Ryan pressed his lips to her forehead.

"But you could have been killed." Tears were burning the backs of her eyes.

"But I wasn't," Ryan countered.

"But you could have been," she repeated. "And if you hadn't been there, then Jack would have been. Is he really okay?"

"Yes, he is," Ryan replied firmly. "And right now, the only thing he's thinking about are Laura and the baby."

Sofia was about to try to convince Ryan to let her go and see Laura, even if it was just for a moment, to reassure herself that her sister-in-law was, in fact, all right, when her phone began to ring. Reaching for the bedside table to pick it up, she cast a concerned glance at Ryan. "Who would be calling me at three in the morning?"

He gave her a small smile. "Why don't you answer it and find out."

Making a face at Ryan, she pressed answer. "Hello?"

"I'm sorry."

The voice sounded odd. It took her less than a second to realize it was a voice modifier. This had to be the stalker, which, if he was calling her, couldn't be good news for Paige. Gesturing at her phone, she mouthed the word "stalker" to Ryan. Her husband bounded to his feet but then stopped. There wasn't much he could do. They could never set up a trace that quickly, and he no doubt wanted Paige in his line of sight immediately, but that was impossible because she was still at the scene of tonight's near carnage.

"I'm sorry I didn't stop her sooner," the voice continued. "But I'm going to stop her tonight. I'm going to make sure she won't ever hurt you again."

Sofia hadn't had an opportunity to talk to the stalker since he had set his sights on Paige. Now she had to make the most of it. "Please don't hurt Paige. She isn't a threat to me. She's happily married; she's not after Ryan."

"She has hidden her true self from you," the stalker sad sadly. "But not from me. I will protect you from her."

Grabbing the phone from her hand, Ryan pressed speakerphone. "Paige and I are not having an affair," he all but yelled at the stalker.

"I saw you with her tonight, outside the hospital, she was crying in your arms," the stalker scoffed.

"Because she was upset. She and her husband are trying to adopt, but she just found out another adoption fell through. I was comforting her. She loves her husband, and she wants a family with him." Ryan sounded frustrated, because he knew that the stalker wasn't governed by logic and wasn't going to be convinced that nothing was going on between him and his partner.

"Please," Sofia begged, "please don't hurt Paige."

"You won't be able to get to her, anyway. We're not leaving her alone. She'll be protected." Ryan's frustration was melting away, leaving behind pure fear.

"Funny, she looks like she's alone right now," the stalker mocked. "She's driving a blue SUV, and I don't see any other cars about."

"That's Xavier's car," Ryan muttered. "She must be driving it back here from the cemetery. She was supposed to stay there, where she'd be surrounded by cops, until I came and got her."

"Don't worry, Sofia. After tonight, you won't have to worry about her. She'll be dead. And you can tell your sister-in-law she won't have to worry either. That so-called friend of yours is sinking her claws into her husband, too."

"Please don't kill her. I know you want to protect me, but this isn't necessary. Paige is my friend. She wouldn't do anything to hurt me. Please just tell me who you are. You say you love me, that you care about me. If that's true, then I should know who you are."

"I wish I could," the stalker murmured softly. "Goodbye, Sofia. After tonight, your marriage will be safe."

Then he was gone. In a blind panic, she turned to Ryan. "He's going to kill her. She's all alone. He's already gone after her twice tonight. He won't stop. Oh my gosh, Ryan, he's not going to stop until she's dead."

If her stalker killed Paige, then Sofia knew she would never forgive herself.

* * * * *

3:58 A.M.

It was time.

And this time around, no one was going to get in his way.

He had already been interrupted twice tonight. Bruce had been positive that he had Paige when he'd driven his car at her. She hadn't really registered what was about to happen until he was almost on her. If it wasn't for Ryan pushing her away at the last second, she'd be dead right now.

And then later after he had circled back to the hospital, he had followed her as she wandered the halls on her own. She had known he was there, not that he'd minded, it had added a little more fun to know that she knew he was watching her. Only then she had called one of her cop buddies to come, and Xavier Montague had turned up just before he had had a chance to grab her.

Nothing like that was going to happen this time around, though.

Paige was alone in the car.

Their cars were the only ones on the road.

It was storming. Rain was pounding down; the wind was howling—both made for difficult driving conditions.

Bruce wasn't concerned about having given a heads-up to Sofia about his intentions. Her cop husband and friends knew he was after Paige anyway. And what Ryan had said was almost definitely true; they were going to be sticking to Paige like glue. If he didn't take her out tonight, he may not get another shot.

And that was unacceptable.

That woman could not be allowed to continue with her vile behavior.

He did wish that he could go to Sofia and tell her who he was.

She would be so surprised.

Everyone would.

No one knew how he knew Sofia.

No one knew their connection.

If he was honest, no one even knew his real identity.

He himself hadn't even known who he really was for the majority of his life.

It had only been a few months before he started leaving gifts and notes for Sofia that he had learned the truth.

Although he wished he'd always known, he understood why his father had kept it a secret.

Upon his father's death, he had received some paperwork from an attorney. Paperwork that his father had had his lawyer keep until his death. Then he had ordered it be sent to his son.

Bruce had gotten the shock of his life when he'd opened the

envelope and read what was inside.

He had been raised by a single father and been told that his mother had died in a car accident.

In fact, she had not.

She had been alive until just a few years ago.

Only it wasn't safe for him to be a part of her life.

For his stepfather was a cruel and vicious man.

When Bruce had been just two years old, his stepfather had plotted to kill him. Somehow his mother had gotten wind of her husband's plan and turned the tables on him.

As the plan to kill him was set into motion, his mother faked his death and spirited him away to live with his father. While she had remained with her evil husband for the sole purpose of protecting him and making sure no one ever knew he was still alive.

Bruce didn't remember his mother and he'd had a good life with his father, even following in his footsteps to become a doctor.

Even after his father had died, and the truth of his parentage had been revealed, he hadn't reached out to the family he had left. It had still been imperative to keep his identity a secret because his stepfather was alive, and thus still a threat to him.

But that wasn't the case any longer.

His stepfather was dead now.

His mother, too, but since he hadn't really known her, he hadn't really grieved her.

He only had one person left in the world.

And he was going to make protecting her his life's goal.

No one was going to mess with his little sister on his watch.

Sofia Everette Xander was actually his half-sister. They shared the same mother, but had different fathers. His father was a doctor who had an affair with Gloria Everette. Sofia's father was the man she had grown up thinking was actually her brother, Logan Everette IV.

Bruce had been christened Logan Everette III—supposedly the son of Logan Everette II and his wife, Gloria. His mother thought no one knew of her affair or that her husband wasn't the father of her child. Only somehow Logan had figured it out. And so, his mother had been forced to give him up.

With both his parents deceased and no other biological siblings, Sofia was all he had. He would do *anything* for her. Not excluding lie, cheat, steal, or kill.

And tonight, his sole mission was killing Paige Hood.

Sofia deserved happiness. She had it with Ryan and their children.

No one was going to take it from her.

So, revving his car engine, he prepared to slam it into Paige's car.

* * * * *

3:59 A.M.

Paige was so tired.

When she got to the hospital, she was going to call Elias and ask him to come and get her and take her home. Assuming Xavier wanted to stay with Eliza until they knew whether or not she was going to survive her surgery, she would get her boss to organize a car to be posted at her house overnight so the boys wouldn't worry about her.

In the morning, she still intended to discuss with her boss her plan to use herself as bait to catch the stalker. Right now, though, all she cared about was going home, falling into bed, and curling up in her husband's arms to sleep.

Her phone, which sat in her bag on the passenger seat of Xavier's car, began to ring.

Paige ignored it.

She didn't want to talk to anyone right now.

She was too tired to deal with anything.

The storm was growing worse, making her glad she'd left the crime scene when she had. She hadn't been able to get warm since the stalker had tried to run her down with his car. Getting drenched in the pounding rain and sleet, with the wind howling, she would have been utterly freezing.

It was only a ten-minute drive from the cemetery to the hospital, but she was driving slower on account of the storm. Their house was only fifteen minutes from the hospital. If she called Elias now, he could start driving before she even reached the hospital. That meant she could be home and taking a steaming hot shower then climbing into bed in less than forty-five minutes.

That sounded like heaven.

Her phone began to ring again.

Maybe she should answer.

What if it was news on Laura?

Hopefully, if indeed Laura was in labor, the doctors would be able to stop it. Paige didn't want anything to happen to Laura or her baby. If anyone deserved some happiness, it was Laura—especially after tonight's events.

Reaching over to pull out her phone, she saw her partner's name on the screen.

"Where are you?" he screamed at her before she could even say hello.

"On my way to the hospital, why?" she asked, confused by his panicked tone. At the crime scene, she had been surrounded by cops. She had agreed to let Xavier stay with her. She was even going to be good and make sure she wasn't alone tonight. There was nothing for him to be panicking about.

"The stalker is following you." Ryan's words tumbled out in a rush, causing the car to swerve as she turned in her seat to search for another car on the road.

Seeing no headlights, she said to her partner, "I don't see anyone. How can you be sure he's following me?"

"Because he just called Sofia and told her he's going to kill you tonight," Ryan yelled. "What road are you on?"

"Woods Drive, down by the river," she replied.

"I'm on my—"

All of a sudden, her car was rammed from behind. The force jerked her forward and her phone flew from her hand.

"Paige? Paige?" Ryan's voice yelled at her from her cell, which was now lying uselessly out of reach on the floor under her seat somewhere.

She had no time to even think about trying to retrieve it because the blows from the other car kept coming. One after another. Her body jerked forward, straining against the seat belt with each hit. She tried to brake, but her tires couldn't find traction on the slippery roads.

Another blow, more powerful than the others, sent the car skidding off the road and hurtling toward the river.

Again, Paige tried to brake, but the wet grass was even more slippery than the wet roads had been.

Her car built up speed as it went down a small decline.

She was bounced about, her body jarring as even the seat belt couldn't prevent her from hitting the door and the steering wheel.

A second later, the car crashed into the water.

The river was deep, and almost immediately, the car began to sink.

Paige knew she didn't have much time to get out.

She fumbled with the seat belt.

But it wouldn't undo.

It was jammed.

Water was quickly flooding into the car.

Freezing water.

So cold it almost stole her breath.

It numbed her quickly, making her efforts at forcing the seat belt undone virtually pointless.

She was going to die.

The stalker had succeeded.

Ryan knew where she was, but he could never get to her in time.

If she had been cold before, it was nothing compared to being trapped in her car that was quickly submerging in the river.

Water continued to pour inside.

Already, it was up to her waist.

She was shaking badly and her teeth were chattering. If the water didn't claim her first and she drowned, then she would die of hypothermia.

The cold became all-consuming.

Paige couldn't think of anything else.

Her whole body was numb.

Her mind was quickly going numb, too.

Her movements as she continued to fight with the seat belt were sluggish now.

The cold continued to seep into her bones.

There was no escaping from it.

The water had risen to her chest.

Paige didn't know how long she'd been in the car.

It felt like hours but couldn't have been more than five to ten minutes.

It wasn't just cold in here, it was dark, too.

Like a coffin.

Which, in a way, it was.

She wasn't getting out of here alive.

Water began to tickle at her neck.

Soon, it would cover her head.

The cold was making her sleepy.

Still, she didn't give up.

Her hands continued to try and pry the seat belt loose.

If she could get it undone, she might still have a chance of getting out of this car alive.

It wasn't until the water reached her mouth and she was forced to take a breath and hold it, that she gave up her struggle with the seat belt.

She closed her eyes.

Sleep was lapping at her mind.

No, not sleep, she thought.

Death.

Death was lapping at her mind.

Ready to tug her under as soon as her starving lungs forced her to take a breath.

She seemed to be immune to the cold water now despite the fact that it filled the entire car and covered her body.

Instead, she felt oddly warm.

A small part of her brain that still functioned knew that wasn't a good thing.

Vainly, she continued to hold her breath.

For what, she wasn't sure.

No one was coming.

She was going to drown.

Paige thought that she saw a light moving toward her, but she was probably wrong.

She wished she could see Elias just one more time. To hold him, to kiss him, to make love to him, to tell him how much she loved him.

Unable to hold her breath any longer, she opened her mouth.

Water filled it.

And then she passed out.

Jane has loved reading and writing since she can remember. She writes dark and disturbing crime/mystery/suspense with some romance thrown in because, well, who doesn't love romance?! She has several series including the complete Detective Parker Bell series, the Count to Ten series, the Christmas Romantic Suspense series, and the Flashes of Fate series of novelettes.

When she's not writing Jane loves to read, bake, go to the beach, ski, horse ride, and watch Disney movies. She has a black belt in Taekwondo, a 200+ collection of teddy bears, and her favorite color is pink. She has the world's two most sweet and pretty Dalmatians, Ivory and Pearl. Oh, and she also enjoys spending time with family and friends!

For more information please visit any of the following –

Amazon – http://www.amazon.com/author/janeblythe
BookBub – https://www.bookbub.com/authors/jane-blythe
Email – mailto:janeblytheauthor@gmail.com
Facebook – http://www.facebook.com/janeblytheauthor
Goodreads – http://www.goodreads.com/author/show/6574160.Jane_Blythe
Instagram – http://www.instagram.com/jane_blythe_author
Reader Group – http://www.facebook.com/groups/janeskillersweethearts
Twitter – http://www.twitter.com/jblytheauthor
Website – http://www.janeblythe.com.au

sic enim dilexit Deus mundum ut Filium suum unigenitum daret ut omnis qui credit in eum habeat vitam aeternam